Verena rose to her knees. Jordan stood before her, suddenly still. Verena captured his eyes and held them, communicating all the pleasure she would give to him as her hands did what they were aching to do.

She touched his abdomen then moved upward to take in the smooth warmth of his chest. She paused, pressing her hand against the place where his life's blood pumped. Then he grasped both her hands, pulling her up and against him.

"You want me. I know you do," he told her.

She nodded. "And I will have you this day." With that her lips went to his. As she channeled the tremendous build-up of pleasure, his lips moved about her, his tongue darted around hers and, without a thought at all, she joined him in this strange ritual without interrupting the channeling, all the while building, building within them both a need for more. When she pulled back his eyes were dazed.

"What are you doing to me?" Jordan questioned aloud. At the same time, he asked himself why he was letting this happen. There were reasons this should not happen. Important reasons.

MISSION

PAMELA LEIGH STARR

Genesis Press, Inc.

Indigo Love Spectrum

An imprint of Genesis Press, Inc.
Publishing Company

Genesis Press, Inc.
P.O. Box 101
Columbus, MS 39703

ISBN-13: 978-1-58571-255-7
ISBN-10: 1-58571-255-8
Manufactured in the United States of America

First Edition

Visit us at www.genesis-press.com or call at 1-888-Indigo-1

DEDICATION

To my daughter Kaitlyn, who is diligently on a mission to create her own "Great American Novel" that I'm sure will be out of this world.

PROLOGUE

"Mighty She-force."

Verena Tovick-Ra's regal head turned in the direction of her explorations officer.

Zytai's confident tone was enough to pull Verena away from the rare cloud of depression that had descended on her a moment before—a depression she would not have allowed to linger in any event, despite the grave situation in which she and her sisters of Vixen found themselves. She had just been informed through a transmission that the very last surviving half-ling, the male of their species, had expired.

"Speak," Verena commanded, blowing the last particles of despair away with that one word.

"I have found a likely planet."

"Speak more."

"It is two light years away and has a blue-green appearance like that of our own planet Vixen."

"More," Verena demanded, forcing down the beginnings of excitement. They were the only ship of the hundreds deployed that so far had *not* discovered anything that might mean success for this vital mission.

"The male species on the surface are of similar form."

"Be more precise."

"They are compatible."

MISSION

After searching far and wide on both charted and finally uncharted parts of the universe, Verena Tovick-Ra of Vixen felt a sense of peace grow inside herself upon hearing the wondrous news.

She and her crew would not return home in shame and defeat. They would do their part to insure that the Vixens of the Roma Galaxy survived.

They had found compatible males.

They would procreate, not bow down to extinction.

"Show me this planet."

Zytai immediately complied. Verena's face stretched into a smile as she viewed a planet so much like her own. Pertinent information flashed in one corner of the viewer: atmosphere, landmass and water content, all so similar to their own lush planet.

Verena held the gaze of each of her officers on deck. Soon they were all wearing the same exultant expression, feeling identical trills of hope.

"Proceed without delay," Verena commanded.

"Without delay!" every female voice echoed as the ship's course was altered.

"To planet Earth," Zytai announced.

"Planet Earth," Verena whispered, "will give us what we need to survive."

CHAPTER 1

"You do not fit the requirements. Begone!" The tall, beautiful woman waved an ebony brown hand at him.

Jordan Mitchell turned in the direction she pointed, toward the door he had entered exactly three minutes and twenty seconds ago.

Swoosh!

He heard and felt another door close behind him. Or what was supposed to be a door. It was stupid of him to have taken his eyes off her. Now the opening and the beautiful woman were gone. The sudden disappearance of both didn't bother him too much. He had seen stranger things happen in the last two years.

Not allowing his quarry to get away was top priority. Dealing with an unknown species left little time to waste. He froze for a moment, his eyes scanning the sparse interior, finding only a metal chair and matching table. The furniture flashed at him, its brightness and strange contours startling him.

"J.M. here. I've entered and interacted." The hidden mike sewn into today's disguise, a flannel working class shirt, transmitted his message.

"Not too friendly," Troy, one of the many ears and eyes of Project Discover, quipped.

"No, but sexy as hell," grunted Jordan, inspecting the metal panel that used to be a door. "My kind of woman.

Better yet, exactly your kind of woman. If we can call her that."

"The way I like my coffee?"

"Close enough, my friend, close enough."

"Status?"

"I've inched my way into what looks like the outer area of the ship. I'm trying to find a way inside. I could possibly use backup," Jordan answered as his hand skimmed over the cool, smooth metal. It felt flexible, almost plastic, but hardened when he pushed the bulk of his weight against it.

"Signal when ready." Troy's voice confirmed that he heard and understood.

It was reassuring to know that outside this strange little chamber were a dozen agents, men and woman awaiting the order to converge, trap and detain the 'people,' if they could be called that, inside this spacecraft.

Project Discover, a little known division of the FBI, had tracked, found and quietly observed this particular visitor. Most spacecrafts that had been tracked in past years were quickly lost or came and left in a matter of minutes, sometimes seconds. These visitors had arrived almost immediately after one of the worst hurricanes to hit the southeast region of the United States, and they had stayed.

Jordan and his team had watched as the craft was camouflaged among the huge oak trees in a deserted corner of Bayou Savage. With half the population still evacuated in the aftermath of the storm, the visitors hid by blending in as just another construction company seeking workers to help rebuild what had been destroyed.

Jordan and his people had watched.

At first nothing much happened beyond a few of them coming and going. What appeared to be an all female crew hid in plain sight for an entire week.

Until today.

A slight vibration thrummed beneath his feet. It was enough to convince him that backup was indeed needed.

"J.M., give status."

"Something's going on. I feel movement."

The second he relayed that message, Jordan heard Troy yell, "It's gone!" in a tone that held an astonishing degree of disbelief.

"What? What's gone? Tell me what you see out there."

"Nothing." For a moment static filled the air, then loud and clear, "The ship's gone."

"Gone? I'm still here."

"If you're there, then you're gone. J.M. lost in action," Troy's voice said over and over again until it faded into static.

"Lost in action?" Jordan said aloud. "Lost in space?"

That was ridiculous. Jordan took long strides across the chamber, patting his side for the gun he had hidden there. "*Lost in Space* was a sitcom, then a movie," he told the empty chamber, determined that it would *not* be his reality.

Gun in hand, Jordan raced to the place where the door used to be. He pushed against the wall, felt it move, then harden. He did this over and over again until perspiration beaded his forehead and ran down his face. Determined not to be a helpless victim, he went to the farthest corner of the chamber, then ran toward the solid wall like a human battering ram.

Instead of suddenly stopping his assault, the wall stretched and thinned, becoming transparent. The gun in his hand poked through the stretchy, plastic-like material. In an instant, it was sucked out of his hand.

His face plastered against a now crystal clear wall, Jordan watched as his only weapon floated away. Watched as his home, his planet, disappeared and faded into the nothingness of dark, empty space and flashing distant stars.

He didn't suffer this devastating view for long because suddenly the transparent wall was no longer transparent. With a twang, it pulled itself back together, tossing him like a cartoon character to the other side of the chamber, where he landed flat on his back.

Dazed, he stared at the solid, shining wall that had once held a door, then a window to a nightmare he had never imagined actually living.

"Get up," he told himself. "Snap out of it and get ready for whatever's coming next." Jordan was sure something was coming next. In nightmares there was always a next. He tried to tap at the seam in his shirt where the tiny radio was concealed but his hand wouldn't do more than move in the general direction of where he wanted it to go.

"Troy," he whispered, sitting up with a grimace. "You there, man? Anybody there?" The sound of voices, female voices, coming closer and speaking in English put a stop to his useless attempt to contact his team. Besides, at the speed the ship was moving, Jordan was sure they had already flown past Saturn, dismantling one if its rings as they zoomed by. Radio contact was impossible.

A sense of helplessness overtaking him, Jordan fell back to the floor, banging his head once again. He had no weapon, no contact, and no way to get home. The voices were coming nearer. Like birds twittering above a fallen cartoon character's head, Jordan thought he saw tiny women, exactly like the one who had yelled, "Begone!" circling around his head chanting over and over again, "Begone, begone, begone!"

Maybe he *had* turned into a cartoon version of himself. Jordan shook his head, trying to clear it. He succeeded only in spreading a sharp, intense pain through his entire brain.

Through the pain and the annoying chants of "Begone," Jordan could hear bits of a conversation right outside the room.

"This should not be," one of the voices distinctly said.

Not having many choices, Jordan opted to assess the situation by lying down and pretending to be unconscious. The sound of the panel opening told him he had made the right decision.

"I see that it *is* so, Rya." It was the voice of the woman who had first said 'Begone.'

They were talking in English, yet he and his team had intercepted only an alien language they had yet to interpret.

"Zytai, he should not be here. I saw you command the male to leave," another voice said.

Names, they had names. Zytai was the 'Begone' woman and Rya was the other voice. Despite the throbbing pain, Jordan kept his eyes closed and his body still, in what he hoped was a convincing pose of unconsciousness as he stored away this bit of information about the aliens.

7

"Your grasp of the males' language is impressive." A new voice, commanding and regal, filled the room.

"We are conversing in their language at all times, as you have instructed, Commander," one of the women answered.

"A little practice and consistent use is all that is necessary to become proficient in such a simple tongue."

At their nod she turned her attention to the situation at hand. "An uncooperative, unwelcome male, my fellow sisters? We are learning firsthand that these males of Earth, though compatible, are quite different from what we are used to," the new voice said right above his head.

A rustling sound and the shuffle of feet tempted Jordan to open his eyes. The firm, sexy voice belonging to the newcomer was temptation within itself. A temptation he couldn't give in to. Not when he didn't have any idea what he was up against. For all he knew, these woman, their voices, their bodies, could be some disguise. He had no idea what they really were or what they wanted with all the men who had been lured here. In order to discover exactly what kind of nightmare he had landed in the middle of, he needed to gather as much information from these aliens as he could. What might be revealed when they thought he was unconscious would certainly not be said if they knew he was awake.

"Mighty She-force," Zytai began, but stopped as if she were at a loss for words.

"We have noted what you have said, Commander, about these males of Earth," Rya finished.

Jordan listened carefully, still amazed that he was hearing English. He and his team had intercepted communications from passing spacecraft on many occasions, but never before had any of them had been in English.

"Commander, what do we do about this strange situation?"

Commander? As Jordan heard that word spoken again by one of the alien women addressing the new voice, he remained still, concentrating on breathing at a regular rate and listening hard, alert for any helpful information.

"Not to worry," reassured the voice that pulled at his eyelids, begging them to open, to connect a face to its seductive lure. "We have time enough to train them all before we get to Vixen."

Train them?

For what?

Were they going to be part of some huge intergalactic zoo?

A circus?

A long silence filled the room and his mind ran wild with possibilities. Jordan reined in his thoughts, forcing his imagination into a dormant state as he felt their eyes boring into him. Had they read his thoughts? Jordan could swear that he felt a thick layer of superiority in the air. These beings acted as if their captives were mischievous children or pets. Jordan took offense, a bit of his male ego rising at the insult, making it difficult to keep himself in check.

"He is alive then?" the commander asked.

"Yes, according to the sensors," Zytai answered with a bit of disgust.

"What do we do with him? Zytai commanded him to leave before we departed from the planet but he did not heed her words. He is one of the watchers from the woods."

"I know this," the commander said, a trace of humor in her voice.

So they'd known that his team was watching the ship but had done nothing. Did that mean they themselves were peaceful observers? But where were all the men who'd entered and never left? And why had this ship taken off so suddenly? Jordan had so many questions flying through his head that he wanted to jump up and confront the aliens with every one of them. There were only three in this room and they were *only* women. Or were they?

"And he's a pale one!" Zytai suddenly interjected with complete disgust.

Pale? Jordan felt insulted again. What did that have to do with anything?

"That is why I told him to go, Commander. We want beautiful children, not pale ones. He has no golden or deep brown tint."

Deep brown? No, he wouldn't fit that description; Troy would, to a T. But golden? Yeah, he could be golden after spending some time in the sun, Jordan thought indignantly. And children? He would make gorgeous children. *He* was gorgeous. At least that's what tons of women had told him. But none of this mattered. Jordan mentally shook himself as the sensible side of his brain made him realize how ridiculous it was for him to be insulted by what was being said about him. His focus was, and should remain, on returning to Earth. Nothing else mattered.

"And that hair? Not much color. It is almost as pale as his skin."

"Enough, Zytai, we must keep him."

Jordan was pleased to hear the commander say this. He had had enough bashing to leave his ego sore and aching for long time. What was it the alien named Zytai had said in between the denouncements of his looks? Jordan felt it was very important but the thought slipped out of his mind as they began to talk again.

"I will not have him. Will you, Rya?"

"No, Zytai. Not with so many more desirable males to choose from."

"Then I will take him."

"Commander, are you sure?" the two other aliens said at the same time, with a mutual degree of shock.

"There is never a time that I am not," she said in a tone that threw the room into silence once again.

The conversation swirling above him was too strange. Its strangeness was the only constant so far. A sense of dread filled Jordan as he felt himself being lifted and carried out of the room. What were they going to do with him? What was going to happen now that the commander had *chosen* him?

Verena stared at the pale one lying on the pallet beside her own. He was different, in that Zytai was right. But things that were different had always intrigued Verena. It was this tendency to seek the unusual that had guided her destiny. She had become a searcher, exploring other worlds, other species. On Vixen there was no female as accomplished as she, which was why she was one of many chosen by the queen to help save her people. Verena had begun to have doubts when all the ships found compatible males before hers did. She had almost had her first taste of defeat. Finding Earth had saved her from that disgrace. In finding Earth they had found what they were searching for. Males.

But not just any males. Males who were strong. New half-lings for the sisters of Vixen to direct, protect and insure the continuation of their race. A simple experiment had confirmed that Earth males were not susceptible to the disease that had killed every male Vixen, both young and old. A sample of an Earth male's blood was taken and exposed to the virus. Earth males had proven to have a natural immunity.

This success had put Verena in a contented state of mind. The unique features of her future half-ling pleased her. She reached down to touch the hair on his head, so different from hers. Its color was a much lighter tint than even her own skin, a tone she had never seen on someone's head. The hair felt slick, smooth, not as hair should feel. It did not matter, for soon it would be no more.

A pair of her fingers joined to make a journey across his face. Starting at the hair above one of his eyes, Verena made small circular movements, creating a downward path to the other side of his pale face. She traced his nose and lips, her fingers finally landing on his chin, which Verena lifted as she spoke directly to him for the first time.

"Come away from your artificial slumber." She paused for only a moment, giving in to a sudden urge to lay her lips on each closed eyelid. "Lift your eyes to your new life."

It took a minute for Jordan to realize that the woman who had laid her soft, warm lips across his eyelids was on to him. His determination to appear unconscious while suppressing the instant reaction to her touch had nearly thrown his mind to another world.

His mind?

He was in another world.

Seeing no reason to continue the charade, Jordan opened his eyes to find a goddess staring down at him. Perhaps a goddess in disguise, he reminded himself, slowly lifting to rest on his elbows, keeping his eyes squarely on her. He rose to his feet, carefully putting distance between them. "How did you know?" he asked when he felt he was at a comfortable distance, able to react to any unexpected threat from her. Not that taking him away from his planet and traveling at a great speed through space wasn't threatening enough.

She shifted with fluid grace before answering, adjusting her long, long legs to regally sit on the edge of an oval-shaped bed pallet elevated from the floor. She was easily the most beautiful woman he had ever seen, her skin a golden bronze, her eyes wide and inquiring. And her lips, the ones that had touched him, were full and wide and holding a funny sort of half-smile.

"Are you surprised that I knew of your artificial sleep?"

Jordan nodded, slowly moving to the other side of the bed, attempting to get a view from behind. He wanted to see all of this creature's body parts. Were there any extras that might shoot out at him?

Her eyes followed him. "Tell me your purpose in that foolish act."

"In pretending?" Jordan stalled.

"Of course."

"After you tell me your purpose in all of this." Jordan spread his arms wide trying to encompass all that he had experienced within the span of his arms.

"You will know in time."

"I want to know now."

The half smile disappeared; her lips formed a straight, uncompromising line. She stood and moved toward him. Had he said she was tall? She was at least an inch taller than his six-foot-two frame. As she stood before him, there was no hiding the fact that he had angered her. Refusing to step back or show any fear or alarm, Jordan braced himself for the unexpected, waiting to see what form of attack her anger would take.

She stopped before him, standing toe-to-toe, eye-to-eye, and laughed.

No.

It was more of a chuckle, directly into his face. She was laughing at him. This was a day for insults. As she reached a hand toward him, Jordan took a step back, prepared to put into action the defensive moves he'd learned in training. However, he wasn't going to beat up on a woman unless she proved herself to be something other than a woman.

Her hand continued to move forward slowly, gracefully. It rested on his cheek in a completely non-threatening way. Despite her careful approach, Jordan's distrust of the beautiful alien automatically caused him to react; he grasped her wrist in readiness to pull and flip her if necessary. The contact of skin against skin stilled his action. They stood this way, assessing, gazing and *enjoying* the moment.

The hand on his face was firm, yet soft, the warmth a living thing that spread far beyond the side of his face where her hand rested. A sense of deep pleasure began to fill him as her eyes held his with a promise of more to come.

Jordan dropped his own hand, releasing her wrist, wanting to do no more than stare into her eyes as an ebb and flow of increasing pleasure spread through his body, washing over him with an intensity that he had never experienced before. Suddenly he felt as if he couldn't breathe, had long forgotten how, as his senses took in the rising tide of incredible feelings.

Was she suffocating him?

Was this how she did away with her victims?

Was she some kind of space siren like the legendary sea sirens who lured men to their deaths with a promise of pleasures beyond anything anyone had ever conceived? At the moment he didn't really care. He began to feel light-headed from lack of air. *If she is a space siren, what a way to go.*

"Release," she said.

Release? He wasn't the one touching her. Release her from what? he wondered as he felt his blood heat and sing, a pulsating wave of pleasure touching every cell in his body. He had never felt anything like this in his life. As the pleasure slowly ebbed away, the blood in his veins seemingly vibrating, Jordan felt her hand gently pressing against his chest.

Suddenly Jordan let out a huge breath he'd had no idea that he had been holding. Her hand moved up and down his chest as if to soothe him. Realizing that the deep pleasure he had experienced was slowly draining from every pore of his body, Jordan heard himself yell, "No!" He was losing the glorious feeling and wanted to stop its escape, yet he was powerless to do anything about it.

But at least now he could breathe. Jordan concentrated on doing just that.

"Commander." A voice invaded the room.

"Proceed." She continued to stare into his eyes, soothing him as she listened to whoever had interrupted them.

"You are needed," was all the voice said.

Needed? He needed her. He didn't want her to go. Her eyes told him she understood. She began making soft shushing sounds. Jordan closed his eyes for a moment; when he opened them, she was gone.

Jordan didn't know how long he stood in the middle of the room feeling bereft and abandoned, but eventually he moved and could do no more than fall onto the pallet where he drifted into a deep sleep—a sleep he did not want to give in to.

There was something he needed to do.
Something he had to find out.
Someplace he was supposed to go.

CHAPTER 2

Jordan felt a hand on his face, lips on his eyelids and words that sent instant dread into his heart.

"Lift your eyes to your new life."

A resounding 'no' exploded inside Jordan's head. "No," slowly echoed out of his mouth. The soft sound of the word to his own ears did nothing to convey the disgust he felt in even considering following the command. Even through the sleepy haze that clung to him like Velcro, Jordan knew the silky, smooth words *were* a command.

"Yes," the voice insisted.

"No," Jordan growled, frustrated with his own constant use of the word, which nonetheless seemed to leave him powerless. The force needed to push out his refusal sent a trembling vibration through him. His eyes flew open and he stood. He was still a bit disoriented but knew he had to move. He had to put some distance between himself and the voice. The goddess stood across the room just as regal and beautiful as before, looking as if she had not a care in the world. She moved toward him.

Jordan took a step back.

Memory of the pleasure of her touch flashed through him. He suddenly wanted to experience it all over again but knew he shouldn't—

No, couldn't. He couldn't give in to the sudden over-powering desire to welcome more of what she offered and fall once again under the debilitating effects her touch had already had on him.

"Don't come any closer," he warned.

She paused, folding her long fingers in front of her, that half-smile spreading across her face, just as before. Jordan got the feeling that she was humoring him.

"How long did I sleep?"

No response.

"What did you do to me?"

Nothing.

"What is going on here?" he asked, this time not expecting a response. Oh, but he needed one. Why didn't this alien just come out with whatever horrible plans they had in mind?

She wouldn't.

Jordan was certain that he wouldn't be getting any answers from her.

He began pacing up and down the room in frustration. Long strides made a path that crossed in front of the goddess, while maintaining a distance. Jordan continued to throw questions at her whether she answered them or not.

"How far are we from Earth? What did you do with the other men? What do you want with us? What do *you* want with *me*?" He turned to face her directly, his eyes demanding some type of response.

"So, you are more informed than we thought," she said.

"What does that mean?"

"The other males are not aware of where they are."

"Not aware?"

"This planet Earth that you are from is where they think they are. Earth is where they will continue to believe they are until the time comes for that to change."

"And who decides that?"

"I do, of course."

"And who are you?"

"Mighty She-force Verena Tovick-Ra of the planet Vixen, commander of the searcher *Vixen II*.

"And what does that mean?"

"It means that I am in command. And I am tired of questions. Answering them grows bothersome. I awoke you so that you may attend me."

"What?"

"More questions." Verena pulled inside the regret and longing she instantly felt, preventing it from showing on her face. As commander she often had to suppress her feelings. And right now she was feeling a need to become more acquainted with her future mate. But he was obviously not ready. She did not have the patience to deal with his questions at this moment, which caused her to respond with more force than she intended. "You are not worth the bother. Go into the side chamber so that I may rest and not worry that you will do something to harm yourself."

Jordan stared at her. She might be a woman used to giving orders but he was no child to be pushed around. "I must not have understood you. Are you requesting that I leave? No problem. Swing back around and drop me off on Earth—in the middle of the Atlantic or Pacific Ocean, on the top of Mount Everest. I don't care as long as it's Earth."

Feeling a small measure of guilt over her choice of words Verena attempted to respond to his outburst in a civilized manner befitting a commander. Besides, he had to understand and accept his present circumstances. "That planet, which is no longer yours, is more than three Earth days away." Her hands parted, spreading out in a gesture that said there was nothing she could do.

"I have been sleeping for three days!"

"Yes, but I have not." Feeling the limited control she had gathered but moments before dwindling away, Verena slowly walked toward him and commanded in a quiet voice, "To the side chamber, unless you would rather…"

Watching the goddess step toward him with her hand outstretched, Jordan took a step back. Having no intention of being knocked out in another three-day coma, he reluctantly backed into the chamber, moving just slow enough so that Verena the commander understood that he was *letting* her have her way *this* time. As soon as he was inside, a transparent door slid closed, locking him in. He stood on one side, she on the other. Their eyes met and held. Refusing to be the first to look away, refusing to give in to what he felt was complete submission, Jordan challenged her with his eyes. As he stared, her mesmerizing deep brown eyes revealed many things:

A strength he had already detected.

A purpose he would soon know more about.

A determination to get what she wanted.

And a promise of the universe if he'd simply give himself into her. Jordan held her gaze, resisting what she silently demanded, holding eye contact until she turned away, her movements so quick Jordan nearly fell back onto the wall behind him.

Wary of her, wary of the unknown, Jordan knew that it was best that he had avoided physical contact. It didn't matter that what she had done to him before was the most gratifying experience he had ever had with a woman. It was a 'once in a lifetime' locker room/ bar room beer guzzling story to tell the guys. And he had been dying to feel it again, but he had to keep his head clear.

His entire body thought otherwise.

He craved her touch.

He wanted to touch *her*.

Jordan was stiff with an aching desire for her. None of which was important.

Getting back to Earth.

Rescuing almost a fifty men from the clutches of aliens.

Those things were important.

Jordan looked around the small room Verena the Commander referred to as the side chamber and realized exactly why he had nearly fallen onto the back wall.

Six paces was all it took to cover its width, and a dozen its length. The rectangular room wasn't a chamber. It was a closet.

Closet or not, it was safer than being in the commander's presence. Jordan sat cross-legged in the middle of the room. Suddenly he was very tired again. The effects of his previous encounter with the commander were not fully out of his system. Not wanting to, but completely unable to resist the urge, Jordan leaned against the back wall and fell into a restless sleep.

Having transferred her message to the pale one, having revealed the rewards of submission, Verena had allowed him his little victory in the 'who-can-hold-a-gaze' game. Awaking him had been a mistake, just as giving him a sampling of the joy they could share before they could be united as mates had been. She simply could not resist and had not anticipated the energy draining effect it would have on him. His slight injury, plus adjusting to being taken from his home, had left him too weak to withstand such joys.

Her thoughts had been with him the entire time he had slept. After days of dealing with engine problems due to their quick departure, consulting with Suvan, her officer directly in command of their new half-lings, and finding solutions to the various problems arising with the Earth men, Verena was exhausted.

Too tired to go on. Too tired to answer questions. Too tired to study the visual cards that would explain more about this species of men they had captured to save their race. Verena only wanted to rest. She had wanted to gaze upon him, watch as he massaged her tired extremities and lulled her body into relaxation so that she might sleep peacefully. Was that too much to ask? Hadn't she seen her own father rightfully cater to the needs of his mate?

But all she had gotten were questions. Still tense but too weary to care, Verena lay upon her reclining pallet and slept.

Jordan woke up suddenly. He'd had that dream again. The one about his father. The teasing and taunting echoed inside his head. As the voices faded away, realization of where he was intensified the effects of the dream. Frustration and anger roiled inside his stomach. Both were feelings he detested. Jordan automatically began the breathing exercises he had learned long ago. Inner peace was what he sought. A clear, strong mind to direct his next action was essential if he had any hope of doing something about the situation he found himself in or of saving the men duped into entering a ship zooming through space and into the unknown.

"Mind and body as one…"

"A spirit of humility…"

"Devoted utterly to the cause of justice…"

The words from Gichin Funakoshi, the father of Karate-do, easily flowed through his brain and out his mouth in firm, whispered syllables. These phrases he repeated over and over again until he could feel frustration and anger ease from his body. Finding the inner peace he sought, Jordan stood. His mind now focused, he was ready to prepare his body for the unknown challenges he must face. He removed the shirt and jeans that would hamper his movements.

In true Karate-do spirit, Jordan focused body and mind to be prepared for any circumstance. *Everything* that had happened to him so far had been an unexpected circumstance. *Unexpected* was a word that was on the top of the list of descriptors for his job. He had never had a problem dealing with unexpected situations, but this was way beyond anything he had experienced before.

Weaponless.

That he was. But he had another resource, himself. Karate-do translated into "empty-handed way." His only weapons now against his foe would be his inner strength and his resourcefulness.

Alone.

He was all he had, his greatest strength, at least until he found the other men on this ship.

Jordan could do no more than rely on himself. "One's true opponent is oneself, " he reminded himself as he warmed up by practicing the basic moves and forms of Karate-do.

Jordan had no idea how long he stood in the middle of the room practicing, but some part of his mind noted that as he began to perspire and overheat, he suddenly became cool once again. This happened a number of times. It had been a long time since he had trained so long and hard, but the presence of a good sweat meant he was moving in the right direction. Only after he had pushed his body to the edge did he sit to contemplate the strangeness of it all. His stomach growled loudly, letting him know that he should be contemplating a way to get some food.

Before any other thought could make its way through his head, a computerized voice threw a series of strange syllables at him. Jordan took in the entire room, studying all four walls. The voice came again, polite, smooth and at times high-pitched, like that of a young boy whose voice had not fully developed. The words were completely unrecognizable.

"What?" Jordan asked aloud. "Who's there?"

More sounds seemed to erupt from every corner of the tiny room.

"I can't understand," Jordan said slowly.

What could it be? The men on the ship somehow trying to communicate with him? Had they find out what these women were about? A long series of syllables rumbled off into the empty room.

Jordan stood and said loudly, "I have no idea what you are saying!"

There was the sound of moving panels and suddenly he was being sprayed with cool water. Suds and a piece of cloth appeared out of nowhere. Jordan stood stunned for a moment before beginning to wash. A warm spray rinsed him, and then a vacuum-like suction of air completely dried his body, as well as his boxers.

Feeling completely refreshed, Jordan stretched and flexed, curious to know how a room could be flooded with water and suds one minute and completely dry the next.

"Strange," he said to himself.

"Strange," the computerized voice echoed.

"What did you say?" Jordan calmly asked. "Who said that?" He was going to get answers from *someone* today.

"Say? Said?" someone or something repeated in question.

"Yes, say. What did you say?"

"Say. Say what? Say," it went on as patient and polite as before.

"Again with the say? Okay, should I say my name? Jordan Mitchell, Jr. Age? Thirty-one. Home? New Orleans, Louisiana, uptown, right next to Audubon Park. Maybe I should have said my home planet. It's Earth, where I wish to return. My mission? To release every Earth man from the clutches of these strange, alien women," Jordan told the voice just as calmly and politely as it had spoken, not caring who on the spacecraft knew of his plans.

"Good."

"What's so good?"

"Thank you. I have now assimilated enough of your language to be of assistance."

"Good! Assist me by getting me out of here."

"I cannot, only your Higher-ling may do that."

"My Higher-ling?

"The one you obey. Your mate."

"I have no mate."

"Somewhat true."

"Completely true. Exactly what are you?"

"Translated in your language I would be called your assistant. Comfort 1 at your service."

"If you can't assist me in escaping this closet, what are you good for?"

"Daily functions, cleaning, a listening ear."

"Sounds like a woman's dream machine."

"A male's."

Jordan brushed that answer aside as he realized that this computer—machine, whatever it was—could be his first step toward getting home. "Tell me, what exactly is going on aboard this spacecraft."

"Going on?"

"What will become of the Earth men on board?"

"They are here to benefit the sisters of Vixen."

"How?"

"To serve."

"Meaning?" Jordan asked, feeling like he was getting nowhere.

"To obey."

"Then we are to be slaves?"

"I cannot see how that could possibly be suggested."

"What else could I assume?"

"Assumptions are not becoming to a half-ling."

"Do you consider the other men and myself half-lings?"

"Almost."

"What are we then?"

"Future half-lings."

"Meant to serve and obey the sisters of Vixen?"

"Yes."

"Slaves, then."

"No."

"You are talking in circles." Jordan forced himself to speak slowly, pulling in a calming, measured breath.

"And so are you."

True, Jordan thought, and directed his questions to discovering other important facts. "Where are we headed?"

"The planet Vixen in the Roma Galaxy."

"What type of power source does this spacecraft run on? Are there any shuttlecraft that are easily accessible? And if there are, how many men can one craft hold?"

"These are questions you should not be asking, questions no half-ling has ever asked before. Do not do so again."

Dead silence filled the small chamber.

"Comfort 1," Jordan called, waiting to hear the voice once more.

"I need a listening ear," he tried again.

"How about some answers?" Still nothing.

Wonderful. His first lead had turned into a dead end. Jordan sat in the middle of the room and sifted through his mind, trying to recall everything that had happened to him, but found there were too many missing pieces to get an accurate picture.

Jordan stood and roamed from one end of the chamber to the other. Twelve steps forward, twelve steps back. He wondered how long the commander expected him to stay shut up in this tiny, bare room. Well, almost bare, he realized, when he noticed strange symbols spread out at various intervals on the three solid walls. Beside each symbol were what looked to be small, oval-shaped buttons. Since he had been put in there to keep him out of trouble, Jordan figured it wouldn't hurt to investigate, and it might just lead to…

Something.

Getting a closer look, Jordan traced the outline of a shape with his finger. A light came on, bright in the dim chamber. Each one he touched lit up until the wall became a colorful, solid brightness.

"May I assist you in making a selection?" Comfort 1's voice filled the room.

"No, go away. I don't need you," Jordan told the computer, still annoyed with its lack of response earlier.

"But you may—"

"I said no, go away!" Jordan commanded, completely out of patience.

"If you insist," the voice seemed to sob.

"I insist." Jordan growled with no remorse.

Turning his attention back to the wall, he saw a flashing blue light on the left that seemed to call out to him. Blue was his favorite color. *Why not try it first?* Jordan thought as he pushed the palm of his hand against the flashing light.

Nothing happen.

Nothing happened for at least ten seconds. Then everything happened.

The entire wall turned, taking with it the flashing blue light as well as all the others. Water began to flood into the chamber. This was no warm, cozy shower. Icy cold water rose, reached his shoulders in no time. There was nothing anywhere in the room to stand on, no way to elevate himself above the flood of water that had now reached his ears.

He could use Comfort 1's help, he realized, as he took a final gulp of air, but it was too late to ask for it. The water now covered his head. Although there seemed to be nothing he could do to help himself, he refused to die aboard this spaceship in such an insignificant way.

He couldn't get out of this jam by himself but the commander was out there; still asleep from what he could see, but out there. Jordan banged his fists and kicked against the clear wall, desperate to get the commander's attention.

It shimmered and wobbled, flexible as plastic, reminding him of the wall that had thinned and created a hole causing him to lose his gun and have a view of Earth he had never in his life wanted to see.

Earth.

Home.

His lungs burning from lack of oxygen, Jordan concentrated. Pressing his palms together in prayer-like fashion, he pushed them forward, then spread them wide, creating a hole in the wall. Water immediately gushed out. Holding the opening steady with both hands, Jordan thrust his head through to the other side, gulping lifesaving air into his lungs. The wall closed in around his neck, stopping the flow of water. His head fit like a cork plugged into a hole of an old-fashioned wooden beer barrel.

Jordan looked across the room to find the commander sitting on the edge of her bed staring at him for what seemed like forever. Jordan knew he looked strange with his head sticking out of the middle of a wall but it *was* obvious that he needed help.

"Freeing me would be appreciated," he told her, blinking water from his eyes.

She said not a word but stood and flowed toward him as if nothing out of the ordinary was happening. She pressed a few buttons. The wall vanished, just long enough for him to fall forward before reappearing in time to hold back the flood of water. She pressed a few more buttons and the water quickly drained from the chamber.

"Some buttons like that on the other side would have been a good idea."

"But unnecessary. You had Comfort 1 to see to your needs," she said without turning. "Why was the cleansing mode activated?"

"Cleansing mode, huh? I guess I just learned what the flashing blue button was for." His body convulsed with a colossal shiver he was unable to control.

"I did not think that you could possibly harm yourself." She paused as she turned around in the middle of berating him to study him with such intensity that Jordan felt like a gigolo on display.

"Go back into the chamber, dry off and request from Comfort 1 some garments to wear." She turned away from him without another word.

CHAPTER 3

Verena was pleased.

Despite the pale one's troublesome ways and the near fatal mishap, she was more certain than ever that her choice in mate would prove satisfactory. Never had she seen a male so completely perfect in his natural state. Of course she had viewed the visual-tapes of the men of Earth and had even seen those aboard the ship from a distance. But to have one so well formed and nearly bare standing a few feet away, and knowing that he was hers, sent a sense of pride and desire through her that she had never experienced before.

"Put your mind to important matters," she reminded herself. "Males are males, a small portion of life. Though essential for procreation, they are not the center of all things."

Still, an anxious chuckle unlike any sound she had made before escaped her lips as she pictured once again her future half-ling's face poking out of the wall, his body surrounded by water and trapped on the other side. Though experiencing humor as well as some other strange emotion from the memory, she was also impressed by the inventive manner in which he had saved himself. If she went by his example, these Earth men were very resourceful. Any other male would have died in such a mishap. But he was not an ordinary male, she reminded herself. He had had enough strength to create a hole in the krylogin, the fiber plastic the wall was made of, so that he could save himself. No male from Vixen had ever done that before.

Not allowing herself a moment more to reflect on him, Verena went to the console designed to keep her abreast of every aspect of the ship. She spoke briefly to the various commanders of each sector, leaving Suvan, the commander of the Earth men, for last.

"How do you fare?" Verena asked without preamble.

"Good day, Commander. All is well, for now."

"Meaning?"

"I have convinced the majority of the males that I am a force to be recognized and that they must follow my orders while working at the construction site."

"You cannot mean that you, a *female*, actually had to prove yourself to these males."

"As I informed you, the males of Earth seem to believe themselves superior to females."

"So you have told me. But the idea is difficult to acknowledge. I realize they are different from what we are used to but have not reconciled myself to the degree that it is so."

"Then you have not viewed the history?"

"No, I have been relying on your expertise."

"That I appreciate, Commander, but your knowledge and input would be most valuable."

"Hey! Susie girl, ain't it time for lunch yet!"

Verna's eyes widened at the sound of a deep male voice coming through the console. "Such insolence. Who is that? I have no doubt that you will see to taking care of the situation," Verena said, appalled at the volume, tone and familiarity of the voice.

"Bruce, the only black hole in our sky of otherwise bright lights," Suvan answered. "He will need special attention."

"Susie!" Verena heard once again.

"Susie?" the commander asked.

"His name for me. He will be taken care of, Commander."

"See to it."

"You are insolent and impolite but clothed, I hope," Verena said to the pale one without turning away from the console.

"I'm dressed. At least I think I am. What language was that you were speaking?"

"Once again insolent and impolite, I see."

"The insolence and impoliteness can be summed up as curiosity."

"Curiosity blew up the crit." She turned to take in his attire, noticing that he stood quite some distance away. The robes given to him did not do much to hide the muscular build she'd had the pleasure of viewing before. The length barely reached mid-thigh and the sleeves did not reach his elbows, leaving in view the sight of firm thighs and strong forearms beneath pale skin that stirred her deeply inside. "Those garments were not made for a male of your size," she said to channel her thoughts more productively.

"I noticed." He looked down at himself, displaying no modestly in the amount of flesh that was exposed.

Of course Verena should not have been surprised since he had shown none when earlier, he stood before her wearing much less.

"Shouldn't you have said curiosity killed the cat?"

"No, I say what I mean."

"On Earth, the saying is 'curiosity killed the cat.' I assume you have crits on this planet of yours."

"Do not make assumptions. But yes, we do have a type of feline similar to your cat."

"Why is yours different?"

"More questions?" Verena asked, not really minding this time. She was in the mood to speak to her future half-ling. He was very entertaining. She busied herself at the console, noting their speed, location in relation to Vixen and the distance they had traveled while she had rested—all information she had already obtained. But she felt the need to appear busy as she awaited his response.

"Questions are the only way one learns anything."

"But they can be dangerous, deadly even."

"You're referring to the crit that blew up."

"Certainly. He gained too much knowledge of things *he* could in no way comprehend or use. His brain filled and exploded."

"*His* brain?"

"Of course."

Without a word the pale one turned away from her, and having had no permission to do so moved toward the side chamber as if he had a right to go, all without uttering one word of thanks for saving his life earlier. With a mere touch of the screen before her, the door to the chamber closed, stopping him from going inside.

"I did not grant you permission to leave my presence," she said to his back, which had stiffened at the closing of the door.

"May I go into my closet of death?" he asked, his back still facing her.

"Did you speak? I did not see your mouth move?"

He slowly faced her. The anger he emitted was a living thing, though carefully held within.

"May I go into my closet of death?"

"You may go into the side chamber if you wish, but only after you have shown to me appreciation for saving your life."

"You can't be serious."

He began the gazing game again, breathing deeply as he kept his eyes on her. Intrigued, she watched as his fist uncurled and his head lowered until his chin met his chest, losing eye contact with her for the briefest moment before he spoke again.

"I thank you, Verena the Commander, for yanking me from my home planet, lulling me into a three-day coma, locking me into a closet without food or water and nearly causing me to drown because I couldn't free myself from the prison to which I am more than happy to return so that I may be removed from your presence."

"Dismissed." She waved a hand at him, both surprised and appalled not only by the words but also the vast number of them he had thrown at her. Of course she could not let him see this. Allowing a male to get the better of one was asking for trouble. They would think too much of themselves and create all sorts of dissension in a union. It was best to ignore his temper as she had seen her mother do in the handling of her father.

Yes, that was what she would do, but something he had said had disturbed her.

No food or water? Verena went to the console and did a diagnostic on Comfort 1's functions, a menial task that a commander would not usually undertake. But she could not have her future half-ling starving to death before providing her with descendants. At least that's what she told herself over and over again until the test proved that no malfunctions existed.

"Comfort 1," Verena commanded.

"Y-y-y-yes," a nervous voice responded.

"Explain my future half-ling's lack of nourishment."

"Commander, he did not request any. He only sat and then moved about with kicks and jumps and various wild movements. I cooled his body with refreshing air and offered a cleansing shower even before it was requested."

"You did not offer food or drink?"

"Commander, I am merely a male's companion and not equipped with advance language functions. I could not speak until he spoke enough of his native tongue so that I might make the offering. Then he grew angry with me."

"Offer him some nourishment now and see that no harm comes to him."

"As you command."

"Comfort 1, if harm does come upon him, disablement will come upon you."

"U-u-understood, Commander."

That bit of benevolence and show of caring for his well-being should put the pale one in a proper mood, Verena thought, feeling quite pleased with herself as she returned to the responsibilities of commanding *Vixen II*.

"Good day, Jordan Mitchell, Jr." The computerized voice invaded what Jordan considered to be his prison.

He did not pause in his workout, continuing the exercises that helped him calm down and collect himself.

"I have offerings of food."

At that Jordan ended the session, bowing to the room in general. "Go on," he told the voice.

"I know you are still angry with me."

"Now why would I be angry? You refuse to answer my questions and haven't been one bit of help. You even deserted me when I needed you the most."

"You told me to go away," the computer squeaked.

"Then," Jordan continued, "you gave me clothes that didn't fit and made me look like a sissy. I felt like a fool in front of the almighty commander."

"Almighty is not necessary. You may say commander," the computer corrected, adding, "the robes were all I had available."

"My own clothes would have been nice."

"I have just finished refreshing them."

Jordan's clothes lay on a shelf that had just eased out of the wall. He immediately changed into them, throwing the ridiculous miniature robe to a corner of the room where it was quickly pulled beyond one of the walls. "What were you saying about food?"

"What is your pleasure?"

"To be taken home."

"That cannot be done. I am to provide nourishment."

"Then provide away." Jordan answered, resigned to getting whatever he could from his supposed assistant.

"If you would please come over to the far-left wall and make certain to avoid the flashing blue light, I can assist you."

"No problem," Jordan readily agreed as Comfort 1 explained the meaning of the various lighted buttons and symbols. Not only was there a machine dispensing foods he was familiar with, but a rollaway pallet that eased out of the wall with the touch of one of the oval lights, a hideaway sink-like bowl to use when needed and an abundance of other gadgets he could not begin to describe.

His hunger taken care of and all the various gadgets put away, Jordan sat in the middle of the room. Resigned to the fact that he was stuck in this room once again and having no other means of obtaining information, Jordan decided to try once more to get what he could out of the only source available to him. "I just might be able to forgive you, Comfort 1," he began.

"Thank you, thank you, and thank you! The commander will be so pleased!"

"Is that so?"

"I have been directed to feed, clothe and keep you out of harm's way."

"By the commander herself?"

"Indeed," the voice threw out with pride. "I have had the pleasure of being personally commanded by the Mighty-one. It is a rare thing for a Comfort model to be addressed by any female. I feel deeply honored to have been recognized."

The ring of pride annoyed Jordan, as if being commanded by Verena the Abductor was a thing to aspire to. "What would happen if you were unable to do as you were commanded?"

"Well, then I would be—"

"Be what?" Jordan asked at the sudden silence.

"Disabled."

This information sparked an idea. He would have to be deceitful, which wasn't like him, but his life and the lives of other Earth men were at stake.

Jordan jumped up from his sitting position, revved and ready to put his plan into action. "So-o-o," he said as he strolled to the wall where the symbols and buttons shone bright. "If I accidentally leaned against," his hand pushed at the flashing blue button, "this button..." Water began to flood the room as before.

"What are you doing?" Comfort 1 squeaked.

The room immediately drained of the water that had already reached his knees. The panel of lights turned into the wall once again, causing Jordan to lose his balance and fall. He easily caught himself, but using the fall to his advantage, lingered on the floor and moaned as if in serious pain.

"Oh no! Oh no! What have I done? My first direct command and I've already failed."

Jordan continued to moan.

"Jordan Mitchell, Jr., what do you desire? A cold compress?"

A cold, thin, rectangular piece of cloth landed on his head.

"No," Jordan answered low and painfully. The cloth disappeared.

"A hot compress?" the computer asked nervously.

An identical piece of material landed on his head. It felt warm to the touch.

"Owww!" Jordan screamed, improvising yet another injury.

"Oh no, did I injure you more? Are you sensitive to heat? Disablement will be my fate for sure."

Slowly, carefully, Jordan inched into a sitting position. "I'll be okay, Comfort 1."

"Thank goodness." A computerized sigh filled the room.

"It is just my wrist." Jordan held it up. His hand flapped uselessly downward. He flipped his hand up a couple of times, allowing it to fall as if he had no control over it.

"Is it broken? Let me scan it."

The room experienced a quick flash. Jordan didn't anticipate this but should have realized that Comfort 1 would be capable of detecting broken bones.

"It is not broken, praise Vixianne."

"But it hurts. What have you done to me?" Jordan moaned, laying it on thick. "Call the commander now. I want to tell her what a horrible, mean computer you are."

"No, you don't want to do that," Comfort 1 said in what sounded somewhat like a soothing tone. "We all know that males tend to get emotional. I believe you should think before doing anything rash."

Males get emotional? The constant put-down on males in general was becoming a disturbing constant with these aliens. Even the computer was infected with it.

Playing along, rising to the role of a defenseless *male*, Jordan asked, "What should I do?"

"Do not say a word to the commander. Allow me to wrap it and I will treat you to anything your heart desires."

"Anything?" Jordan asked, satisfied with how easily his plan was working.

"Anything."

"Okay," Jordan agreed, hoping the reluctance he tried to portray didn't sound as phony as it felt.

The worry and panic in Comfort 1's voice miraculously transformed into a relieved, "Good."

As instructed, Jordan placed his perfectly well hand into a small circular opening in the wall. He felt something wrapping it and in a matter of seconds, removed his expertly bound hand.

"Now when the commander requests your presence, we will quickly remove it and pretend that there is nothing wrong."

"If you say so," Jordan whined.

"Good male."

"Now tell me, what is your desire?"

Jordan had many answers for that question.

First and foremost he wanted to get himself and every Earth man home.

He wanted to know where they were located.

He wanted to know how to run this ship or any other kind of vessel he could get his hands on.

He wanted many things but he was sure Comfort 1 would not part with such information despite the secret between them.

No, he had to shoot for something simple that would help him to gain knowledge of the things he wanted most.

"I want you to teach me the language of Vixen."

"Teach you? I do not know. You may not be capable of learning. That is why all the Sisters of Vixen are knowledgeable of your native tongue."

"Are you saying I am too dumb to learn? There you go being mean all over again." Jordan put into play his acting skills. "I'm going to tell the commander this and everything else you've done."

"No, no. Don't do that. You are not dumb, but the language of Vixen is not a simple thing to learn."

"Then you're not smart enough to teach me?"

"Of course I am smart enough."

"Okay." Jordan sat cross-legged in the middle of the room. "Let's start."

And so Jordan's first step toward getting what he needed depended on him pretending to be a senseless, bubble-headed blond. Never in his life had he acted less like himself.

Never in his life had he needed to rely so heavily on the philosophy of Karate-do, challenging himself to be self-disciplined enough to be something other then himself so that justice could prevail.

CHAPTER 4

Verena sat before the viewer, her pride in finding the best compatible species quickly shrinking as she observed the history of the Earth men. Physical attributes and the immunity to the unknown plague that had killed all half-lings of Vixen had been the priority in the mind of every sister of Vixen. No consideration had been given to the traditions and habits of Earth men. They were, after all, only males.

Disturbed by what she found, Verena immediately called a meeting of her most trusted officers.

She waited on their arrival, moving across the floor in one direction and then the other. Realizing what she was doing, Verena halted in the middle of the room. She had been doing what the pale one had done many times when he was angry or nervous.

Verena was neither.

And most importantly, it was unbecoming to adopt such habits from a male, no matter how attractive he looked as he moved about before her, the bulges on his arms and legs most noticeable and calling for her touch. Verna glanced at the transparent door of the side chamber. There he sat in the middle of the room, most probably conversing with Comfort 1 as she had noticed him doing often in the past. Males were so easily occupied and enter-tained, as the sisters' creation of the Comfort series proved.

Males had, at times, demanded more of a female's attention than it was possible to give. The computer was designed as a toy for males to keep them busy and happy and females free from their demands. Everyone had been pleased.

Verena tilted her head to get a better view of the pale one. He was wearing no more than the short cloth that covered his private parts. She wanted to summon him to her, but knew it would only be another meeting of frustration.

He still did not understand or in any way accept his fate with her. And she did not wish to use force or punishment upon him. Verena wanted the pale one to come to her willingly and with gratitude for all the wonders she had to offer him. He would have a life of privilege and comfort if he would only willingly submit. It was the strange ways of his planet that were at fault.

"You have summoned us, Commander?" Zytai asked, surprising Verena, for she had not heard the signal that usually announced any arrival.

Taking her eyes from the pale one, she turned to address Zytai, Explorations Officer; Rya, Engine Master; and Suvan, Species Expert.

"Yes, we must plan what direction to take to insure the submission of our future half-lings."

"What is wrong, Jordan Mitchell, Jr.?"

"Nothing, and stop calling me that."

"You have told me this before. That is your name. If I do not call you Jordan Mitchell, Jr., what shall I call you?"

"J.M.," Jordan answered, a distinct warmth spreading through his veins. If he looked up, Jordan knew who he would see at the crystal clear wall, but he refused to look in the direction of the gaze that was demanding his attention. Instead, he turned his attention to Comfort 1's lesson.

"Shall we continue? I congratulate you, for you must be an advanced male. You are learning the language quite rapidly."

Jordan ignored the off-handed compliment, having heard so many like it from Comfort 1 in the last week. "Let's get with it."

"Get with what?"

"The lesson, let's continue," Jordan explained, forgetting how literally Comfort 1 took slang. He had already learned words and phrases for everyday items that were similar to Vixen and Earth, general terms and various space-related words. He had practiced using them in sentences and tried his best to speak in the language of Vixen whenever possible. Jordan was slowly inching toward using his lessons as a backdoor to getting answers from Comfort 1.

He rotated his shoulders and adjusted his sitting position as the warmth and a rushing flow of blood made its way downward. He glanced at the instant hardness between his thighs. Why didn't she just leave him alone? Jordan preferred to be ignored.

"Why do you squirm? Do you need to wave, jump and throw your arms and legs about?" Comfort 1 asked.

"It's called karate, a form of exercise. I've already told you that."

"This I know, J.M., but I like to say it my way."

Hearing Comfort 1 use his nickname soothed him. Whenever Comfort 1 used his full name, unwanted memories connected with his father flashed inside his head. "Sure thing, C1."

"C1? I like that shortened form of title."

"It's called a nickname.

"You may use this nickname, refer to me as C1 at all times, if you wish."

"I wish. Now, let's continue."

Jordan attempted to get back into the lesson, but the persistent hardness between his thighs and *her* eyes on him were too much of a distraction. "Why does she do that?" Jordan asked, interrupting Comfort 1's translation of body parts.

"Stare at you?"

"Yes."

"Because you are hers to stare at."

"No, I am not."

"Must we go through this again, J.M.?"

"No." Jordan did not want to hear about serving and following orders. He didn't want to hear about being a slave. It wasn't going to happen. Jordan rejected every attempt of C1 to inform him of his role to Verena the Commander.

"This is why you cannot concentrate on the lesson. Her look has left you wanting."

"Not at all." With those words the intensity of Jordan's desire for her eased to a banked ache. He relaxed, attributing his decrease of sexual frustration to his own willpower, but soon found out otherwise.

C1 issued a computerized version of a patronizing sigh. Jordan relaxed a bit more despite the sound.

"As you say, J.M. It is only a matter of time before—"

"Look, someone's come in." Verena the Commander's attention was no longer on him. So much for willpower easing his suffering; her sudden change of focus was what had done it. "She's never had company before."

"Not since I have been activated to serve you, no."

"I know these aliens, at least two of them." Jordan thought a minute. "Zytai and Rya."

"You should not refer to them by their first names. How *do* you know their names?"

"That's not important. What are they saying?"

"That is another thing you do not need to know."

"Are they speaking in Vixen? Let me hear what they're saying. It will give me a chance to see how well I understand the language."

"Allowing you to hear will only get me disabled."

"A lot of things can get you disabled." Jordan remained on the floor, pretending an outward disinterest in a scene that couldn't interest him more. The alien called Zytai was speaking. He was dying to know what was being said.

"You are no longer in pain. You have used that hand in your karate. And *I* have been very nice to you."

"True, but…" Jordan searched his mind for something to blackmail C1 with. *Anything.* "You have never given me my favorite food," he threw out.

"I have given you everything you desire."

"Not my favorite."

"Tell me and I will provide it," the computer squeaked, a bit of desperation tinting its voice.

One of the aliens was speaking, the only one in the room he did not know by name. Jordan had to know what was going on. This was too good an opportunity. Slipping into the role he hated he wailed, "You mean you don't know? I shouldn't have to tell you! You are supposed to know these things! I'm going to have to tell the commander."

"No, no, J.M. Do not," Comfort 1 said in a high-pitched panic. "Maybe…"

Jordan held a pout and issued a steady whine, disgusting himself completely as he waited for the computer to continue.

"Maybe I should let you listen. It will be a productive lesson. Does that make you happy?"

"Yes," Jordan sniffed. "Quick, let me hear." Every trace of Jordan's whiny facade disappeared in an instant.

"The males will be difficult to control," Verena the Commander was saying.

The words of her own native tongue rolled off the commander's lips, holding a musical quality that Jordan found…

…sexy?

He shook his head. She had to have done something to him that caused him to find everything about her sexy as hell.

"But we must find a way," Rya said to them all.

51

"Agreed, we have all viewed their history. It is a good thing we chose this America to visit." Verena was saying.

Visit? Jordan thought. *More like pillage and steal human slaves.*

"Their thoughts on females are more agreeable then some other places on Earth," Suvan agreed. "But still very much opposite to our own."

"Completely so," Rya agreed.

"Intolerable," Zytai added.

"Suvan," Verena spoke again. "You have had much more contact with them. Would training be impossible?"

"Training," Jordan whispered, holding himself very still as he listened. Maybe they *were* going to be part of a circus.

"It would be difficult."

"But not impossible."

"That, I can not be sure of. These men of Earth are most unpredictable. Perhaps if they had the right incentive..." Suvan paused. "They are becoming restless and complain of boredom. The men work all day and recline to the temporary houses we have replicated on the site. But that does not seem to be enough."

"Work them harder and longer then."

"That will not work, Commander, unless we reveal ourselves to them. They are all part of some union—"

"They already have mates?"

"No, a group that makes rules on how much time they should work and how much money they are paid."

"Then we may have to reveal ourselves to them."

"With all respect, Commander, how has that worked for you? The future half-ling you have chosen is the only

Earth male who knows who we are. Has he willingly come to accept his fate?"

All eyes turned to him.

Jordan knew they were focused on him.

Not only because he saw them turn as one, but because he felt *her* eyes and *her* effect on him. Jordan closed his own in feigned meditation.

"No," Verena answered.

"Commander, you have chosen well," Rya said. "I feel his response to you."

"And your mark on him," Zytai added. "He was meant for you."

His response? These women knew how sexually frustrated he was. It was bad enough that *she* knew, that C1 knew. Jordan squashed an urge to place a hand over his lap. That action would not hide whatever it was that they sensed and would only reveal that he could hear and understand every word that was spoken.

"He is trying to ignore us," Suvan remarked.

"That is the response I get often."

"If this is a common reaction, then we cannot reveal ourselves to them yet. We do not wish the males to ignore us," Rya observed.

"Not as sisters of Vixen," Suvan slowly announced. "But we can pretend to be Earth women and in the meeting make our future half-lings true half-lings and announce it to them all once we have reached Vixen."

"I do not wish to pretend to be an Earth woman," Zytai protested.

"It will only be temporary," Verena assured her.

"They are bored and seek entertainment. We will be their entertainment."

"This may all be a waste of time," Zytai suggested.

"But necessary, I believe," Verena insisted. "Rya, how long before we reach Vixen?"

"In about thirty Earth days."

"Proceed with the plan. In the meantime I will see if I can gain some insight on the men of Earth from a direct source. Good day."

"Good day, Commander." Each of the aliens, with a graceful twist of a wrist, bid Verena the Commander good-bye.

She was coming toward him.

"Are you happy now, J.M.? Please tell me that you are happy."

"I am happy, C1." As happy as he could be knowing that fellow Earth men were about to be duped even more than they already were and eventually trapped on a planet that was even further from home than he realized.

The panel opened.

"Come," she said to him in English. The sound of his own language was not as pleasurable to his ears as the language of Vixen. She sat on the edge of the large oval bed and motioned for him to do the same on the much smaller pallet beside it.

"Tell me of Earth," she requested.

Keeping hidden all that he had heard, keeping hidden any outward sign of his desire for her, Jordan told her of Earth.

"Earth is the third planet in our solar system. It is about ninety-three million miles away from the sun."

She nodded and smiled at him, so Jordan went on.

"Our solar system is located in the Milky Way Galaxy. Bet you didn't know that the Milky Way is a spiral galaxy with about a ka-billion stars. But then you probably did, considering the fact that you searched out the planet with intent to steal men, or is abduct a better word?"

Verena the Commander ignored the jibe, her smile actually growing, "Tell me more."

So Jordan threw out tons of facts about the solar system, the continents, oceans and as many different kinds of land forms as he could name. After about an hour of talking, Jordan was at a point where he was searching his brain for any bit information.

She stood, and laying a hand on his shoulder said, "Thank you, pale one. I would like to know more about your planet. We will continue this conversation at the same hour tomorrow. Good day."

Jordan stood there, uncertain as to what he was supposed to do.

CHAPTER 5

"Commander!" Rya stormed into the chamber. Verena once again had not heard the signal for her arrival. She had spent another hour listening to the mundane monologue of the pale one as she gazed upon him, just as she had done every day this past week. Her need to make him hers had grown as she spent more time in his direct presence.

"Verena!" Rya skidded to a halt before her. The absence of her usual grace and use of her first name before the pale one indicated some terrible misfortune.

"Rya, become calm," Verena demanded in their native tongue.

"It is most difficult, Commander, when the men have formed a force that could ruin all our plans." Rya followed her lead, answering in Vixen.

Sensing the pale one's intense interest despite knowing that he couldn't understand the language, Verena commanded him to leave with a flick of her wrist. He stood beside her, a look of incomprehension on his face as Rya stood on her other side panting. "To the side chamber."

"Pardon me?" he boldly asked.

Making the easiest choice, Verena folded her arms. "To the side chamber," she repeated, then slowly pushed past her lips the word she knew he wanted to hear. "Please."

He nodded and quickly did as he was told. Seeing him obey the command eased her frustration at somehow being tricked into falling into the Earth custom of *manners,* as the pale one called them. Her second day into questioning him, he had somehow extracted from her a commitment to use words such as *please, thank you* and *excuse me* when speaking to him.

"Commander, the males!" Rya urged.

"Inform me of what has happened."

"Let's hear what's going on out there, C1," Jordan said as soon as the door to the chamber the commander had so politely demanded he go back to slid close.

"Disablement, disablement will come to me for sure," the computer moaned but did as was requested.

"The large male named Bruce with the loud resounding voice has threatened to leave the construction site and take a large number of the other males with him." Rya's voice came into the side chamber.

"Why is that a matter of concern? Allow him to leave. Where can he go?"

"He can go nowhere, Commander, which is the problem. He wishes to walk back to the city, this New Orleans, if that is the only way to get there. He will surely discover that the construction site is false and we have no means to develop the entire city he wishes to relocate to. We have already diverted too much power to creating the exercise gym and the sports area for entertainment and a meeting place."

57

"I see your point," Verena said, folding and unfolding her arms.

I see your problem, Jordan grinned, taking pleasure in the view. Arms crossed meant the commander was worried.

"Our plan had been going so well. We cannot relinquish it. We cannot allow one male to ruin our progress. This Bruce, hasn't Suvan controlled him in the past?"

"Yes, but she is ill."

"We will need a show of force to calm him."

"He does not think much of females."

"Then we need a male to intervene."

"So you women of Vixen are finally realizing that men are more useful than just as baby-making machines." Jordan paced, voicing the words he had been dying to say to the commander's face since he first learned the true purpose for the Vixens' visit to Earth. He would have never considered the possibility of an alien species invading his planet and stealing men for procreation. It was such an improbable idea that it had taken this past week to thoroughly sink into his brain.

Hours of meditation and an intense willpower he had not known he possessed kept Jordan sane enough to sit through the daily, hour-long questioning sessions with the commander without confronting her. Giving in to the urge would reveal the only upper hand he had—knowledge of their language. It would also guarantee disablement for C1.

That, Jordan could not have. C1 was his best source of information.

His ally.

His friend.

His only team member.

His team. Jordan hadn't thought about his team in so long. He missed them, the comfort and security of knowing they were there for him. C1 had somehow taken their place. The computer was much more than a machine. C1 provided comfort for his everyday needs, companionship and the security of knowing that he could get almost any information he needed.

Information.

He had gotten a ton of that.

And that wasn't all. C1 would eventually provide him with a way back home.

All Jordan had to do was get access to the men aboard the ship, open their eyes to what was happening, incite a riot, take over the ship and fly them all back home.

Not easy, but not impossible either.

"What of your half-ling, Rya?" The commander's voice rose. "Tell him to intervene." The two women stood staring at each other, looking less like commander and officer and more like equals.

Jordan had settled into a meditation pose that would allow him to listen without being noticed. Rya, so far, was the only Vixen who had successfully snagged an Earth man as her mate, though the poor sap didn't know it. C1, still unable to provide Jordan with his favorite food, had allowed him to not only hear but see it all happen, providing a personalized version of a monitoring screen that Jordan was able to hold in the palm of his hand.

MISSION

It was like watching a blossoming relationship on a movie screen. Jordan had written it all down in a journal he had begun when the commander started her questioning sessions.

Day one: They met at the new gym the aliens had created. Rya. She was the only one of them I sort of liked. She portrayed herself as sweet and innocent. Michael Joseph ate it all up.

Day two: Rya brought that poor sap a picnic lunch at work. He got ribbed. Michael didn't care. He was hooked.

Day three: Rya convinced Michael to experience a special treatment in a room in the back of the gym. He went. C1 refused to let me see what was going on inside, saying that the Ceremony of Unity was sacred and could not be witnessed by an outsider. But when the couple came out, both were full of smiles as wide as the arcs of Uranus. Michael's head was shaved except for the smallest bit of hair at the back of his head in the shape of a diamond.

This first fall of my fellow Earth men worries me. Though the men teased Michael, I could sense a bit of jealousy. They wanted what Michael had. Being away from home, family and friends, they will more easily fall in with what the women of Vixen have planned.

"I have suggested to Michael that he do something to quiet this Bruce," Rya finally answered.

"Suggested? He is your half-ling. Command him to do as you say!"

"Just as you command your future half-ling, Verena?"

Arms folding and unfolding, Verena twisted her lips. "You can get away with speaking so freely because our mothers are kin sisters and we have spent many years together."

"And because it is true."

"That as well, Rya. We may have to follow the ways of the Earth men during this journey, but when we get to our home planet this situation will be rectified."

"I hope that is true. But what do we do about this loud Bruce man?"

"We will have to use the pale one." The commander looked over at him. Jordan felt her eyes and his instant reaction to her focus on him.

"How will we ensure that he cooperates?"

"We will provide a few promises to appease him. It won't be difficult to outwit him. I had at one time begun to think that he was different from other males, more intelligent than the males of our planet. I was almost certain of this, but after spending a great deal more time with him…"

"You have discovered something?"

"Yes, that I must have been mistaken. The other Earth men seem to have more intelligence than my future halfling."

"You seem disappointed by this," Rya said.

Through stilted eyelids, Jordan watched as Rya placed a comforting hand on the commander's shoulder. The almost human interaction began to soften the sting of the insult to his intelligence.

Why *should* he be so insulted? Jordan tossed the prick of offense aside. He had succeeded. The image of a dumb blond, the one he had worked hard to present, had stuck.

"I am not disappointed. The pale one is only a male. What more should I expect?"

"From these Earth men? I would expect the unusual."

"I will keep that in mind. Now, sit with me and let us create a plan."

As they sat on the edge of the bed, their voices lowered in a conspiratorial manner. The sight of their heads pressed together reminded him of an advertisement he'd seen in one of Troy's *Jet* magazines. Beautiful and sexy, they looked like models. But Verena, of course, was the more beautiful of the two.

Not caring for the direction of his thoughts and the fact that he was missing out on important information, Jordan stood. "I can't hear, C1. Amplify."

A low whine preceded his request. Jordan began to pace as bits and pieces of the conversation filled the room. He had missed it all. He had no idea how they planned to use him. Disgusted with himself, he moved across the room at a faster pace.

"Pale one."

Jordan was surprised to see Verena and Rya standing before him, the side chamber door wide open.

"Come." She waved a hand forward. "Please," she added when he stood without moving. Jordan caught an "I-told-you-so" look Rya tossed at Verena.

Jordan's hesitation hadn't been an effort to force pleasantries from her but a reaction to their sudden presence. He eased through his nostrils a steadying, mind-clearing breath, not liking that he had no idea what was coming next. But this could be the chance he had been waiting for, he reminded himself. *They* needed him.

As he stepped out of the chamber, Rya turned to the commander. "I will take my leave of you, Commander. Good day."

"Good day," the commander answered half-heartedly, her mind obviously occupied with how she was going to trick him into complying with her wishes.

The signal declaring Rya's departure was a distant sound as she gazed upon the pale one standing before her expectantly. If only his expectations included her right to touch and feel his body pressed against hers, she would be pleased. *Cease these thoughts*, Verena admonished herself. The entire mission was at stake.

"You *commanded* my presence?"

The pale one's voice interrupted her thoughts. Verena nodded, offering him a seat next to her on her own luxuriously soft sleeping pallet, an honor given to half-lings who had pleased their mates. He sat without a touch of appreciation showing on his handsome pale face or coming from his lips. The honor had obviously escaped him, for his face was completely blank.

How was it that she had once thought his face full of wondrous thoughts and secrets yet to be told? Who'd have thought that she would be disappointed because it was not so?

"What is it you want of me, Commander? More stories?"

More stories? Sisters of Vixen, save her. Verena did not think that she could suffer though another long tale told in the most deathlike voice that never seemed to cease. At least not until she had been away from him for a full day attending to her duties as commander with thoughts of the pale one floating into her mind like space dust at the most inappropriate times. She must speak to her mother about this strange happening. Was it normal to think so much about a male? Could it be because Verena knew him to be her future half-ling and had not yet claimed him in the Ceremony of Unity? Yes, that had to be it.

"Commander." He was standing before her wearing the strange Earth clothing she had become accustomed to. Verena found herself wishing that he had chosen to wear the new robes C1 had assembled for him. "If all you choose to do is sit and stare I would gladly return to my chamber."

He stood without asking, left the comfort of her pallet she had so graciously offered and was ready to leave her presence when all she could think about was being in his. Ungrateful male. "Back to the side chamber!" Verena wanted to order, but instead went on with the plan that she and Rya had created, that she had nearly forgotten. "Sit." When he did not comply, Verena softened her voice. "Sit." Then she remembered to add, "Please, I wish to do you a kindness."

He sat.

"A—kindness? Give me something that I want? Something to make me happy?"

This was going well. A smile stretched across her face, and her hands relaxed on her lap. "Yes, a kindness. I wish to make you happy," Verena allowed, feeling magnanimous.

"Release me. Take me home to Earth."

Verena's certainty of the ease of her plan deflated upon hearing the request. "Surely you have come to understand by now how that is impossible."

"No, I don't understand."

Of course not, his mind was much too simple and full of male thoughts to comprehend the gravity of the situation, the distance they had traveled and the complexities of space travel. Staring into his eyes, Verena felt sorry for him. "Maybe I will explain it all to you someday."

"I don't want it explained. If you want me to be happy, then take me back to Earth. Take every man on this ship back to Earth."

His face had changed. It was no longer blank. A passion and intense wanting had filled every inch of his skin. "And that would make you happy?" she asked, intrigued by him all over again.

"More than happy. Ecstatic!"

A light shone in his pale eyes of gray. He was so close. Happy? Yes, Verena would like to make him happy. Ecstatic? Yes, she wanted to fill him with ecstasy. Without taking a moment to think on her impulse, Verena reached for his face.

He did not pull away.

He didn't avoid her touch.

That simple act reminded Verena to tread slowly, to share her pleasures carefully.

The thrust of desire poured into her fingertips. Her eyes held his, first with a touch of unwillingness, then an equal degree of desire as Verena eased his entire body onto the pallet. Her other hand caressed the strange texture of his hair before she brought her lips to meet his.

Space and plans.

Vixen and survival.

And all other Earth men were distant, unimportant fading lights as the pale one did a strange act.

His lips moved upon hers.

His tongue went into her mouth.

Verena almost bit it, but the warm, gentle brush inside her mouth was stunningly pleasing, until he rolled upon her, pressing more firmly into her mouth.

The pleasure of what he was doing—

The shock of what he was doing—

—left her motionless for a moment.

What was he *doing* to her?

Whatever it was, it was not right. Verena pulled herself from under the pale one and stood staring at him as he lay upon the pallet, the strange light still in his eye. She folded and unfolded her arms as she tried to slow all the unsteady movements of every body part.

"You started it," he had the audacity to say as he eased into a sitting position.

"Remove yourself from my pallet," she ordered in a low, commanding tone.

"Sure," he told her easily. He stood and began walking back to the side chamber.

"Where are you going? I am not done with you."

"You aren't? But *you* were the one who ran away."

"I did not run. I was merely trying to make you happy. To give you pleasure." Verena stopped herself from explaining. She need not explain. He needed to do some explaining. "What was that you were doing to me?"

"Kissing you. I kissed you."

"You *kissed* me?" Such a strange word. But she had heard it used somewhere before. From her memory, a brief flash of a couple in a similar embrace ran through her head. She had seen it as she studied the records of Earth's history. She had not studied that portion for long. The act of copulation was the same, Suvan had assured her. There were obviously some subtle differences. She *must* speak to Rya.

"Yes, Commander, *we* kissed. As a matter of fact, you kissed me first." His tone of accusation pulled Verena out of her musings.

"I do not know of kiss. I was merely using your mouth as a channel to give you pleasure."

"So was I."

"But then you grappled me."

"Grappled?'

"Took over in a most unnatural way."

"Unnatural for who?'

"Any male. Males do not lead in the act of pleasure. You accept it. You receive it and are grateful for it."

"And happy?"

67

"Of course."

"Do me a favor? Please don't try to make me happy ever again." He turned once more to the side chamber.

His mention of happiness forced Verena to remember the plan and the problem of the loud Earth man. "Where are you going? I have not allowed you to leave my presence."

"Why should I stay? There is nothing you can do to make me happy."

"What of a visit with the other males? Would that please you?"

Verena had meant to throw it out as a treat, not a desperate plea. She wanted him to feel grateful for her great kindness. She wanted him to gush with his thank yous and make promises of undying gratitude for this favor.

The pale one turned to her and simply said, "Okay."

The one word answer was far less than what she had expected. A flood of disappointment rolled over her but Verena hid it well as she took command of the situation once again. "You may visit with one male."

"Fine."

"I must be present, and the conversation must center on work."

"If you say so. Can we go now?"

"There is one more necessary task. Come forward."

Cautiously taking the few steps to reach her, Jordan stood before her. Turning her palm upward, she revealed a tiny dart-like object resting on the tip of her finger.

"What's that?"

"A number of things," she answered, lifting her hand toward the side of his head.

Jordan laid a hand on her arm to stop its ascent. "What things?"

"This device is a locator as well as a communications system."

"You want to keep track of me. That makes sense, but what good's a communication device? Who would I communicate with?"

"Your Comfort Model."

"Oh, so this is a way to keep men happily on a leash."

She didn't reply, simply stared at his arm. Jordan removed his hand, immediately missing the pulsating warmth beneath his palm, somehow knowing that she had told him the truth. The commander had no intention of hurting him. If she had such an intention, she could have done so any number of times in the past week. Jordan stood still as her finger grazed a spot behind his ear. A sharp, needle-like pinch indicated that device had been attached.

"Are we ready to go now?" Jordan asked.

Verena issued a slight, superior nod, reminding both him and herself that she was in charge, though the plan had somehow taken on a mind of its own. Never had a situation been so completely out of her control. At the very least, the outcome was close to what she and Rya had planned. He was willing to speak to the male trouble-maker, but only about work. She of course would be there to help direct the conversation if necessary.

"You may lead the way, Commander."

MISSION

"Yes, I will," a perplexed Verena said, leading the pale one out of her chamber. The signal announcing their exit sounded loud to her sensitive ears.

CHAPTER 6

Jordan didn't know why an invitation to sit on her bed had shifted his focus from freedom to desire.

He had no idea why *he* had kissed *her*.

None of this made sense. All he wanted from her was a way back home.

Not kindness.

Not pleasure.

And definitely not an opportunity for her to take his sperm for procreation.

Jordan Mitchell Jr. was not leaving a half-earthling, half-alien baby to be raised without a father, because one thing was certain: He was going back home to Earth.

Following the commander past crystal-like sparkling walls, Jordan pulled from within himself his meditation techniques. A few moments of concentration and he felt better, more focused, though his eyes could do nothing but admire the proud, graceful female form walking a few paces ahead of him. She hadn't even glanced back once, so certain she was that he would follow, that he would obey.

Obey.

Jordan was getting a little tired of obeying. And a little tired of the bronze controlled commander whose mission of kidnapping had thrown him into a near helpless situation.

That was it!

That explained it all!

That's why he had kissed her!

He had kissed *her*! And when he did, *he* had been in control. He had gained the upper hand and she had run away. That small triumph was what had made the touch of her lips so exciting.

No, the commander did not like his take-over. Jordan wasn't surprised that she didn't. These Vixens were so backwards in their thinking. Jordan paused mid-step, sensing rather than actually seeing the commander stop. They stood before a huge oval door shimmering with a dull gray luster. Jordan should have been paying more attention. This was his first venture into the space ship and he had wasted it on thoughts of her.

She turned. The commander's clothing had somehow changed during the time it took for them to walk from her chambers to this door. She was professionally yet sensually dressed, the business style attire clinging to her curves and accenting her long, beautiful legs. Her movements were so soft and feminine that for a second Jordan had to fight the urge to pull her into his arms again. Her words soon knocked that urge clear out of him.

"Speak only of work. This male works as a laborer of construction. You will have thirty minutes in which to visit. And remember, I will be present."

"I could not forget that, Commander."

Seeming to get the answer she wanted, the commander turned to the door once again.

"Before you do me this wonderful honor of a visit, can you tell me the name of this person I have the pleasure of speaking to?"

She paused as if to think. "I do believe he is called Bruce."

Jordan nodded in reply and the commander walked in ahead of him.

"Well, it's about time!" a loud, rumbling, slightly slurred voice called out.

Jordan took in the man overpowering a small round table. He had one arm slung behind a sturdy wooden chair he was sitting in, the other fisted around a half empty mug of beer.

"You're not Susie!" he bellowed in almost the same breath, throwing his body from the chair to confront the commander.

For the moment Jordan ignored the obviously drunk man. It was his first contact with one of his own species in weeks and this was what he got. Jordan should let the commander deal with their "problem," as Rya had called it.

Drunken or not, their problem was also his own, and how he handled it might mean the future salvation of every man on this ship. Pretending to wait for direct orders from the commander and enjoying the telltale sight of arms folding and unfolding as the commander spoke to Bruce, Jordan looked around, hardly able to take in the sweet, familiar sight of the room. It resembled the back room of any bar, in any city on Earth: a pool table in the center of the room, small round tables with dark wooden chairs, peanuts on the tables, empty mugs scattered here and there.

"I was told I could talk to the person in charge of this so-called business!"

The drunk got even louder as he yelled directly in the commander's face. Jordan found that he wasn't enjoying the sight of her obvious discomfort as much as he'd thought he would. She took a step back before answering. "This is so," she told him with quiet steel.

A strange sense of pride rose inside of him as he watched her stand toe to toe with Bruce. He recognized the unexpected feeling, then forced it aside. The feeling was unreasonable, unacceptable considering the circumstances; it's Earth men verses aliens, Jordan reminded himself.

"Then what are you waiting for? I don't have all day. I've got some serious drinking to do before I march out of here with half the crew right behind me, sister girl!"

The breath of space from the step the commander had taken back was no longer in existence as Bruce stood face to face with her. Jordan noticed that Bruce had to lift his head a few inches to meet her eye to eye. Jordan also noticed that though the commander did not back down, did not flinch or show any fear whatsoever, her folded arms gripped her forearms to a point that Jordan was sure she was doing damage to herself. Bruce didn't know it, but he was upsetting her. Jordan knew it and it bothered him. He was getting no joy from this confrontation.

"Don't just stand there as if you're in charge. Get your butt moving!"

Jordan saw Bruce's hand rise, saw his gaze trained on her tight derriere as he tried to twist behind the commander. If he made contact, Jordan wasn't sure what form of retaliation the Vixens would have for him. Would they reject him as unsuitable? Throw him out into space to die?

That act would definitely ruin his plan to get every Earth man home alive and whole. Jordan rushed forward, grabbing Bruce's hand as it began its downward swing. "Jordan Mitchell, Jr., pleased to meet you."

"Where the hell did you come from?"

"The city." Jordan frowned at the man. "I was taken from an important meeting, forced to drive way out in the middle of a swamp to address the concerns of one of my workers. To stop a riot, I was told." Jordan had heard enough to know that this guy was causing some kind of trouble and hoped this would work. Maybe by pretending to be the owner of the company he would have an excuse to visit the site, wherever that was, and have contact with the other men.

"Oh," Bruce said as he plopped down into the same seat he had jumped out of earlier, downing the remainder of his beer in one huge gulp.

Jordan glanced over at the commander. Her fingers had relaxed, no longer gripping her forearms. She gave him a slight nod, moving a few tables away to a chair within hearing distance. He joined Bruce at the table.

Bruce swallowed loudly. "I'm surprised."

"You're in for a lot of surprises," Jordan whispered.

"What was that?" Bruce asked.

"Nothing. Why are you surprised?"

"You're white. I would have thought a black man owned this company. All the crew's black; the only women

I've seen are black. Never figured a white man was in charge."

I'm a mistake, Jordan wanted to tell him. These women hadn't wanted him. He was too pale. Which was why the commander called him the pale one. But if he was so unattractive, Jordan wondered, why did she want him?

"Not that I have a problem with working for you," the man continued. "The pay's good, and after the hurricane this job was a blessing. It's just strange. You want a drink? Sister girl, go get the boss a drink," he called over to the commander.

Her face tightened, holding the same look she usually wore when gritting out the pleases and thank yous Jordan had tricked her into using. For a moment it looked as if she wasn't going to move, but Jordan knew better. If nothing else, he had learned that the commander would do anything for her planet. She stood, then called into what had to be the main bar room. Almost immediately another beautiful woman appeared, an alien he had not seen before. She looked much younger, radiating an eagerness to please. She stared at him with wide eyes. Too eager, too young, Jordan thought, unconsciously comparing the girl to the commander. The commander spoke to her. The girl left and returned almost immediately with a mug of beer in her hands. Before she could move forward to place the mug before him, the commander took the drink from the girl's hands, splashing some of it on her very earthlike office attire in the most ungraceful movement from her Jordan had ever seen.

As she put the beer before him, Jordan caught the commander's eyes, the deep brown of them pulling at him, promising him so much. Jordan blinked. "Thank you," he told her, returning her small smile which showed she understood that he was teasing her by his use of manners.

"Look, Mitchell."

The sound of Bruce talking brought Jordan back to what was important. What was wrong with him? Making eyes at the commander, sharing secret messages, those were all signs of some kind of relationship.

They had none.

There would be none.

What he had was a relationship with the men on this ship, a kinship.

"Like I was saying…"

"What were you saying?" Jordan asked, determined to get the most out of this meeting. "Is there a problem with *work*?" Jordan emphasized the word, letting the commander know he was obeying her order, reminding himself that he was a captive following orders.

"I didn't mean to drag you down here." His voice had lowered a bit.

"So you've wasted my time. There's nothing wrong here?"

"No, not really."

"Then why have you insisted that you would walk away, taking half the crew with you, if there is nothing wrong?" The commander stood as she asked the question, her hands at her side.

"Listen, sister girl, stay out of this. This is between the boss and me."

The commander stared holes into the man, folded her hands, and Jordan had the joy of seeing her defer to him. "He has made such threats and *should not* get away with them."

"I understand." And now Jordan got the whole picture. They needed his help to calm the man down. His pretending to be the owner was exactly what they had wanted. Fine, since that was exactly what he wanted.

"Pipe down over there!" Bruce yelled at the commander. "Who is she anyway?"

"My secretary, or second in command," Jordan happily invented. Verena's arms folded and unfolded.

"Sure." Bruce looked from him to the commander and said again, "Sure. Look, I didn't expect you to come down here. I wasn't serious about all that." He leaned in closer, as if they shared an embarrassing secret. "I wanted to see Susie."

"Susie?" Jordan asked.

"My species offi—," The Commander paused, "Our foreman," she corrected.

"Yeah, the beautiful gal who loves to boss us around. She's got some gorgeous eyes. They tell me things. But she hasn't been in to work for almost a week. Nobody will tell me where she went or when she's coming back."

"And you thought by causing trouble she would show up?"

"That's pretty much it."

"I should fire you on the spot."

"No, you shouldn't. I'm a good worker. The hurricane flooded and destroyed my home and I was lucky to get this job. And like I said, I work my butt off. Ask Susie, if you can find her."

"I think I'll do that. Get Susie. Tell her I need to see her right away." Jordan was enjoying this whole bossing around business.

"Her name is Suvan and she is not available. She is ill."

"Susie's sick? Why didn't you just say that? I would have gone to see her, take her some flowers or something. Nobody told me she was sick. What's her number, sister girl?"

Jordan sat in wonder. The big burly man who had looked so tough had now turned into a lovesick man. Another one was falling under the Vixens' spell. Jordan wanted to warn him, to tell him to stay way from Susie, resist her until they got back home to Earth. But the commander was standing too close. Whatever he said would be heard, and a warning now would only ensure that he would have no further contact with his people.

Another call into the room brought forth a telephone and the beautiful young alien. This time she got past the commander and stood over him with the phone. Jordan felt her eyes run up and down him, felt her interest, then a second later heard her shriek when her hand grazed his as he took the phone from her.

Jordan passed the phone to the man across from him. "Here you go, Bruce."

Jordan barely registered the thank you Bruce muttered because the scene at the other end of the room had caught his attention.

"Forgive me, Commander," Jordan heard the girl whisper.

"Only your youth and inexperience keep you from punishment, but I understand." The commander looked directly at him after saying this, then continued to speak to the girl. Her voice was suddenly drowned out by the lovesick troublemaker.

"Sister girl? What's Susie's number?"

The commander held up a silencing hand and continued to speak to the girl. Now was as good a time as any to get something into Bruce's head. But what would he remember? The man was getting agitated as he stretched his neck in the commander's direction, mumbling under his breath.

"Do you know Susie's number?"

"No, my secretary will help you with that. But in the future, if you need anything, *anything* at all, call for me." Bruce nodded, still distracted because the commander was ignoring him. Telling Bruce to contact him wasn't enough. "Look, you seem like a good man. You say you're a hard worker."

"Susie will vouch for me. I've got a good reputation."

"I believe you. I can see that you're a leader. This is what I want you to do. Every week I'd like to sit with the men, talk about your concerns, see how we can make this site run better, smoother. A group of you can meet with me in this same room every Friday, starting next week. You can be the leading voice of the men who work for me."

"I don't know. That sounds like Susie's job. I don't want to step on her toes. I'm more interested in stepping somewhere else, if you know what I mean."

Jordan only stared at him in response. It was a repeat of the Rya and Michael situation.

"There's no rule about fraternizing with your boss, is there?"

"No such rule exists." The commander, standing behind him, answered before Jordan could tell him otherwise.

"Good. How about that number, sister girl?"

The commander called out a few numbers, Bruce punched them in and Jordan sat through another love scene as Bruce gushed with sympathy for Susie. The Vixens were ahead by two, Jordan realized in frustrated silence as Bruce promised to meet Susie at the gym the next day. Jordan had no doubt another Ceremony of Unity would be performed.

Bruce hung up the phone looking like a man who'd died and had gone to heaven. "I'm gonna go sleep off this beer so I can be nice and fresh for my Susie tomorrow. Sorry about making you come out here, but it all worked out." Bruce rose on unsteady feet.

Jordan stood to grab the big man's wavering hand. "Yes, it did. I'll be seeing you next week," he said in a low voice, "no objections. And no need to worry," Jordan said loud enough for the commander to hear, "Susie's job is not on the line."

"Then I look forward to it. Good night. See you around, sister girl. You know, you need to loosen up a little."

As Bruce ambled out of the back room, a hearty laugh burst out of Jordan's chest. He couldn't contain it. Despite his less than productive encounter with his fellow Earth man, his distracted attraction because of the commander and his losing fight to keep the men unattached, ununified, Jordan found himself laughing at the horrific look of indignation on the commander's face.

"There is no humor here. I am most displeased with you, pale one."

Jordan tried to rein in his laughter but found that he couldn't. He heard the commander call into the bar once again. Not long after, two of the aliens stood at each side of him. The laughter froze inside his throat. "What's this, Commander?"

"Security forces."

"Feeling insecure again?" he asked, reminding her of her flight from the pallet earlier.

"Do not speak to the commander with such insolence, male," the alien on his right growled in a most unladylike way as she gripped his arm.

"Do not handle him. I will do so without an insecure thought." The commander's straight stare told him that she knew exactly what he had been referring to.

"As you wish, Commander."

Jordan's arm was released, though each woman stood so close he felt the aliens held him upright on both sides. He was escorted out of the room, down the crystal hall and back into the commander's quarters. His escorts left so abruptly Jordan stumbled at the sudden lack of support.

Catching himself, he stood in the middle of the room. The commander came in behind him, staring at him for a long moment, arms folded. Her clothes had reverted back to the robes he was accustomed to seeing her wear. She began pacing up and down in front of him, long, graceful strides that exposed her curved legs through the parted robes.

She suddenly stopped before him. "You have told me falsehoods. You are not a simple male with a simple male mind," she accused.

"So you've noticed."

"You have intelligence and a keen sense of knowing when to act. It was evident in your handling of Bruce."

"Am I to assume that intelligence is not a quality a good male, a simple male, should have?"

"That is correct."

"Then take me home where my talents are appreciated, expected and extremely common."

"That I cannot do. You are mine. You will live your life on Vixen. You understand that, I know you do. We will have the Ceremony of Unity to bind us, we will mate and have beautiful offspring together."

"Why not mate with your own men?" Jordan knew the answer to this question but she didn't know he knew.

"They are all gone. Extinct now because of a strange plague we could not find a cure for until it was too late."

"So, you fly in, steal men from their own home planet to take back to your world, a foreign place, so that you can make babies!"

"Of course." She looked at him in amazement. "That is exactly what this mission has been about."

"And do you think fifty Earth men are enough to keep extinction at bay?

"*The Vixen II* is only one of many ships on the same mission," Verena answered, her surprise in his complete understanding of the situation causing her to reveal information she had not intended to share. "You have grasped it almost completely on your own. It is like speaking to Suvan or Rya or any sister of Vixen. I am not so sure I like the idea that my half-ling is so intelligent."

"I think it's about time you stop with the insults. I've heard enough."

"I have offended you?"

"Only on a daily basis."

"But you have offended me as well."

"You mean I have done something worse than ripping you from your world?"

"A necessary action," the commander quietly told him, obviously having no remorse for having done just that. "You, though, have offended me greatly by allowing another to touch you."

"What are you talking about?" She seemed to be jumping from one offense to another.

"You made contact with Tora through your eyes, showing your interest, and then you allowed her to touch you."

The offense was incomprehensible, considering what she had done and was still doing to him and every Earth man on board. "I am the victim here. You have no right to be offended. I have no interest in that girl. She looked at me. I noticed that she was attractive, that's all." Jordan paused. Why was he explaining himself as if they were in a relationship? He owed her no explanation. She owed him answers. "That's how you Vixens plan on trapping us all. Right?" Jordan remembered to add, realizing he wasn't supposed to know all this.

"Trapping is not the appropriate word. Obtaining is a better choice. And you are changing the subject. If you were a male of Vixen you would be punished for allowing another to touch you."

"She touched my hand while giving me the fake phone you were using to dupe one of my people into believing he was still on Earth."

"That is not the issue here."

"I can see our situation is of no concern to you."

"Your situation is as it should be and will remain as you see it now. Now explain to me why you allowed another to touch you."

Frustrated with finding no way for the commander to understand what her mission was doing to his people, Jordan sat on the pallet and rubbed a hand down his face.

"I did not give you leave to sit on my pallet."

"I did not give you leave to snatch me from Earth. My sitting here doesn't even begin to even the odds."

She paced in front of him once, twice, then stood before him, her arms folded. "Speak of this situation with

Tora or I will have my force return to take you to the brig where you will be secured for the remainder of the voyage."

Jordan couldn't have that. He wouldn't be able to meet Bruce this Friday. Being locked up would kill his chance to make contact with the other men. "Alright," he answered, pausing to think about what to say. When nothing more came to mind, she glided to the entrance of the chamber where Jordan got a glimpse of his escorts still outside.

"*Alright*! Like I said before, I did not invite her to touch me. She looked at me, and I looked at her. She touched me and shrieked. That was it."

The commander looked at him for a long time and carefully unfolded her arms before speaking. "Despite the many falsehoods you have told me I believe you have spoken the truth."

"Great. Does that mean you won't imprison me?"

"For now, I will not. But you must not repeat the mistake of attracting another. You are mine."

Tried of being referred to as a possession, Jordan pulled himself from the pallet. "I belong to no one but myself."

"I'm afraid that is another thing you must get accustomed to. You are mine. I have marked you. Recall the shriek Tora issued. She sensed that you were taken and knew that you were mine. You are so much a part of me that I am in your very skin."

"So that's why she was apologizing all over the place."

"Certainly."

"I don't know exactly what you've done to me, but if you've marked me, the very least I can do is repay the kindness." With that Jordan gave in to the banked desire he had been feeling for her since she had run away from him earlier today. He wrapped his arms around her, pulling her into him until they stood flush against each other. Staring into her eyes, Jordan saw once again the promises, the pleasure she could give but chose to close his eyes against it. He didn't reach for her mouth but instead tilted his head so that he had perfect access to her neck, and without a bit of gentleness, used his mouth to suckle her tender skin, pulling harder and harder, not releasing her when her hands pulled at his shoulders, only to relax down his back. He suckled until he was sure that his mark would be visible on her beautiful bronze skin.

Jordan stepped back to examine his handiwork. The mark was there, barely visible on her brown skin, but it was there, glistening with moisture from his touch. He grazed the oval mark with his fingers, then lifted her hand to touch it as well. "How do you like being branded, Commander?"

She gazed at him with uncertainty and was about to reply when a voice interrupted them. "Commander, you are needed."

Her hand still touching the mark he had given her, she answered in her most commanding way, "I will be there." To him she said, "We will speak more of this. Return to your side chamber." She paused, then added, "Please."

Jordan nodded in reply and made his way to the chamber, which opened automatically. He turned to find her at the door of her quarters.

"Until I see you later, pale one."

MISSION

Her door slid shut just before his own did. "The name's Jordan," he yelled to the closed door, wondering exactly what would happen later.

CHAPTER 7

Verena's hand once again moved to the mark on her neck as she surveyed the report Zytai had prepared. Her mind was scattered. It was most difficult to respond with more than an affirmative wave indicating she saw no problem with their current speed and course.

Verena forced her hand to move away from the mark, though the action did nothing to erase the memory of his mouth, the moist heat, the tingling pressure and intoxicating pull of that small part of her skin into his mouth. That mouth of his could perform amazing acts.

"Commander."

Zytai was still standing before her, a rare look of concern on her face. "Is there more you need to relay?" Verena asked.

"Some good news, yes."

"Proceed."

"I have chosen a male to pursue."

"That *is* good news." The faster they obtained mates, the stronger hold they would have on these males.

"He is healthy, with a face of good quality and will provide beautiful offspring."

"An excellent match, then," Verena said, thinking of the pale one and the odd turn in their relationship. Her thoughts directed her finger as they caressed the mark on her neck.

"Yes, but…"

"Go on, Zytai." Verena's hand dropped to her side at the unusual sound of worry from her explorations officer.

"He is so large. Larger than the loud one."

"Bruce," Verena said, remembering the name of the man the pale one had dealt with.

"Yes, that is the one. I had expected these males to be larger than our own, but the one I have chosen is very much larger than all the others."

"Are you certain that he is the one for you?"

"Yes, there is something about him that has called out to me."

Verena understood that well. Everything about the pale one called out to her: his unusual features, his strange movements, his defiance, his recently revealed intelligence, his unnatural tendency to take the lead in pleasure-giving activities.

"I have marked him as mine."

"Good, but tread carefully, Zytai," Verena felt it necessary to warn. "I have learned that these Earth men are unpredictable. Until we have them home we must keep them cloaked in ignorance. That is the easier course of action."

"As you say, Commander. Before I leave, that mark on your neck. If it is bothering you, should you not the seek the counsel of Sister Denee?"

"There is no need to bother the healer. It is simply a slight worry. Do not concern yourself," Verena told her, wishing she could really brush it aside as easily as the words she had spoken implied.

"Good day, then. I have a meeting with my future half-ling now." Sounding more like her confident self, Zytai left her alone.

Verena raised her hand in dismissal, wishing with all her being that the pale one was cloaked in the same ignorance as all the other males. Yet some miniscule part of her rebelled at the wish, for in ignorance there would not exist the secret excitement she felt at not knowing what to expect of him. There were also some thoughts in her head that she had never voiced aloud, had even tried not to think too often. However, the feelings the pale one stirred within her caused them to rise to the surface.

The relationships she had witnessed, that of her parents, relatives and friends, had always left her sad, for there seemed to be something lacking. A half-ling was joined to a sister of Vixen for life with a pledge to obey and serve, just as the sister pledged to protect and cherish. The rites of Unity had been the same for thousands of years and would remain the same, as they should. What could be missing when each brought a pledge to the union? It was senseless to dwell on negative thoughts.

Verena's fingers grazed the tender spot once again, her mind returning to one particular Earth man. She was anxious to go back to him now that she was no longer needed, but nervous at the prospect. She swiveled in her chair, her eyes landing on the small portal that gave her a breathtaking view of the lights of millions of far away stars.

Verena decided to sit for a time, to calm herself, to collect her thoughts. She should not allow a male to upset her so.

But he did.

The mere thought of him should not excite her so.

But it did.

Being apart from him should not make her long to be in his presence.

But she did.

Verena forced herself to stay planted in her seat, reminding herself of tradition, of her mother and how she would have handled her father in such a situation. But, she realized, her mother would not have faced this situation. A male would not have thrown her mother into a state of confusion. She decided she should not rush back to her quarters. That would only lead the pale one to believe that she was anxious to see him.

Verena folded her arms and was able to maintain a calm outward appearance as she relived the tantalizing moments in his arms when he had left his mark on her.

He had marked her.

Suddenly the full significance of what he had done spread through her like an exploding star, a burst of outrage expanding outward, reaching the tips of her fingers, pulsating to every cell within her.

An hour's worth of Karate-do, an hour's worth of meditation, and Jordan still felt a knot of frustration in the pit of his stomach.

He hadn't meant to kiss her.

He hadn't meant to hold her in his arms.

He hadn't meant to mark her.

But it had all felt so good and so right. What was wrong with him? Nothing was more important to him than getting back to Earth with all fifty men aboard. Was there some flaw in his personality, some dormant awakening of his father's genes that threw him off balance?

No! He wasn't a womanizer out to get whatever he could from any woman he made contact with. He didn't use people. That was Jordan Mitchell, *Sr.* The only thing he shared with his father was his name, which was unfortunate enough.

Jordan continued to sit in his meditation pose, though his mind raced with thoughts of the commander.

Where did she go?

Why hadn't she come back?

Why did he want to see her so badly?

What was it she had done to him to make him want her so much?

"J.M., are you ill?"

Jordan heard C1's voice but wasn't in the mood for company. He wished the commander would bring herself back.

"J.M., I am concerned. Your pulse rate is high, and there is moisture on your body. Do you need a refreshing shower?"

Knowing the computer wouldn't leave him alone, Jordan answered, "No, thank you. I'm fine, C1."

"Though I do not believe you, it is good to hear you speak. I am sure that now that you have completed your movements about and quiet breathing, that you would like some conversation."

"Not really."

"A lesson then?" C1 asked hopefully.

That was the last thing he wanted, but seeing no reason for both of them to be miserable, Jordan decided that conversation was better than a lesson. "What do you want to talk about, C1?"

"Anything you wish."

"The location of an escape shuttle."

"That is classified information."

"Schematics of the ship?"

"No can do."

Jordan laughed at C1's use of slang. "You are picking up some bad habits, my friend."

"Friend? You think of me as a friend, J.M.?"

Jordan paused in thought. "Yes, my only friend for the moment."

"I am honored, but you have other companionship. You have the commander."

"I don't want to hear another word about that controlling, over-dominate alien."

"True. But that is the nature of a sister of Vixen, and you must realize that you are considered an alien to her."

Jordan hadn't thought about it that way but the point was irrelevant. "What about me? What about my nature?"

"I am not as sure of it as I once was, J.M. You are no ordinary male. Neither are your fellow Earth men. I believe I will have to do some research."

"That would be an excellent idea." It would be nice to know that somebody around here understood him. The commander couldn't care less about the effect her mission was having on its victims. The men he hoped to save and make contact with on a regular basis would think he was crazy if he started babbling about aliens.

"For now let us continue to converse. We will not speak of the commander."

"You choose a topic then."

"Let us speak of Earth and your kinships. I will begin my research with you. Tell me about all the males in your family."

"C1, you just had to pick the sorriest subject, didn't you?"

"If it makes you uncomfortable…"

"No, there was only one male in my life and he's been on my mind so I might as well talk about him. If anything, it might help to get him out of my mind. I was starting to think that I was falling into his shoes."

"Earth males fall into shoes? Why do you not simply put them on?"

"No, I mean, following his example. I was worried about turning out to be exactly like him."

"But you should. A male should model his father."

"Not this one."

"Am I to understand that he did not display obedience, kind acts and a gentle touch?"

Raw laughter grated past Jordan's throat. "He had the gentle touch down pat. Obedience? The only laws he obeyed were the ones he made as he sailed through life without a conscience. Kind acts? The kindest thing he did was divorce my mother."

"I am uncertain of the 'down pat' and sailing reference, but I am understanding that he was not a very nice male."

"Nice enough to get what he wanted. All charm when he chased women, a buddy to all as he stole money right under the noses of the people who trusted him, a company he worked for well over fifteen years."

"Such horrid behavior. Did he not get punished for such offenses?"

"He was sent to jail for embezzlement, his name dragged through the mud. My name was dragged through the mud. I still hate being introduced to new people. I never know when someone will recognize the name, forcing me to relive the shame all over again."

"I will never use your entire name again, J.M."

"You know, I like to hear you call me J.M. All my friends do—well, did. Plain Jordan is fine too. My mother used to call me Jordan."

"Used to. She is no longer living?"

"No, but she had a good life after all the scandal with my father died down. I made sure of that."

"Am I to believe that you think yourself like this male?"

"Look at me, C1. I'm panting after the commander like a desperate fool when I should be—" Jordan stopped.

Though C1 was his friend, he was also a Vixen computer. Despite all that he had done for him so far, Jordan didn't want to do anything to risk his meeting with Bruce and the other men.

"Should be? Yes, you should be. You two should have performed the Ceremony of Unity at least a week ago. You have been marked and your need for conjugal union has heightened."

"I knew it! She did something unnatural to me to make me want her every waking moment." Jordan was so excited to learn that he was not like his father that he could barely sit still.

"That is not what I said."

"What are you saying then?"

"You and the commander were meant to be together. It is Vi-she, destiny. The marking merely heightened your awareness of each other."

Instantly deflated, Jordan digested this information as his mind worked through C1's logic. "What you're saying is that I was meant to be kidnapped. That I was meant to mate and have babies with an alien, live my life on a planet that's not my own."

"Yes, J.M."

"That is not what I want."

"Vi-she is not always kind. Destiny is not something we can control."

The door to the commander's quarters opened with the commander and her robes flying through. Jordan didn't so much as lift his head.

"She does not seem to be in good spirits, J.M."

"I've noticed." *She* had taken her time in returning and *she* was peeved. "Vi-she or destiny, whatever you call it, might have brought me here, but I've got a thing a two to add, a thing or two to teach the commander."

"Do not do anything foolish, J.M. An angered Vixen is not a pretty sight," C1 warned.

He had marked her! The thought screamed at her over and over again.

Such a thing was unheard of. It was a great insult for a male to take it upon himself to claim a female's privilege. Moving through the ship with the speed that only an offended sister of Vixen could manage, Verena burst through the entry of her chamber. Through the clear wall she could see him sitting and talking. He was calmly entertaining himself with Comfort 1, no doubt, when she had been struck with worries as numerous as the stars.

"Bring yourself forward!" Verena's voice rang loud in her own ears. Not surprised when he did not readily obey she thundered, "Now, pale one!"

He stood slowly, not an ounce of concern on his too-handsome face. She waited for him to walk through the door she had unlocked. Her legs took control, moving her to and fro about the room. She stopped as soon as she realized that she was once again duplicating his strange actions.

"The name's Jordan. And I can only assume this is the later you mentioned."

"Later? What do you speak of?"

"When you left over three hours ago you said that we would finish this later. I was looking forward to it. Not so much now."

"Do not be so insolent, pale one—"

"The name is Jordan."

"You have marked me!" she went on as if he had interrupted with some insignificant noise.

"Say my name. Say, 'You have marked me, Jordan.' "

His softly spoken words interrupted her thoughts, elevating her anger to a point where she could not concentrate, could do nothing but dwell on his offense. Laying a hand on each of his shoulders and using the inner strength which had grown with her anger, Verena tossed him across the room and onto her pallet, a feat that was not as easy as she had thought it would be, reminding her once again of the differences of Earth males. She followed, placing herself upon him, holding his wrist within her palms, using her strength to subdue him.

"Be silent! Listen to all I have to say to you, pale one!"

"My name is Jordan. I will listen only when you've used my name."

"What?" Verena asked, amazed at his audacity, flustered at his cool, quiet response. This was not how events were to proceed. She was to show her power over him. He was to submit.

A computerized voice entered the room. "If I may intervene—"

"Go away, C1. I can handle this all by myself," Jordan spoke to the computer.

"Of that I am not so sure, J.M.," it responded.

99

"Trust me," Jordan answered.

"How dare you have a conversation in this room as if I were not present. Begone, Comfort 1, or disablement will be yours within the hour."

"I do apologize, Commander. It is just—"

"Go away, C1. I told you, I have it." Jordan paused before adding, "Friend."

"If you say so, friend."

The room went silent. The pale one lay under her as if he were gaining great enjoyment. He should be riddled with fear, worry and anxiety by now—she had seen so with her father. This was not going as she had planned.

"You are not frightened."

"Try saying, 'You are not frightened, Jordan.' "

"*Jordan*, what is this *Jordan*?" Verena asked, confused enough by his reaction that she didn't expect him to add to it.

"My name."

"Your name? I call you pale one."

"That is not my name. You may call me Jordan."

"There are many things that I may do. My least concern is what I will call you."

"If you, a mighty sister of Vixen, do not posses the mere courtesy to speak to someone using their given name, then you are a backward race of people."

"You go too far, pale one."

"Did you speak, Verena?" he said, using her given name as if she had given him leave to do so, as if he were not lying beneath the heated surge of an exploding star.

"You need to be taught a lesson, pale one." Her hands tightened on his wrists.

"You *are* strong, Verena, " he told her in that same soft voice, somehow converting her name as it passed his lips into a soothing stroke that eased into her anger.

"As I should be." While Verena gloated at her strength over him, his fingers reached like warm tentacles to brush her hand, warming her skin, sending touches of joy throughout her being—neutralizing the anger. Verena attempted to pull back, but the anger was slowly turning into stardust. "This is not as it should be," she whispered.

"Everything is not as it should be. Nothing is right, is it, Verena?"

"Do not use my name. That is not a privilege I have given you yet."

"You have the privilege of using mine. Call me Jordan."

"That is no privilege, that is my right. I will call you what I wish, my handsome pale one." The anger that had once been inside her was now a nonexistent thing. Verena's plans shifted. She decided to enjoy the moment, to give and take a bit of pleasure. Her body and her mind had been calling for it. By all rights, they should have been joined by now. Leaning into him, placing all her weight onto his hard body, Verena pressed her mouth onto his. The connection was a warm melting need as she channeled all of her cravings to the surface, to their joined parts. Before the feeling could fully penetrate, Verena felt a tremendous force thrust her onto her back. She opened her eyes to find the pale one lying upon her. They had reversed positions.

"How?"

"You may be strong, Verena, but I am just as strong as you."

"Just as strong?"

"Possibly stronger."

"That cannot be."

"But it is. Try to get up."

Staring up at him, feeling helpless and lowly, Verena did try. She attempted to move her wrists but could barely twist them within his grasp. She attempted to throw him off her but her upward thrust only forced her to connect with the hardness between his legs that for the moment she wanted nothing to do with. At least that was what she told herself.

After a few minutes of struggling, Verena lay still, her body drenched in perspiration. The anger that had disappeared but a few minutes before returned when she found herself held in such an undignified manner. Now she felt disbelief, exhaustion and defeat. Not wanting to face these strange feelings, Verena closed her eyes, hoping that all would change in a few moments.

"Have you had enough?" she heard him say. She opened her eyes to find his strange gray-colored eyes staring at her.

"Have…you…had…enough?" he asked slowly, as if *she* had a simple mind.

Though shame at her present position filled her, Verena stared into his eyes as she nodded in response, unable to answer aloud. What would her mother think of this? What would her crew think if they knew she had been subdued by a male?

"Do you feel the shame, the frustration, the powerlessness of your situation?"

"Yes, I do," she forced herself to say, "and when you release me you will suffer the consequences of your foolish actions."

"I expect to. But you, Verena, will remember the few moments when I overpowered you and held you against your will. You will remember the feeling and possibly think before you act in the future."

Verena listened to him without actually listening. She heard his words, but a dozen possible punishments were racing through her mind as well.

"You've got nothing to say?" he asked her, interrupting her pleasurable thought of assigning him to the duty of waste retrieval for the remainder of the voyage.

"You are perspiring," she told him, noticing the moisture on his arms, his face and his neck for the first time.

"So?"

"That means you had to work very hard to restrain me. You are not stronger than me. We are of equal strength."

"Maybe, maybe not."

"There is no maybe. It is so. Release me and stop this foolish game. Use your intelligence to save yourself more punishment."

"I'm ready to quit and take my punishment like a man."

"Then like a male you will beg for forgiveness and mercy," Verena told him, unable to imagine such a thing. It was not a thing she wanted to see. The thought of him begging was extremely distasteful.

"You will see."

"Remove yourself from me."

"After you say my name."

"What?"

"My name, Verena. Say Jordan."

Verena lay motionless beneath him. Now that she had discovered their equal strength, she no longer felt so deeply humiliated, only mildly embarrassed. He was staring at her again, willing her to do this thing as if it were of great importance, such a little thing. She would give in to him if for no other reason than to end this foolish game so that she could issue her punishment. "I am waiting for you to remove yourself." Verena took a breath before adding, "Jordan."

He released her wrists, his entire body backing away, brushing against her, leaving her with a craving to call him back. Almost.

"You have no idea what you have done, pale one," she told him as she slowly stood before him.

"Forgotten already? It's Jordan, and I know exactly what I have done," he told her, staring pointedly at her folded arms as if they held some great secret. "I await your punishment."

His bold declaration should have been another offense but Verena was not offended. She found that she was very much excited. She should have been offended. He needed to know that his actions were offensive. "You seem much too prepared to accept punishment."

"I am only doing as a good half-ling, excuse me, future half-ling should. Quietly accepting my fate. Quietly obeying orders."

"As if you could."

"It is Vi-she, is it not?"

"What do you know of Vi-she?"

"Only what C1 has told me. He is forever insisting that I must accept my fate, that you are my destiny."

"I may not issue an order of disablement for this faithful computer of Vixen. He speaks the truth. Vi-she has directed me to your planet, to this New Or-leans place which you come from and Vi-she has decided the direction your life will take."

"Destiny or Vi-she might have brought me here, but the future is not set. I intend to have a say in what happens in my life."

Verena laughed at this. "As if you could." The humor of his words died in her throat as he stepped forward. A single fingertip brushing against the tender mark on her neck stilled her.

"Have you ever been marked before, Verena? Have you ever done anything against your will before?"

Remembering the mark thrust renewed anger to the surface, compounded by the reminder that he had held her, then forced her to use his given name when she had no wish to. "Guards!" she called, wondering why she hadn't called them to her before.

"What's the matter, Verena? Can't you handle your own male?" he whispered in her ear.

"Commander?" The guards stood in question at the entrance of the chamber.

Looking at them, she realized why she hadn't called them earlier.

Pride.

A sister of Vixen should not need aid when dealing with her own male. Verena threw a smug smile at him before turning to say to the guards, "You are relieved of duty. Good day."

"Good day," they answered in unison.

"Good move, Mighty-one. Show your might. Issue forth this grand punishment." He folded his body forward as he said this. Verena was certain that he was mocking her.

She was at a loss as to what to do. A commander of her own ship for five years, a sister of Vixen who had never paused in making a decision, she was now indecisive. Punishing him would be too easy. He wanted punishment. Should she assign him to waste retrieval? No, she did not wish him to reek. Lock him in the side chamber? No, he seemed to find ways to entertain himself. Take Comfort 1 away? That would not be wise. The computer seemed to be the only channel to accepting his fate.

"I am respectfully waiting."

"The punishment is that you will receive no punishment."

"What?"

Verena took great joy in seeing the look of surprise on his face. "For now. I will reflect on it. Your punishment will be forthcoming, be assured of that, pale one."

He stared at her.

Verena stared back.

When neither gave in, he said to her, "I see what you're doing. You're thinking, 'Let him stew. Let him wonder.' Now you're the one playing games."

"This constant display of your amazing thought processes truly intrigues me. As for games, if this is a game I am playing, then it is one I will win."

Verena left him in the chamber to speculate and agonize on that. The problem was she had no place else she wanted to go or where she wanted to be. He had driven her out of her own chamber, which had her wondering who was punishing who.

CHAPTER 8

Six days.

Jordan lay in the side chamber. He had awakened with the thought that it had only been six days. Yet so much had happened.

He had gotten the best of Verena by escaping punishment.

Correction. He had escaped the kind of punishment he had expected.

His pride had pushed him to risk his only hope of salvation, his only plan—his prearranged meeting with Bruce and what Jordan hoped would be at least a dozen more men. But it had been worth it.

Verena had not imprisoned him as she had threatened before, but quite the opposite. She no longer locked the door to the side chamber or so politely requested that he stay inside. Jordan smiled at the mental image of her doing just that. He actually missed the look of pained tolerance she had worn every time the words *please* and *thank you* were forced past her lips.

One loss was another gain, for now he had free rein of her chamber, everything from the crystal walls of her bathroom to the symbols on the doorway. He was very careful of what he touched, however, especially when she was not around. Jordan was sure that somehow he was being watched, that maybe this new freedom was some kind of trap or simply part of the game.

Whatever the case, Jordan took advantage of this time, fiddling with gadgets, memorizing Vixen symbols and learning their meanings. The strange symbols, reminiscent of Egyptian hieroglyphics, reminded him that though he was becoming proficient in speaking the Vixen language, being able to *read* the language would be essential if he was going to take control of a shuttle.

"Think big," Jordan told himself, "the entire ship." His voice in the quiet room rang loud, echoing inside his ear. It was going to happen. He would make it happen. Part of that involved the reading lessons C1 was now giving him, no longer through trickery, but out of friendship, a friendship that seemed to have overridden C1's fear of disablement. This warmed Jordan's heart, and the fact that they were doing so right under the commander's nose warmed his pride. Jordan counted it as a five-point advantage each day. This game they played was in full swing. Verena was in the lead, having control of her space vessel and everything in it.

Jordan sat up, releasing a grunt. He thought of the half dozen more men who had fallen under the spell of the Sisters of Vixen. With the help of C1, Jordan kept track of the Ceremony of Unity victims. There was Bruce, who he had already known would be taken in by Susie, and five others. One, a huge man, had the horrible luck of attaching himself to that Vixen called Zytai, the one who first called him the pale one. Suddenly Jordan realized that Verena rarely called him that anymore. She didn't call him anything.

Strange.

Jordan shook off the memory that realization triggered, not allowing himself to relive the little scene that had him brooding much too often. What he needed to concern himself with was the game they were in the midst of. Verena was ahead, but he was still in it. His intelligence, the one thing that she both admired and was appalled by, was his only resource in this game they played. And he was using it to good advantage, despite the promise of punishment still ringing inside his head. Verena made sure he never forgot.

Since the day he overpowered her, giving her a taste of how powerless her actions made him feel, Jordan would often awaken to the feel of her eyes on him from across the room as she lay stretched across the pallet. She would question him, the same as she had every morning since their confrontation. "Should your punishment be issued today?" After a long pause she would say, "I will think on it." Then she would undress, parting with her pajamas or her sleeping robes as C1 referred to them, piece by piece until she was completely naked.

Amazingly so.

Jordan would pretend not to notice, but his eyes strayed as she sauntered away to shower. His gaze followed her direction much too often, leaving him completely aroused, of course.

Unforgettably so.

The arousal, a constant all day ache, reminded him of an all-day sucker he once had as a kid: huge and lasting, tempting and delicious; it had nevertheless left a pain in his gut. Now the pain he was experiencing was much lower, intensifying when she changed from daytime attire to her sleeping robes every night, gracing the pallet with her too-perfect body.

Today Jordan was going to switch things up a bit. Today was going to be different, a turning point in many ways, he hoped.

First Verena. He enjoyed thinking of her as Verena instead of the commander. This name change made her seem less powerful, less intimidating. Yes, Jordan could admit that he had been intimidated by her. Not anymore. He had learned a great deal about her from watching her and from C1. It was the most recent revelation from C1 that had Jordan rising long before her this Friday morning.

"You are both nearly bursting with overheated desires," C1 had told him, as if Jordan hadn't already known exactly why falling asleep was so difficult.

"No kidding," Jordan had sarcastically answered.

"The commander is tossing and turning just as much, no, I would say much more, than you. At least twenty percent more."

"Impossible," Jordan had told him.

"I have concerns for you both, but more so for the commander."

"Oh, so you like her more than me now?"

"No. How could you say such a thing, J.M.?"

"Ignore me. It was a little shot at humor. Laughing is better than suffering in silence."

"Suffering is what you are both doing. It is said that a sister of Vixen cannot withstand such onslaughts of desire. They must be eased."

"Aw, that's just a Vixen myth, I'm sure. We have similar ones on Earth. But of course it's men who claim they'll explode. I haven't exploded yet and this is the worst case of—"

"Suffrage."

"No, in America that's a women's movement for voting, but like I told you, I am suffering."

"The commander suffers even more than you."

That news from C1, given to him in a matter-of-fact tone in the middle of the night had set his mind churning. He'd watched her the rest of the night, only dozing when his body allowed him to relax enough to take a short nap. All night long she tossed and turned. C1 was right. She *was* worse off than him. That was the moment he decided to rush ahead in this game of theirs to gain a few points.

Verena had been lying on her pallet for the last twenty minutes without moving. For the first time all night, she lay in restful slumber. But not for long, Jordan decided. He opened his door and removed every stitch of clothes from his body. Though he had not exercised in the nude since long before leaving Earth, the freedom of bare skin had always been a gratifying experience.

After meditating a few minutes, Jordan eased into the Karate-do movements with slow, precise gestures, practicing the careful breathing techniques he knew so well. Focusing so squarely on his routine, feeling so free, so unrestricted, Jordan soon forgot the point of the entire exercise until out of the corner of his eye he caught a movement.

Verena was instantly awake, though uncertain why. Maybe it was the dream stemming from the conversation she had had with Rya days ago. It had replayed in her sleep for the past few nights. She had gone to Rya that day when Jordan had marked her, not as the Commander, but as a sister needing to confide. Rya, the only sister of Vixen who at that time had an Earth half-ling, was the only person equipped to understand what was troubling her. Upon leaving Jordan, Verna had gone straight to the dwelling that Rya was now occupying with her half-ling.

"Rya," she had called after hitting the palm of her hand on the door in traditional Vixen custom. There was a scuffling noise, a banging sound and soon a breathless Rya at the door.

"Co—I mean—"

"Verena. Call me Verena," she reminded a flustered Rya, not wanting her mate to wonder at the title of commander.

"Verena," Rya repeated.

"Who's there?" the male inside had asked.

Rya glanced back, "Verena, my kinswoman," she said in answer to her half-ling.

"Kinswoman?" the voice asked.

"Our mothers are sisters."

"Your cousin, then."

"Yes, my cousin."

"Nosy little things, these Earth males," Verena commented.

"Sometimes," Rya admitted as the male belonging to the voice squeezed his way between Rya and the door, brushing his entire body against her before pressing his lips upon hers for such a long time that Verena wondered if they would perform the act of pleasuring right before her very eyes.

As the kiss went on, Verena considered intervening, maybe calling the guards. Before she could decide, he released Rya in a slow smooth motion, then returned to her with smaller pressing and pulling of the lips.

"I love the way you talk. The way you say things is so cute. I'll see you later," Verena heard him whisper to Rya. Then, "Oh, hi there, Verena. Nice to meet you." He nodded as he passed her.

Verena moved into the dwelling with Rya following behind her. "Sorry about that, Commander," Rya fell back into a more formal address now that Michael was not present. "What has drawn you here? Is there something amiss? Some emergency?"

"No, it's that thing I just witnessed."

"What thing?"

"That pulling and pressing of lips and other mouth parts. That's why I am here. That's what I want to talk to you about."

"Oh."

"*Oh?* What is *oh?*"

"An Earth word of reaction to something that is unusual or surprising."

"Unusual and surprising, that is what this act is."

"At first, but then it becomes the most amazing type of sharing."

"Like channeling? That is what I was attempting to do when—" Verena paused at Rya's gasp.

"You have performed the Ceremony of Unity?"

Before Verena could answer, Rya continued, "That is wonderful! We will have offspring near the same age. I did not want to say until I was certain but I suspect that I am holding a child within."

"That is good news, Rya."

"It is wonderful news! The sisters of Vixen will live on. We have strong males to mate and live with. And you, by now, have discovered how strong our Earth men are," Rya told her with a knowing look in her eye.

Verena had discovered this, all right, but not the way Rya meant. Verna sat upon the wide structure called a sofa and waved a hand for Rya to join her. "I have not performed the Ceremony of Unity with the pale one." Somehow saying 'the pale one' sounded odd to her ears.

"You mean that you have performed the act of pleasuring before the ceremony?" Rya stood in stunned surprise. "Have you? That would be an insult to the pale one. It would show that you think less of him then a selog."

"I know this," Verena explained. The image of the slimy insects they lived deep in the caves of Vixen popped into her head. They were not an image she would associate with her future half-ling. "And no, I did not perform the act of pleasuring, though it nearly did occur."

"But you stopped yourself."

"Almost not. It was the shock of the kiss that did that."

"Verena," Rya smiled at her, "you mean kissing."

"I suppose I do. Speak more of this kissing."

"It is a sharing."

"Like the channeling of pleasure."

"Somewhat, but it is more."

"More?"

"With channeling, sisters give pleasure to excite the male so that he is ready to participate in the act."

"Every adolescent of Vixen knows that, Rya."

"But kissing…Kissing is a sharing by both male and female. Both give and receive pleasure in the kissing. "

Verena sat in thought for a long moment. Had she enjoyed the kissing? She was not completely certain. Had he? She was not so certain of that either. Verena had never been so uncertain in her life. "So, you are saying that the pressing, the pulling, the movements are pleasurable to both?"

"Yes."

If the word was not an affirmation, then Rya's eyes truly were. "Good day then," she told her kinswoman before leaving to roam the ship for many hours before returning to her chamber.

Now days later, having awakened after too little sleep once again, all she could think of was Jordan and his kiss and the possible pleasures they could invoke. There was also the dilemma of what punishment to deliver when punishing him was not what she wanted to do to him at all.

Denied cravings making her restless, Verena turned her body upon the pallet hoping to find a more comfortable position. What she saw caused her to sit up in pure fascination. Facing the side chamber, she sat in the middle of her pallet to watch as Jordan moved about in all his bare glory. Jordan was beautiful. It was almost too much for her to bear.

Verena rose, crossed the chamber, disrobing as she went. She stood just inside his chamber door.

He was the something that had awakened her from the first bit of rest she had gotten this night. Verena had no inkling as to whether it was his measured breathing or the soft friction of his feet as they moved about the floor. Maybe it was the short grunting vibrations that escaped his lips every few moments.

Yes, that had to be it.

No, it was all of it.

All of him.

All of Jordan.

How she loved his name.

"Jordan," Verena whispered so low that she herself could barely hear his name as it left her lips. She entered his chamber, a practice frowned upon. Her mother's voice rang inside her head. 'Males come to you. You do not lower yourself by going to a male.' Verena pushed the voice aside, sitting on the floor to enjoy the beauty before her.

She needed to come.

She needed this.

For days she had secretly watched him move about the chamber, performing this strange ritual. A few hands throw away from him, she had rested without truly resting. Having marked him yet unable to truly have him, unable to have the freedom to claim him when so many of her own crew had claimed their mates, united and were now enjoying their men, she had simply watched. Why did she have to suffer?

She shouldn't, not when he was performing just for her. On previous days he had not known that she was watching, but now, without clothes, he moved with pride, knowing that she was watching. The bulges on his body excited her as he turned with swift sure movements. What movements they could make together!

Verena allowed her eyes to roam every glorious inch of him. Her hands itched to touch him. He would not be soft, she knew. Jordan's bulges were firm, hard, though he was not as huge as Zytai's male.

Forget Zytai's male.

Her male stood before her.

He was showing his need for her by this act of sensual movement. Though they were not united she would take what he offered and forget the consequences.

Having made that decision, Verena rose to her knees. Jordan stood before her, suddenly still. Verena captured his eyes and held them communicating all the pleasure she would give to him as her hands did what they were aching to do.

She touched his abdomen, then moved upward to take in the smooth warmth of his chest. She paused, pressing her hand against the place where his life's blood pumped. Then he grasped both her hands, pulling her up and against him.

"You want me, I know you do," he told her.

She nodded. "And I will have you this day." With that, her lips went to his. As she channeled the tremendous build up of pleasure his lips moved about her, his tongue darted around hers and without a thought at all, she joined him in this strange ritual without interrupting the channeling, all the while building, building within them both a need for more. When she pulled back his eyes were dazed.

"What are you doing to me?" Jordan asked aloud. At the same time he asked himself why he was letting this happen. There were reasons this should not happen. Important reasons.

"Giving you pleasure."

"No, you're trying to kill me," Jordan told her.

"Never," she said, leading him toward her sleeping pallet. Jordan followed, wanting what she offered. She eased onto the soft pallet, pulling him down with her. "Cover me with this beautiful body you possess."

Jordan didn't argue but did as she requested.

"Teach me more of the ritual of the kiss, please, Jordan."

The use of his name brought back to him his purpose. He was going to arouse her, leave her wanting and panting after him. But the use of his name, "Jordan," a breath of a word, just two syllables floating out of her mouth, caused him to question his need for one-upmanship. Was that what he still wanted? Should he give her what she wanted?

"Anything you want," Jordan whispered, answering his own question, holding his mouth directly over hers barely touching hers. Tiny waves of electric shocks caressed his lips, pushing his level of excitement up with each little pulse. "Now," he held his breath a minute as he took in a particularly intense wave, "use your tongue to touch any part of my mouth."

Slowly she did, tracing the outside of his upper lip, the bottom. Jordan groaned as the tiny shock waves increased.

"Was that good?" she asked him, truly wondering if she was handling the kiss correctly. She had enjoyed it. Did he?

"Wonderful! Amazing!" Kissing wasn't enough! He had to feel her. His hands moved downward to find her shapely, soft hips. They then traveled upward, brushing the sides of her breasts. He repeated the caress as she played with his lips, pressing her mouth against his. She darted her tongue inside and he captured it with his own for a brief second before she pulled back.

"Teach me more, Jordan. What of the pulling and pressing?"

"I'll do better than that, Rena. I'll show you." Just one more kiss, he told himself, to make her want him more. Then he'd leave her panting on her pallet as she had left him every morning and night.

A hand on each side of her elegant face, Jordan claimed her lips, her tongue, her entire mouth. His body pressed into her; his hardness brushed against the smooth velvety softness that he knew he shouldn't want any part of. Yet he wanted it more than anything else at this moment. This kiss was saying everything he couldn't say because he wanted this woman, even though wanting her was ludicrous. Somehow, despite kidnapping, she had done more than mark him. She had touched something inside him.

Jordan lifted his mouth. "Rena, Rena, Rena," he moaned, not wanting to admit the things he felt for her. Resting on his forearms, he looked down on her. She was his enemy, but that important fact didn't seem to matter.

"Why have you stopped the kiss?" Verena was confused. She must have done it wrong. "Why have you pulled away from me? Come back." She placed both hands on the back of his neck, pulling him back toward her.

"Rena." Jordan needed to leave now or he wouldn't be able to. He no longer wanted to leave her panting; he just wanted to leave her while he still could.

Verena paused. "You have called me this name before." She yanked him to her chest, rolling across the pallet so that their positions were reversed. "Why?"

"Another name for you." Teeth clenched, he released a long, slow breath. "Shorter," he told her. That it was more personal he kept to himself. Not at all surprised at how easily she had rolled him across the bed, this pause, this intermission or whatever, was the perfect time to ease himself away from her. But then the sensation of her breasts pressed against his chest warred with his intentions.

"Oh." Verena said, using the expression she had heard Rya use. She had no words she wanted to share with Jordan. What she wanted to share was more kisses. They were as wonderful and amazing as Jordan said. Though she could kiss him all day, slowly channeling her own excitement and passion into him, kisses were not all that her body craved.

The completely Earth-like 'oh' she had uttered was so unexpected and surprising to Jordan that his heart churned with emotions he refused to acknowledge. Allowing his

121

feelings to take control he pulled her head down, taking the perfect O of her full brown lips between his own and kissed her with soft, careful touches. "My beautiful Rena," he whispered.

The softness of his touch—

His words—

They pulled from Verena a sudden surge of pleasure. It rushed through her, channeling into Jordan as he kissed her. Verena felt him stiffen beneath her, heard him calling out with a joyous moan. She had expected it. She knew what would come next. The demanding hardness of him against her told her this, but she no longer wanted it. She could not take what he was so ready to give to her.

Jordan didn't know what hit him with that last kiss, but whatever had possessed him to hold back from making love to Verena had died a sudden death. He wanted her and she was willing. Rolling across the pallet until he was now on top, Jordan rained kisses all over her face, her neck. He nibbled there, pulling the tender skin into his mouth, leaving another mark where the other had faded. He worked his way down, claiming each bronze colored breast with his mouth. He reached lower, kissing his way down until she stopped him with a loud shriek.

"Jordan, cease, I command you! This cannot happen. This will not happen today!"

Jordan eased his body off the pallet, leaning against it on his knees. The view was so enticing he could almost ignore her words. But cease meant stop, and when a woman said stop Jordan knew better than to force her. He took in a steadying breath. "Is that a command?" he asked in a deadly quiet voice.

"Yes," she told him, seeing that answering in the affirmative was the best possible course. "Step away so that I may clothe myself."

Jordan stood, taking two steps back, each movement a painful ache of unfulfilled need. He stared in disbelief as she stood and without uttering another word, turned her back on him to cover her body. No explanation, no apologies for letting things go so far, just a command for him to cease, to step away. "So," he said aloud, suddenly realizing what this had all been about. "I've finally received my punishment." She had done to him what he had hoped to do to her.

"This had nothing to do with punishment." Verena could barely believe her ears.

"I believe that it does."

"Then you are mistaken," Verena told him. The pulsing of her heart and the throbbing of her mouth, her entire body, was proof enough of that. To have let the act of pleasuring take its natural course would have been most gratifying physically, but she couldn't go through with it. Not after hearing the sweetness in his voice when he called her Rena, beautiful Rena. It was not fitting to take him before they were united. She could not dishonor him so.

"There is no other reasonable explanation."

"There is. We had to stop for your own protection."

"Protection!" Jordan shouted.

Verena stayed where she was, her admiration for him growing even more. He was unafraid to stand up to her.

Naked and uncaring about it, he began to move from one end of the room to the other, the word *protection* echoing inside his head.

He paused.

Protection!

Jordan suddenly realized that he had had no protection. If he had made love to her, he could have very well made her pregnant, done exactly what they wanted him to do. It was those pulsing shock waves that had pushed him over the edge. "Well, all I have to say to that is, thank you for protecting me. This punishment did exactly that for me."

"You are ranting. What we just shared was no punishment."

"Sure the hell feels like it!"

"Do not elevate your voice. Also, stop this senseless moving about and cover yourself."

"Are those all commands? Must I obey them as part of my punishment?"

"You are being emotional and very unreasonable."

"Unreasonable? No, not unreasonable," he quietly told her. "Angry. I am angry."

"Then please clothe your angry body." Verena could not take much more of his naked flesh mocking her.

He marched to the side chamber, threw on some robes C1 had left for him and turned to her. "My angry body is clothed, Commander."

"Then calm yourself. I do not understand your anger. I have done you a great courtesy."

"That you have, by stopping me. Making love to you would have been the worst thing I could have done."

"Are those words some punishment you have for me?" Verena asked. If they were, they worked quite well for she found that what Jordan thought of her had some import.

"Just as much as yours."

"Then it is your anger that talks."

"There's been enough talk. Your actions show me how you feel about me. I have been punished. Be satisfied."

"There has been no satisfaction in any way this morn."

"I agree with you there."

"I will have you know that this degree of sharing will not occur again until we have performed the Ceremony of Unity."

"Another command?"

"A matter of inevitability. We will be united. It is Vi-she."

"As you believe. I believe that I still have some say in the matter."

"Then come to terms with what shall be. I will wait for you to realize where your future lies. Until then, we will not share such intimacies."

"Good. Thank you. I won't have to worry about leaving a child of mine inside of you to be raised by Vixens." Moving closer, standing directly in front of her, Jordan softly whispered, "My only disappointment will be in knowing that I will never feel your softness against me ever again. But I can live with that. Just know that there won't be any kind of ceremony between us."

Watching her arms fold and her fingers tighten on her forearms should have stopped him from saying anything further, but Jordan heard himself say, "Finding a way home is much more appealing." What could have been hurt flashed on her face before she answered.

"You *are* going home, Jordan. You're going to a new home, the planet Vixen. Understand that and life will quickly fall into place."

"As you see it, Commander."

"As I know it."

"We'll have to agree to disagree on this. Time will tell."

Verena was about to question his strange words when a voice invaded the room.

"Commander, I beg your pardon."

Verena forced herself to focus on Suvan's voice coming through the ship's communications system.

"The guards are here to escort the pale one to a gathering with the other men."

Verena eyed Jordan before answering in the language of Vixen. "For what purpose?"

Suvan in turn answered in their native tongue. "Bruce, my half-ling, has stated that this was a meeting arranged when the pale one was sent in to—"

"I recall why he was sent. This meeting cannot be."

After a pause Suvan asked, "May I speak with you more on this, Commander?"

"Meet me in the conferring room."

Verena had sensed Jordan's eyes on her during the brief conversation but was not concerned. Though every sister of Vixen spoke the Earth's English language fluently, the Earth men could not understand theirs.

"Have a nice chat with one of your sisters of Vixen? Did you discuss the crimes of injustice you are all guilty of?"

"We are guilty of nothing more than saving our species. Please, go into the side chamber and speak to Comfort 1. He will explain it all to you. A male of your great intelligence will surely realize that there is no use fighting what shall be."

"So, Verena, once again, I am your prisoner." Saying her name somehow steadied the growing powerlessness he was feeling. From the sound of it, he was losing his chance to have contact with the men.

"Until the time that you willingly step forward to perform the Ceremony of Unity, becoming my half-ling, binding us for life."

"Don't hold your breath."

"Holding our breath is a skill in which we sisters of Vixen are extremely proficient," she told him before walking out of the chamber.

CHAPTER 9

Suvan and the guards were waiting for Verena outside the conferring room. Suvan followed her inside.

"What is this of which you speak? What meeting is there for Jordan with the other males?" Verena asked.

"Jordan? Who is Jordan?"

"The pale one. Jordan is his given name. That is what he wishes—I wish for him to be called."

"Certainly, Commander." A slight smile interrupted Suvan's somber expression. "I am concerned that you did not know of this meeting. It has been arranged to be a frequent occurrence. Were you not you present when—um—Jordan went to Bruce to counteract those ridiculous threats when I was ill?"

"Yes, but so much occurred that night that I do not recall an arrangement of a meeting. Could your Bruce have created such a story?"

"I doubt that. He was very pleased to have 'the ear of the boss,' as he called it."

"I am sorry, Suvan, this meeting can not be. The security of our mission is at stake. It is not safe for Jordan to be near any Earth men at this time."

"If I may say so, having studied our new males extensively, Jordan's absence from this meeting will result in dissatisfaction among the males. They thrive on being heard, on having a 'voice.' Bruce is most excited about being able to air his concerns."

"You are beginning to sound like them, Suvan." Verena folded her arms, deep in thought. "We will simply say that he is ill."

"Will that work for the remainder of the voyage? There are at least fifteen long Earth days of travel before we reach Vixen. We must keep our males content until then."

"I understand this. This mission, I am beginning to see, is more complex then any of us expected. I wonder how our other sisters are faring with their mission."

"Perhaps better for they are not dealing with Earth men."

"Perhaps," Verena mused, lost in thought.

"Commander, maybe some interaction with the other males would keep your Jordan content. I do not know what troubles you are having with him—"

"Troubles? I am having no troubles." Verena denied her fingers digging into her forearms. Her male had been giving her nothing but trouble, but to admit that to another sister would fill her with shame. On reflection, she thought that time spent with the other males might make Jordan more manageable. Seeing Bruce and the other half-lings happy with their mates could possibly direct his thoughts to acceptance of his fate. Satisfied with this idea, Verena announced as she strode toward the door, "If a meeting with Jordan as 'the boss' will keep the males content, then he may attend. Make certain every male who has performed the Ceremony of Unity is in attendance.

The guards must be present at all times. I will be joining you as well."

"As you wish, Commander."

"Tell the guards to escort Jordan to the construction site in the next quarter hour. I will meet you there." Verena made her rounds throughout the ship, inspecting every aspect of her command, before making her way to the prearranged meeting of the males.

"J.M., are you still all together and in one complete piece?" A quick flash in the room told Jordan that C1 had scanned him.

"What was that for? Other then being frustrated more than any man has the right to be I'm perfectly okay."

"No, J.M., what you are is courageous and strong. Your boldness knows no bounds. Your intelligence is immeasurable, although I doubted it a few times."

"Stop with the compliments. I'm starting to take them as insults."

"No insult intended, J.M."

"Wait a minute. You were eavesdropping on us out there."

"I kept my circuits open in case you needed me to intervene. Many times I thought you did indeed need my services but then it became obvious that you did not."

"I did not need your services and I will never need your services in that particular area, C1. Next time stay out of my private business."

"According to your own words there will be no more private business between you and the commander."

"You're right, there won't be any." The reminder did nothing to put him in a better mood. Changing the subject, Jordan asked, "How would you have intervened, if you'd needed to?"

"I could have caused a slight malfunction in the side chamber, brought forth a bit of smoke so that it appeared that something was amiss."

Jordan tucked that information in the back of his head. Right now his mind was on the meeting he might not have. "Tell me, C1, where is the commander now?"

"Leaving the conferring room, I believe."

"Then I missed what happened."

"Not to worry, two guards and Sister Suvan are coming for you. I must tell you, there were four more Ceremonies of Unity last night."

"Great!" Feeling bad about how short-tempered he was being, Jordan added, "Thanks for the information, C1." He quickly changed out of the robes he had been ordered to wear and dressed in the suit C1 had provided. Adding up the number of victims in his head, he realized there were now twenty-five men united to Vixen women.

"They are nearly here for you, J.M."

Jordan was straightening his tie. "I'm almost ready. I hope they're taking me to the meeting and not some holding cell."

"They will not harm you in any way."

"How do you know that?"

"Because you are revered; you are honored by your future mate."

"Could have fooled me," Jordan told C1 as the signal announcing the arrival of Suvan and the guards filled the room.

"We will speak on this later. Enjoy your meeting."

The door to the side chamber opened. The guards stood on each side of the opening and Suvan smiled at him, beckoning him forward with the graceful wave he found to be common among the women of Vixen. Suvan was as beautiful as the other Vixens. Her short hair close to her head formed a low bush with tiny tight curls framing her face. Verena's hair was a bit longer than Suvan's and had even more curl. Jordan found the curly look quite sexy.

"Come, the men await," Suvan told him, making him realize that he had been mentally comparing her to Verena and that Verena had come out on top. None of these women deserved to occupy that much of his mind. "Nothing beyond freedom," he told himself.

With Suvan walking beside him and one guard at each of their sides, Jordan exited Verena's chamber for the second time since becoming trapped on board. He paid more attention this time, noting the same crystal-like walls that seemed endless and smooth as glass.

"The men are anxious to talk with you."

"You called them men, not males," Jordan told her.

"I find that Earth men prefer that reference."

"That's probably because when a sister of Vixen says *males*, it's uttered with a touch of inferiority."

"True, that is why I prefer to say men when speaking to the men."

"I guess it helps to stroke their egos and keep them in line, as well as making it easier to continue to dupe them into believing that they're still on Earth."

"All for a very good cause."

Before Jordan could comment on that, Zytai, the Vixen who had implied that he was ugly, came walking toward them. Unfortunately, he couldn't say the same thing about her. Every one of the Vixen women he'd seen were gorgeous. And gorgeous in such a different way than what he had been raised to believe was gorgeous. Not one of the women had long hair and fair skin, but they were beautiful just the same. They had smooth, brown skin and almond-shaped eyes. Their long sexy bodies moved with a fluid grace that reminded him of giant waves crashing on a beach, powerful and strong but holding a rhythm, a beat, a movement all their own. No wonder twenty-five men had surrendered to them. When a Vixen crashed into you, she was hard to resist. And the men on this ship weren't resisting because they didn't know their true circumstance.

Thinking of Verena, Jordan knew there would have been no resistance on his part if the wool was being pulled over his eyes.

Zytai hailed Suvan with a firm yet ladylike wave, speaking to her in her own tongue. Jordan caught every word as he stared blankly ahead.

"Bringing the pale one to the grand meeting?" she giggled.

The woman giggled. Jordan hadn't thought she was capable of such a thing. As he continued to listen, his hackles went up at her growing derisive tone.

"My half-ling was so excited. This meeting was all that he could talk about. He said he had a thing or two to tell the boss. Such simple things make them happy, don't they?"

"Sometimes," Suvan answered. "We are late. I'll bid you good day."

"Good day," Zytai answered, turning to stare at Jordan. "He is not as unattractive as I once thought. I suppose paleness grows on a person. But the hair, I cannot get used to it."

She had carelessly insulted Jordan without realizing he had understood every word. He watched as she walked a few steps away, stood before an area of the crystal wall and disappeared through it a moment later. As they passed the spot where she had vanished, Jordan did not see any indication of a door or portal. Did they have some strange powers he had yet to learn about? No, more likely, the secret lay in the smooth crystal-like walls.

Suvan did not speak to him again. At the end of the hall, they stepped into an oval-shaped compartment almost too small for the four of them. Their shoulders pushed against each other.

"This is a bit tight, don't you think?"

"Be silent, male," one of the guards told him.

"Commander's orders," Suvan said without apology.

The crowdedness wasn't a problem, for no sooner had Suvan uttered the word, "Holo-level" than they were squeezing out of the tight compartment to move down a dark hall. Suvan quickly punched in a sequence of symbols. Jordan caught only the number of beeps emitting from the touch pad.

Seven.

He'd counted seven.

They entered a room that was the great outdoors.

Before him lay a construction site that could not be considered anything but what it appeared to be. Machinery, equipment and a scaffold towering at least five stories high. A cement truck was spinning and pouring out its contents while another truck with a shipment of lumber was being unloaded by men wearing hard hats. There were trees and birds and clouds. The Vixens had replicated everything.

Jordan sniffed.

The smells were those of a construction site: sawdust, cement and overturned earth. A huge pile of sand and a partially constructed building sat right on the edge of a bayou.

"That looks exactly like Bayou Savage."

"Therefore it is," Suvan told him.

Jordan felt an enormous weight of resistance land on his shoulders. How could he convince the men that *all of this* was fake?

Bruce was walking toward them. He had a new look. His head was shaved clean. Before even acknowledging him, Bruce went straight to Suvan. "You left your hard hat, Susie girl." He kissed her as he placed it on her head.

Jordan was able to see the back of Bruce's head where the only bit of hair was sculpted into a lightening bolt.

Bruce stepped back to pat her hat. "Safety first. Here's one for you, Mr. Mitchell."

"Call me Jordan," he told the big man, catching the hard hat tossed at his stomach. He noted the look of adoration on Bruce's face as he looked at Suvan, as well as the one Suvan wore herself. Jordan was almost certain the tint of her skin hid a blush. This was getting more and more complicated.

"You're late," Bruce told him, donning his own hard hat.

"Got tied up," was all Jordan said by way of explanation. "How about we start this meeting?" Jordan rubbed his hands in anticipation. Verena was nowhere around. Suvan was easy company. He could even say he liked her a little. The guards? They might be a problem.

"You're joining us, right, Susie? After all, you're the foreman." He turned to Jordan. "She keeps these men in line, runs a tight ship. You need to give her a raise."

"A raise? That's something to consider after such a glorious report. As a matter of fact, that's something I'm going to consider," Jordan announced, hoping to score some points with Bruce.

"You heard that, baby!" Bruce grabbed her around the waist and swung her around before gently landing her on her feet. "Check it out." Bruce took his eyes off Suvan to say, "Your secretary's here."

Jordan turned to see Verena gliding toward them. She was wearing a very businesslike, extremely Western and

Earthlike skirt and jacket, the skirt showing way too much of her never-gonna-stop sexy legs. Jordan was itching to tell her to go back to the chamber to cover them. But he caught himself. What she wore should not concern him.

But it did.

"Sorry that I am late," she said to everyone in general.

"Not at all, we're just getting started," Bruce answered. "Susie, why don't you show Mr. Mitchell—"

"Jordan."

"—Jordan and his secretary to the trailer. I'll call the men in."

Suvan nodded, taking her position beside Jordan, guiding him toward the trailer. Verena went to his other side as the guards took their places on each end. They were like a straight line of soldiers standing shoulder to shoulder with Jordan stuck in the middle. The image of an Oreo cookie flashed in his head. If his freedom and that of the men he was determined to rescue weren't at stake, he wouldn't mind being the creamy center surrounded by such rich, dark beauty. But this situation was so much more.

Jordan looked to the left of him and then to the right where Verena stood, her aura of command in no way diminished by the clothes she wore. Still, they had to look as ridiculous as he felt. "Is all this necessary?" Jordan asked Verena. "What do you think I'm going to do?"

"I have not one thought on that, which is why this is necessary," she told him and proceeded in a very low tone to talk to Suvan in their native language, a conversation he easily eavesdropped on.

"Did he cause you any problems?"

"No, he has been most cooperative and pleasant."

"Have you done what I asked?"

"Jordan has been no trouble and yes, all the men you requested have been included."

"Excellent."

Wondering what that meant, Jordan entered the trailer, found a seat and put on his most welcoming smile in hopes of relaxing the men. First impressions mattered. Jordan was determined to gain their trust. Being the only white man didn't help matters, but there was nothing he could do about that. As the men came in one by one, lifting the hard hats from their heads, Jordan soon realized what it was Verena and Suvan had been talking about. Every man who entered had a shaved head. Every man, it appeared, Verena wanted him to see. She didn't know that he knew the significance of the shaved heads.

What was she trying to do?

Did she know about C1 helping him keep track of the men?

He hoped not. Jordan would hate to lose C1. He was much more to him than computerized company.

Jordan's smile did not falter as he shook hands with the men who were now attached to the sisters of Vixen, whether they knew it or not.

Over a dozen men with glistening heads in several shades of brown sat before him. If the situation weren't so serious Jordan would be laughing. "You guys part of some club?" He had to ask, needing to know what they thought about the common baldness surrounding them.

"Naw," the biggest man answered for them all. "Our girlfriends, the women you've got working here, they like the look. We do what pleases our women. Is that a problem?" he asked before Jordan could get a word in.

"Not a problem at all. I'm here to alleviate any problems." Kidnappings from Earth, fake construction sites, sperm-starved females from another planet…

The list in his head could go on and on. Of course inside his head was where all those very real problems had to remain for the time being.

"We'll see," the big man answered.

And so the meeting began with Bruce officiating. The main concerns centered on safety issues, though they were few. The discussion was boring and getting him nowhere. The guards stood at the door, Suvan sat next to Bruce, giving her input when necessary, and Verena sat behind him.

Having no way of changing anything, Jordan found himself diving into the role of business owner. He particularly enjoyed the added perk of giving orders to his 'secretary.'

He had commanded Verena to take notes, get him a cup of coffee and to call his office to let somebody know he wasn't coming in. The last Jordan wished he could actually ask her to do. "Mr. Mitchell won't be in today, Troy. He is flying through space on a Vixen spaceship, under duress, of course, because he's been kidnapped."

Refocusing, Jordan thought about each of the men. Bruce was still loud, but likeable and conscientious now that he was sober, and he seemed to know the construction

139

business. Michael, Rya's pick, was quiet, his only concern a mix-up with his schedule that didn't give him regular days off, days he probably wanted to spend with Rya. There was Joe who kept rubbing his head. One of the new victims, Jordan guessed. Marcus and Earl kept looking at their watches. Impatient. That might be helpful. The other guys, Briceson, Nick, Calvin, and a few whose names he couldn't remember, all appeared to be hard working men out to make a living. It was their right, but a freedom they would soon be denied. The injustice of it all rankled him.

As the meeting wound down, Jordan stood to thank the men for coming and to remind them that there would be another meeting again next week at the same time to voice their concerns. Everyone was rising to leave when the big man, Big John, they called him, threw out a question that Jordan wasn't sure how to answer.

"Something's been bothering me." Big John stood, his width and height an intimidating force.

"Tell me about it." Jordan sat on the edge of a small desk, attempting to look as boss-like and un-intimidated as he could.

"This construction site is the cleanest, smoothest run organization I have ever worked for."

"That's Susie's doing," Bruce called out.

Jordan smiled and nodded. "Go on."

"There's no complaint here. The pay's the best I've ever had, the benefits and medical coverage are more than I ever expected. You provide us with homes to live in, a gym to work out in and a bar to have a little bit of fun in."

"Go on."

"You tell us that we're not to have contact with anyone until the project is completed since we're building some secret government building, a prototype of a level five hurricane resistant building. Am I right?"

Jordan nodded, though this was news to him.

"All the men working here are black, the only women the most gorgeous black women I've ever seen in my life." Big John paused, an expression of suspicion on his face.

Jordan saw where he was going. All black crew, gorgeous black women, yet a white boss. "And this bothers you?" Jordan asked as Big John continued to stare.

"Hell yes, it's bothering me! What bothers me more is that there is not one other white man working on this crew, not one Hispanic or Asian either. Why is that? What's the catch? What's really going on around here?"

A perfect opening, but one Jordan could not fall into. Every man in the room was staring at him expectantly. What was the catch? What was really happening? What Jordan wanted to say was, "At this moment you're being whisked through space billions of miles from Earth to be used as sperm donors on a planet that view men as second-class citizens."

"What can I say?"

"Excuse me, Jor—"

"Mr. Mitchell," Suvan provided.

Verena was standing behind him, her mouth very close to his ear. "May I have a word with you," she stated, making the common question a command.

"Of course. Give me a minute, Big John." Jordan turned to face her, taken aback again by the perfect fit of the business suit, the perfect fit of the woman herself in anything, including the Vixen robes he was used to seeing her wear or nothing at all, like the passionate moments they'd shared before she backed away, saving him from making the mistake of his life.

"Take extreme care in how you respond," Verena said into his ear.

"Is that a warning?" Jordan asked.

"Indeed."

Jordan turned back to the men. The tension in the air was as thick as the hair missing from their heads. "Thank you, Verena, for reminding me of the many benefactors who have contributed to this project," Jordan said out loud for the benefit of the men.

"Project? We're part of some project?" Big John repeated.

"Exactly."

"With a white man in charge?" someone else said.

"Looks that way," Jordan answered, his arms open wide.

The room went silent, then exploded with a wide variety of reactions.

"It don't matter to me as long as I get paid."

"Better not be anything illegal going on. I'm not for going to jail."

"It's a conspiracy, that's what it is."

"I knew this job was too good to be true."

"Someone's always out there trying to keep a brother down."

"Do something to calm this room," Verena hissed into his ear.

Jordan was about to do just that but felt the men needed a minute or two to vent. A loud whistle pierced the room before he could even begin to get their attention. Jordan looked out in the crowed room to see that the whistle was coming from Suvan.

"That's my girl," Bruce bellowed, the only voice resounding in the now quiet room.

"Let me explain," Jordan began. "There is nothing illegal going on here." Jordan paused. *Unethical and illegal,* a voice inside his head corrected.

"That's something," Big John said.

"This is not a conspiracy." *Not one against black men, just Earth men,* that little voice couldn't help saying so.

"As if you would tell us if it was," someone else said.

I wish I could tell you everything. The inside of his head echoed with the responses he wished he could openly relay. "All I can tell you is the truth. As you already know, this complex is being built in secrecy." True, this whole situation was one big secret.

"Why not use those navy builders, those Seabees?"

"This is the FBI, not the armed forces. And this is a two-fold project," Jordan created from the top of his head. "We wanted men to build this complex, but we also wanted to take a statistical count of the race of the men who qualified to work on this project. We were looking for fifty workers. It just so happen that the first fifty men who were interviewed and qualified for this job *were* black men."

Jordan wasn't sure if his off-the-top-of-his-head made-up explanation would be enough to quell their suspicions. The last thing he wanted them to be was suspicious of him. His eventual goal was to direct the suspicion to the Vixen women.

"The interview for this job *was* like nothing I've ever been through before," Big John said after a long silence. "I started to walk away but then I saw Zytai. You could say she helped me to change my mind."

I bet, Jordan thought as he plastered a smile on his face.

"I can see whatcha saying," Briceson said.

"Makes sense to me," another man answered.

"Yeah, I feel like I'm doing something good for my country," Michael called out.

"Proves the talents of the black man," was Bruce's remark.

"And that everybody's not out to hold a brother down," Calvin added.

Brothers. Jordan looked around at the men before him, their shiny heads an in-his-face reminder that he had his work cut out for him. But he would do anything in his power to get them all back to Earth because they were all brothers, men of Earth. He would not allow race to be an issue. He might be the only white man on this ship, but he wasn't the only Earth man.

"One more question," Big John said.

"What's that?" Jordan waited, hoping he would able to answer this one as well.

"Where the hell did all these gorgeous women come from?"

If only he could answer that question. "These gorgeous women," Jordan paused to look at Suvan, the guards at the door and Verena behind him, "come from an isolated area, a place that you probably won't be able to find on a map. A place called Vixen."

"Jordan," he heard Verena say behind him.

"They got hit by the hurricane?"

"Yes, and we have suffered greatly, just as you have," Verena interjected.

"Then they came here looking for jobs?"

"Exactly." Jordan watched Verena out of the corner of his eye. She was wearing that superior half-smile. She knew what she was doing. That little tidbit she had added was enough to give the men and sisters a common ground to build on. As if the sexual tension they created wasn't enough.

"That explains why they live on the grounds."

Jordan nodded, satisfied that he hadn't exactly lied since he was unable to tell them the truth with so many Vixens surrounding him.

"I guess we're done," Jordan reluctantly announced as the men filed out. "Call if you need me," he said to each and every man.

The room was finally empty of everyone except Jordan, the guards and Verena.

"Escort him to my chamber," she told the guards who were walking to the trailer door.

She glided back to him and said in a voice only he could hear, "You, Comfort 1 and I have many things to discuss. Prepare yourself, Jordan."

145

MISSION

And then she was gone, leaving him to wonder exactly what that meant.

CHAPTER 10

"What does she know, C1?"

"That is a question I cannot answer. But if being of service and a friend to you has brought on disablement, then I welcome it," C1 told him without a squeak or a whine.

"You will not be disabled. I won't let it happen."

"J.M., J.M., J.M., a male has so little power. But thank you for your concern."

"A *Vixen* male *had* little power. I am not a Vixen male."

"That I am aware of, J.M."

"And for that, I am most thankful," Verena said as she entered the side chamber.

"Welcome, Commander," C1 one greeted. "It is an honor to have you visit our dwelling. I would have told you so early this morn but your mind was otherwise occupied and—"

"That's enough, C1," Jordan interrupted as his mind flashed with a vision of Verena naked and proud as she walked toward him this morning, reminding him exactly how preoccupied they had been.

"I do understand your earlier dilemma," Verena told C1. "Do not be troubled by it."

"May I offer you a seat? J.M., you should have offered your future mate a seat."

"No, he could not, Comfort model. He is still angry with me. At least he is not angry and *naked*. I will not take offense, and the floor where Jordan reclines on a daily basis is where I shall sit."

In one smooth motion she sat on the floor before him. Unsure of how to react, Jordan didn't say a word. She patted a spot beside her, inviting instead of commanding him to join her. Jordan sat across from her. "You're here, C1's here and I'm here. What is it you want to discuss?"

"C1, that is an interesting name you have for your Comfort model. You have become close, have you not?"

When Jordan didn't answer right away, C1 jumped in. "We have become friends, Commander."

"Unusual."

"What's so unusual about that?" Jordan asked.

"It is an occurrence that has not happened before. Comfort models are rarely given to a male, but those who have had the privilege simply accepted the services, never forming a bond."

"Isn't that something?"

"Your tone implies that you believe that it actually is *not* something."

"It is called sarcasm, Commander," C1 explained.

"C1, will you please stay out of this?"

"But, J.M., I am in this. The Commander wants to speak to me as well."

"You see, this is precisely what I speak of. I have never witnessed such interaction before. I never saw my father speak to his Comfort model in this way."

"So?"

"So, one might deduce that your unusual connection to your companion is similar to our unusual connection."

"Verena, you can't call what we have friendship." Jordan leaned back on his hands, the familiar sexual tension rising as he sat before her. He needed to put a little space between them without looking, as if he needed to put a little space between them.

"No, but friendship is what I am seeking."

"Are you crazy?" Jordan leaned forward, forgetting about distance. In a harsh whisper he said, "The main reason C1 and I have formed a bond of friendship is because of you and your sisters of Vixen." Finding himself so close that he could feel her soft breath, Jordan slowly leaned back again.

"The main reason you have formed a bond is because of you, Jordan," Verena told him, looking in no way bothered by his nearness to her.

"The commander is correct. I have never served a male like you before."

"Then there was something lacking in the Vixen male," Jordan surmised.

"Exactly, which is why our connection is so different. We are not moving along as I had expected."

"You mean I am not doing what you expected."

"Exactly."

"What does this all mean, Verena?" Jordan stood.

"That I will have to forget the ways of Vixen courtship," she said, standing beside him.

C1 gasped. "Commander!"

"Silence, C1," Verena commanded and the computer immediately obeyed. "You and I will have to find our own way," she told Jordan.

Surprised, Jordan controlled his facial features. Mentally his eyebrows raised at her answer. "It will be a way that will lead nowhere. I do not want to be here with you. I don't intend to live the rest of my life on some strange planet. My goal is to return myself and all fifty men to Earth."

"I understand you well, Jordan, but this shall not happen. I am hopeful that C1 will help you to adjust, that your friendship will guide you to accepting what *will* be. That is your mission, C1."

"Yes, Commander."

"So you're using my friendship with C1 against me?"

"No, I am seeking a way to help you to adjust."

"Which is an unusual and gracious thing for a sister of Vixen to do, J.M.," C1 interjected.

Jordan ignored C1, concentrating on Verena instead. "How kind. But you have to realize that whatever you do you can not, will not, change the fact that I was stolen from my home."

"I realize that one necessary action—"

"Necessary action!"

"—did not endear myself to you," she continued, "but I am still hopeful that we can begin to find our own way."

"You said that already."

"But I was not heard. If you could build a bond with C1, could you not consider building a bond with me?"

"My enemy?"

150

"Your future mate."

"My enemy."

"Time will tell. I have thought on these words you spoke once before. Time…will…tell," She said the words slowly, eloquently. "I understand them to mean we will know the outcome in time. So I will say to you again, time will tell."

"Time will only show that you will remain my enemy."

"Time will show that you will become my companion. I propose that we come together peacefully, share meals and conversation. Real conversation. I could not endure one more of those monologues you had a tendency to bore me with."

Jordan didn't want to, but the memory made him smile. A smile that implied they had a history, a connection. She smiled back at him. He didn't want this, but then again, what could it hurt? Maybe by getting to know her better he could catch her off guard, learn something important. There was only so much C1 was able to provide. "Fine, but I will not touch you again. I won't make love to you."

She raised her head at this, her shoulders lifting, her pride evident. "As I have said once before, there will be no more intimacies until the Ceremony of Unity."

"As I have said more than once before, there will be no Ceremony of Unity."

"Time will tell." She walked to the door of the side chamber. Jordan did the same. "I have duties to attend." She laid a hand to his cheek. "Until this eve," she told him. "I wish to dine with you."

Jordan nodded, watching as she went to the outside door. "You may roam about and study anything inside the chamber at your leisure." The door closed as she stood smiling at him.

Jordan stepped back into his chamber. "Close my door, C1. She has been watching me. She knows I've been poking around. I wonder what else she knows?"

"I am not sure but I do not believe that the commander is aware of your lessons in speaking and reading the Vixen language. We have only done so in the side chamber. It is soundproof for a male's privacy and has never held a monitoring device."

"Why not?"

"The sisters of Vixen never thought the things a male would do could be of any concern."

"I like that answer, but still, it rubs me the wrong way."

"You sound frustrated, J.M."

"I am. My abductor wants to date me."

"Your future mate, your destiny."

"There you go again with that! What kind of friend are you?"

"A true friend. Does a friend not speak honest words when the need arises?"

"Yes."

"Then listen to a few honest words, J.M." C1's voice deepened as if he were maturing. And maybe he was because the words he spoke were not words he would have thought the C1 of a month ago would say. "The commander honors you and thinks highly of you."

"Sure she does."

"Sarcasm again, J.M.?"

"Sorry, go on, tell me exactly how she has honored me," Jordan said with disinterest.

"She could have taken you in the act of pleasuring this morn, causing you to be ridiculed, branded as a low being for giving of yourself without benefit of ceremony."

"I wouldn't have been the only one giving anything away."

"Yes, but it is the male who has to remain pure."

"That is so backwards."

"It is the way of Vixen society."

"Well, Earth society sees it the other way around, though we are not as stringent as we used to be."

"Also…"

"There's more?"

"Yes."

"Go on, I might as well hear it all."

"A sister of Vixen has been known to take what she wants."

"They've taken, alright."

"In the beginning, but the commander is no longer taking. Didn't you hear her words, J.M.? She has turned her back on her customs in regards to obtaining a mate, all for your benefit."

"If she had my benefit in mind I would be on my way home by now."

"The commander cares for you deeply, J.M."

"Actions speak louder than words, C1."

"Another Earth expression. I find that I enjoy them. Let me guess. This one means that what one does means more than what one says."

"Exactly."

"Then you are blind, J.M., if you are not seeing what she has done for you."

"I have seen it all."

"Not everything."

"Say that again."

"Not everything, J.M."

"Something seems different about you. Is your voice changing? It sounds deeper."

"It does?"

"That's strange."

"Yes, but I believe our friendship is the result."

"I'm not so sure about that. You are a Vixen computer, I have to remember that."

"Are you questioning my loyalty to you? Our friendship, J.M.?" C1 sounded hurt, insulted.

"I guess I am."

"This saddens me."

C1 sounded more than sad. His voice held a despondency that had not been there before. Jordan wondered if he was barking up the wrong tree, but so many things were out of his control he felt as if he had a hold on nothing at all.

His future.

The men.

Verena.

C1.

Nothing.

"It doesn't make me feel too good either."

"At least listen to the dire consequences the commander will suffer by not following Vixen tradition."

"I don't want to hear any more, C1. Leave me! Go away! I need to meditate."

"As you wish, J.M."

When all was quiet, Jordan sat in the middle of the chamber. "It's not as if it was going to kill her," he whispered.

"Are you certain of that?" C1 asked.

"I told you to go away," Jordan said as calmly as he could, digging deep to hold to the Karate-do values he had been taught. When the room was silent once again, he pulled in a deep, cleansing breath, soothing his spirit and clearing his mind.

After an hour of meditation, Jordan exercised in Karate-do fashion. His body was cooled and refreshed as usual by C1 but they did not share a word between them. Later, Jordan sat on his pallet to add a few words to the journal he had been keeping. He was much too relaxed to write, and with the past week's sleep deprivation taking its toll on him, he soon fell into a deep sleep, providing his body with some much needed rest.

Having spent most of the day on the main deck, Verena sat in the conferring room examining the events of the day. She was pleased with the outcome of her meeting with Jordan and C1. This surprised her. She had thought that ignoring Vixen tradition would leave her in a state of unease. Instead, she found it quite easy to lay aside such traditions as they referred to males. Always in the back of her mind was the idea that males should possibly be treated better. Allowing this thought to surface and remain at the forefront of her mind was something else that surprised her.

Everything she was doing in regards to her future mate surprised her. No tradition, no rules were being followed. Her mother would be most displeased, shocked at her actions. But her mother was not there. Verena could not worry about her reactions. She had to follow her instincts and her instincts told her that though the direction she chose to follow was not traditional, and somewhat dangerous, it was what *should* be done.

This realization had come upon her as she sat in the meeting with Jordan and the men. In the beginning she had experienced an overabundance of contentment as she looked out at the many shiny brown heads symbolizing the continuance of the Vixen race. But as she listened to the men, their opinions, their ideas, contentment turned into concern. These were not Vixen men. These men had thoughts of their own, goals of their own, and would not take kindly to falling in line as a male of Vixen was expected to do.

In a way, they were falling in line but with no knowledge of it. What would happen when these men discovered the truth? A great deal, Verena had begun to understand. Her dealings with Jordan was proof of that. But if she found a way to reach Jordan, to have him understand his place, giving him a bit of leeway of course, then maybe she would have some insight on how the other sisters of Vixen should proceed when the time came.

But then, the sisters already had some advantages over her. Twenty-five and soon all would be united, not one suffering the pains of suppressed pleasuring. They could all possibly have a child within long before they reached Vixen. What male could resist or ignore such a wondrous thing?

A child. Something Jordan did not want with her. To think he hated her that much sent a twinge of hurt through her. No, not hate. Things would change between them. So much was at stake. They had to change.

"Your meal is ready, Commander," Tora's voice announced at the open door. "It is your favorite dish."

Verena had taken to eating her evening meal in the conferring room, all alone now since Rya, Zytai and Suvan had mates. No longer. "I will dine in my chambers. Please provide a meal for two."

"Yes, Commander."

"Be certain to bring a bottle of Vixen Toca," Verena thought to remind her.

"As you wish."

Verena walked to her chamber, immediately scanning the room for Jordan, surprised at not finding him wandering about. He liked to move about she had discovered when she had watched him through a viewing monitor these past days. He was always touching and examining things, an innocent and amusing pastime. There was nothing in her chamber that he could harm or that could harm him and nothing he could use to escape.

157

She went to the side chamber, opening the door to find Jordan asleep on the pallet.

"Welcome," the computer greeted her.

"Fall silent. I wish to wake Jordan." Verena went to the pallet and sitting on its edge, touched the face that intrigued her asleep or awake. Why was he her destiny when there was a choice of so many others? Why someone whose looks were so different? Why was she destined to have what other sisters of Vixen would consider an unattractive half-ling.

Verena did not care.

Also, it was wise not to question Vi-she. Jordan was hers for reasons they were not meant to understand. Besides, it was those differences and difficulties that intrigued her, that gave him an endearing quality. "Open your eyes to a new beginning," she whispered to him.

His eyes opened immediately, as if he had been awake for some time. "What exactly am I opening my eyes to?"

"A meal and conversation," she responded, silently hoping that he would not protest.

"I can handle that." He sat up wearing the robes he'd had on earlier and walked to the door of the side chamber. He folded one arm in such a way that his elbow stuck out at the side of his body.

Verena followed, no longer insulted when he did things without her permission. Now it would seem strange for him to ask permission to do something as simple as walk away from her. How foolish to have required such a thing. "What are you doing, Jordan?" she asked, studying his stance.

"Waiting to escort you to dinner." He took one of her hands and placed it in the bend of his elbow and nodded to her. His hand upon hers was a contrast that highlighted their differences, differences they would overcome for her people's sake, for her own sake.

They walked the five steps it took for them to reach the table Tora had set up for them. Oval-shaped bowls were filled with a delicious Vixen dish, a combination of tender meat similar to Earth's chicken, a mixture of diced roots and a savory sauce made from the pulp of the olinda bush.

Jordan released her hand, moved behind her and then proceeded to pull the chair away from the table. Verena, not sure what he expected, sat and was almost unseated when he began to push the chair and herself forward. "Jordan, please tell me what you are doing."

"Being polite. It's customary for people who are dating."

"Dating?"

"Dinner. Conversation. On Earth that's called dating."

"Let us proceed with the custom, but warn me of any unusual actions."

"That could be almost anything."

True, Verena thought. Despite viewing the tapes of American customs of Earth, there was still much she did not know. "Tell me more of these customs," Verena suggested, thinking this was the perfect beginning.

"Normally," Jordan sat across from her, "a man or male, as you love to say, would drive to the woman's house and take her to a nice restaurant. Instead, you picked me up and took me a few feet from my prison."

159

"Your chamber."

"Yes."

"We would have some chit chat," he continued. "Talk about the weather, look at the menus."

"Explain menus."

He paused, his face a picture of the many thoughts flowing through his head. Watching a male think was a novel experience she found that she enjoyed. "A booklet with a list of foods that can be provided."

"Continue," Verena told him, enjoying the picture he was presenting.

"We would talk about the food, make a selection, but I see mine has already been made for me with no consideration for what I might enjoy."

"Yes." Verena ignored the sarcasm, as C1 had called it. "This dish is one that you will enjoy. It is my favorite."

"Then being the gentleman I am, I must try it."

Jordan took a spoonful and Verena did the same, the utensil gliding to her mouth a second time before she noticed that something was wrong. Jordan swallowed loudly before pulling in a huge draught of air.

"I hope the olinda sauce is not overpowering," she commented.

"Not at all."

"There is moisture collecting in the corners of your eyes." Verena told him, amused by his denial.

"No kidding. Has to be because I was surprised by the taste. Warning your companion about the intense heat of a dish is required on a date."

"Then perhaps—" Verena began as he lifted the tall glass to his lips. Too late. He placed the glass back on the table almost immediately. His tongue pushed past his lips coated with the brown liquid.

"What is that?"

"Toca, a fine liquid delicacy served with olinda stew. I did attempt to warn you."

"Liquid? I could have sworn it was a solid. It tastes like molasses with a kick."

"Has your mouth cooled?"

"As a matter of fact, it has."

"The stew and Toca complement each other, much like we are capable of complementing each other."

He didn't respond to her words, but Verena felt Jordan's eyes on her as she continued to eat.

"I don't see you reaching for the Toca—to cool your mouth."

"I have become accustomed to and am enjoying the heat of this dish."

His eyes went from her bowl to his. Verena could read the challenge even before he voiced it.

"I bet I could eat more of this stew without a drop of Toca than you can."

"A wager? A test? I have never had one with a mal— man before," she corrected, thinking that using the term he preferred might make him feel more comfortable.

Yes, comfortable.

She wanted Jordan to enjoy being in her presence, to feel comfortable. There was rarely a time when Verena could remember her father being comfortable—with herself and her kin sisters, yes, especially when they were grown. Her mother? Never. How sad.

"There's always a first time," Jordan was saying, bringing her attention back to him.

True, Verena admitted to herself. There were many firsts that she was experiencing with him, firsts that made her want to be in his company, that pushed a thrill of excitement into her heart whenever she thought about him, firsts that her mother would frown upon.

"What's the matter? Had too much of the spicy stuff already? Are you dying for some Toca?"

"No." She smiled at him, tossing her mother's face of disapproval to the side. " I would enjoy having a wager with you. What will you give in return for your loss?"

"Loss? I won't lose. I have battled the mighty habanero, the hottest pepper on Earth. This is nothing."

"Evidence I have seen tells me otherwise. What shall I rightfully win?"

"When I win, you will allow me to spend every Friday, all day, on the grounds with the men."

Verena took a second to think on that. "The guards will be present at all times."

"I know you wouldn't have it any other way."

"When I win—"

"If you win."

"A sister of Vixen never loses," Verena told him. "When I win, you must put aside your anger, meeting me with an openness to share."

"Not an easy thing to do, but since I'm not going to lose, it's a deal. Let's shake on it." Jordan thrust his hand out to her. When she simply looked at it, he took her hand in his and clasping them together, he moved them upward and downward.

"We must also contact within." Taking their hands apart, Verena turned them palm side down, intertwining them so that their fingers rested on top of each other's hands, fitting together snuggly, perfectly. Verena brought their joined hands to her breast, touching her heart, before moving their hands toward him, touching his chest in the same manner.

She caught his gaze. The connection that was always there sparked between them.

Jordan cleared his throat, his attention turning to the dish before him. "Let's get started," he announced as if the spark had not been lit. His voice was full of play and excitement, bringing a feel of liveliness into the air.

"Yes, let's."

Verena ate, unable to enjoy the meal as much as usual while watching Jordan suffer through each spoonful. His eyes became small pools of water, and his pale skin soon held a reddish tint, but he did not stop. He did not even waver from spooning the stew into his mouth until it was completely gone. The glass of Toca remained untouched beside him.

"Done!" he announced, releasing a huge breath of air.

"I am done as well." Verena placed the spoon beside the bowl.

"I haven't touched my glass of Toca," Jordan told her.

"Neither have I," Verena calmly said, keeping hidden the smile that wished to present itself.

163

"I know you want some, go ahead and drink."

"I believe it is you who not only want to drink but are also desperate for relief."

"Not at all." He released another lengthy breath. "I can go all night without touching the stuff. How about you?"

"That is possible for me as well."

"So, it's a tie. Nobody wins."

Verena nodded, the smile she tried to keep hidden finding its way to her face. "I agree," she said, taking pity on him. He was in great distress and was going to great lengths not to show it. He could not help the water falling from his eyes or the tint of red on his face. "Shall we drink the Toca together as one?" she asked.

"If you insist."

"I insist." The smile widened on her face.

"We both won, so each of us has to stick to the bet. I will stay all day every Friday at the construction site."

Verena nodded. "And you will be more open, less angry."

"Agreed." Together they lifted their glasses, Jordan tapping the side of hers with his own. "Another custom, a toast. Let us drink to a new—"

"Alliance."

"Alliance," he agreed though he looked reluctant to do so.

Verena tapped her glass to his and together they drank.

An instant relief seemed to take over his face. Jordan stood, came behind her and slowly pulled the chair in which she was seated outward, offering her his arm once again. "It has been a lovely evening. If you will walk me to my—"

"Chamber," Verena supplied, not wanting to hear the word prison again.

"—my chamber," he repeated, "I will say goodnight."

Verena hooked her arm into his, walking as slowly as she possibly could. She did not want this *date* to end. She did not want to leave his presence, but a few steps and they were there. He turned to her and lowering half of his body forward said, "Until tomorrow," and went inside his chamber.

"Good day," Verena told him, wondering if he felt the same sudden loss that she was feeling. Making her way back to the table, Verena felt a hand on her shoulder. She turned to find him standing behind her.

"There is one more custom. A date always ends with..." He stopped, leaned forward and laid his lips upon her forehead, "...a kiss. Good day," he said before going back into the side chamber.

CHAPTER 11

Unable to sleep after his 'date' with Verena, Jordan opened his journal and began to write.

Documentation.

He needed to put everything down on paper: this new swing in his relationship with Verena, C1, and any progress made toward freedom.

Everything.

Friday: The Date

I don't know why I kissed her! I almost felt as if I was on a real date. I almost felt like I was having a good time. Who am I kidding? There was no almost about it. I was on a date. I did have a good time and I didn't want to leave her. That's why I kissed her. Sad, but true, this attraction is bending my judgment. But it seems that I'm not the only one bending, if I am to believe both Verena and C1. Verena's so-called bending of Vixen customs could be a plus, possibly leading to a way home. And bending has already gotten me an opportunity to spend an entire day with the men. Once a week, only on Fridays, but it's a lot more than I had before, which means that I can and should bend some more. I'll do anything in my power to get back home. Spending time with Verena, getting to know her, enjoying her company, even going as far as kissing her good night won't deter me from my mission.

Saturday: The day after The Date

I ate breakfast with Verena today. She woke me again with those same words, "Open your eyes to a new beginning." I have to keep reminding myself to keep my eyes open, to stay focused each time I am with her. It seems easier to be with her. After all that we have been through, our opposing goals, lying naked in each other's arms, this impossible attraction we can do nothing with, last night's sweet kiss, sweeter than I want to admit. I thought there would be some awkwardness between us, but there wasn't. We talked with a sense of freedom I couldn't have ever imagined existing between us. Who would have thought a bet would make the difference? And what did we talk about? Food. Remnants of that powerfully hot dish, I guess. Seems silly I know, but in sharing my favorite dishes with Verena I was also sharing my memories of cooking with my mother. When I was little and my mom was upset with my father, she would cook to keep her mind off him. She'd cook and bake for the whole neighborhood. I would help, wanting to do something to make her happy. And it worked. I made her happy. Lunch and the evening meal with Verena went exactly the same. We talked and we smiled. I kissed her good night again. I had to. All this conversation with Verena and barely any with C1 *feels strange. He's still upset with me. I really hurt C1's feelings, as much as you can hurt a computer's feelings. We haven't had another lesson, but C1 has informed me that five more men have become attached to sisters of Vixen. I'm not surprised. These women are beautiful—gorgeous—almost impossible to keep your hands off (a personal observation). When one claims you, it's almost impossible to resist (another personal observation). Why would any one of these men resist? They have no idea that they're not safely on Earth, living their normal lives (as normal as they could be after the hurricane), earning a living. I am the only one who knows the truth. I have to keep a clear head.*

Sunday:

I thought about church today. I haven't been in ages, having become an occasional practicing Catholic. My mother is probably frowning down on me from heaven. Hey, I'm in the heavens. She's closer to me than I thought. Thinking about church and my mother led me to ask Verena about Vixen religion. According to Verena, we have a similar belief in one benevolent being. My religious curiosity further led to a stimulating debate about God's gender. Male or female? Man or woman? Verena and I debated through the morning and evening meal and well into the night, agreeing to disagree on this issue. Amazing that I could compromise with my enemy. Yes, enemy. I have to

*remember that important fact. Verena's beauty
and the attraction between us have been constant,
steady challenges. But now, adding her unique
charm to the package is making keeping a clear
head even harder. Verena. She has a spontaneous
humor. Yes, believe it or not she can be funny,
something I discovered when she gave up on
expecting me to act like a Vixen male. Or maybe
this was a ploy to sucker me into giving in to her.
Is she more than an insensitive kidnapper? Even
with these thoughts flying through my head like a
comet trailing with uncertainties, I couldn't resist
kissing her good night. It was a simple ending to
the day. What could it hurt?*

Monday/Tuesday

*I had it out with C1. I had never had a full-fledged
argument with a computer before, but hey, I've
never flown through space before either. My suspicion that C1 was maturing was right on target.
C1 sounded exactly like a rebellious eighteen-
year-old know-it-all, so different from the uncertain squeaky-voiced computer I first met. This
change makes me so suspicious. It's as if C1 has
been given an upgrade. If so, who gave it to him?
Verena?*

Jordan paused in his writing. It was the middle of the
night, hours since he had eaten dinner with Verena and he
was still awake. Yesterday and today had not begun or
ended well. The argument with C1 replayed in his head so
much that it kept sleep away. His eyes drawn to Verena,

Jordan watched as she tossed and turned on the pallet. C1 insisted that the sisters of Vixen couldn't care less about a male's computer, but Verena did. She asked about C1 every day.

"Her interest in me only proves how much she has come to steer away from the Vixen traditions!" C1 had said.

"It proves nothing," Jordan had insisted.

"What other Vixen would even care about a Comfort model?"

"One who will use any means to get what she wants, and what she wants is a Ceremony of Unity."

"What she wants is your love!" C1 had actually shouted at him.

"Ha! She's after one thing, my sperm, and she can't have that without my permission."

"Of course she can."

"What?"

"There are procedures, J.M. But a sister of Vixen needs a mate. You are hers and she could die before you are ready to admit it."

"Right, she'll die of unrequited love," Jordan had sarcastically drawled.

"You are still blind. I will not speak to you again until your eyes are opened."

"Opened to what? Opened to following a life that's not my own?"

"The commander is your life."

Jordan continued writing.

170

*Whatever happened to C1, I can no longer trust the
    computer. I have to make the most of my time
    with the men this Friday. Somehow I have to let
    them know what's happening. Evidence is what I
    need.*

Jordan looked though the open door of the side
chamber into Verena's. He was sure he could find something he could use to prove to the men the truth about
where they were, something that was completely alien to
Earth. Movement and a soft sound coming from the
pallet drew his attention. She was constantly distracting
him.

*I didn't give in to the urge to kiss her yesterday or
    today. Our meals were quiet, our conversation
    quieter. The change in atmosphere was obvious to
    both of us, but neither one of us commented on it.
    Strangely, I enjoyed the quiet with Verena, even
    with C1 and escape on my mind. I'm not sure
    what was on Verena's. She seemed sad, tired,
    almost sick. Verena sick? A germ wouldn't dare to
    invade her body. That would be as ridiculous as
    her dying if I did not give in to performing the
    Ceremony of Unity.*

Jordan put the journal away and lay down on his
pallet, only to open it a moment later.

I missed kissing her.

He closed the journal for the final time as sleep finally
removed him from his frustrations.

He did not kiss me.

This somber thought went through Verena's mind as she rolled across the pallet unable to sleep. She moved her limbs outward, stretching them in an attempt to draw from herself some of the energy that had been building inside of her, the unsatisfied longing to join with Jordan. This energy, the natural effect of marking a mate was meant to ensure a successful pleasurable mating experience for both. It was now having the opposite effect because it had not been allowed to be released through its natural course. The consequence of denying her body that release had turned the energy against itself, clashing with and slowly draining her life force.

The pleasures she was unable to share with Jordan without the rightful Ceremony of Unity were beginning to build, weakening her from the inside. Without a sharing, without a release, eventually the energy would consume her.

But it would not come to that. Jordan *would* come to her. They would unite before that happened. She was strong. If Verena did not appreciate any other of her mother's attributes, her strength was one Verena was grateful to know she had inherited.

Jordan was awake as surely as she was. Verena could feel his eyes on her every few moments. He was scribbling in that thing he called a journal once again. She was pleased to know he could not sleep, but curious to know what it was he was writing. Though Verena could speak the language fluently, she did not understand it in its written form, but maybe she could learn.

Another detour from Vixen tradition. To learn something new for the sake of a male was unheard of. To suffer unshared pleasures and long for what was rightfully hers was also unheard of.

Verena touched her forehead, longing for the brief physical connection of his head pressed against her own, that breath of a kiss, so little that meant so much. She wondered what stopped had him from giving her the kiss the night before as well as this night. He'd wanted to. Verena could see it in his eyes. But she did not wish to force him to do something he did not want. Jordan must come to her.

For hours she lay on her pallet, tossing and turning, gazing at him from across the chamber, knowing when he finally rested peacefully. Peace was not possible. Verena rose to take an early morning tour of the ship.

Upon evaluating each command sector and receiving satisfactory reports, Verena ventured onto the construction site. She walked about gazing upon the beauty of Earth's male species and wondered again at her choice of a male, the path of Vi-she that had directed her to Jordan, of her foolishness in allowing herself to care for him so deeply. A directive her mother constantly drilled into her head presented itself: 'Do not allow emotions to tie in with the relationship you have with your half-ling. You will risk your pride and honor if you do so.'

Pride and honor, were they so important? Verena was beginning to realize that they were not. These two virtues, while they had their place, were, Verena suspected, detrimental to their society. If the Sisters of Vixen had had a closer relationship with their half-lings, would they not have noticed sooner that the males were suffering? Nothing unusual had been noted until all males, infants to adults, began to die with such swift succession that the healers were unable to help them.

The situation she found herself in was as it should be. It was unwise to question Vi-she. Verena stood next to an artificial tree and looked up at the beauty of the artificial sky so much like that of Vixen. Her path with Jordan would eventually lead to happiness, she was certain of it. She had to persevere. Her thoughts led to Verena picturing Jordan's face in the clouds. She could almost feel his lips pressing against hers, his warmth melding with her own. Suddenly Jordan's face within the wispy white clouds disappeared. Verena glanced down, directing her focus to the ground, pressing her body against the tree in an attempt to steady herself.

"I am strong, I will not falter," she whispered, her pride ringing through as she silently admonished herself for not eating something. Keeping her body nourished was important in keeping up her strength, in holding back the passion-filled energy that fought to consume her. When Verena's knees threatened to buckle, she stiffened them and pressed closer to the tree. The bark dug into her skin from the pressure.

"Verena?" she heard a male voice say. "That is you, right? Rya's cousin."

Michael, Rya's half-ling, Verena realized as his face hazily came into view.

"Something wrong? Do you need some help? Some water? Something?"

What she needed was Jordan and a Ceremony of Unity. What she needed was what Michael and Rya had together. "Rya, bring her to me," she said in her most commanding voice, draining herself even more as she fought to stay in an upright position. 'Do not show weakness to a male.' Her mother's voice rang inside her head, proving that pride was still very much alive within her.

"Sure thing. Don't go anywhere."

Verena watched his hazy form move away from her, stop to speak to another questionable shape before doing what she asked him to do. A moment later Verena was not surprised when Suvan stood at her side.

"Commander, what are you doing here?"

"Visiting," Verena said in what she hoped was a strong, steady tone.

"Are you well?"

"Certainly, why would I not be?" For her fellow sisters to know that she suffered this way would not do.

"Michael seemed concerned."

"I asked him to find Rya. I wish to speak to her." Verena leaned more heavily into the tree, determined to maintain her stance. "Do not concern yourself with me. Go about your duties. I will await Rya."

"Good day then, Commander," Suvan said, but only after studying her fully.

"Good day," Verena remembered to say, relieved as Suvan walked away. She was a very perceptive sister of

Vixen, which made her excellent at her job. Verena was certain she had not fooled her.

"Verena." Rya ran up to her.

"Do not run in your condition."

"Do not concern yourself about me."

"Condition? What condition?" Michael asked two steps behind her.

"Verena's condition," Rya quickly answered. "Are you well?" she asked.

"Almost," Verena answered. "Walk with me."

"If you wish," Rya said, concern on her features.

"Do you need me to carry her?" Michael asked.

Detecting Rya's concern for her was bad enough, but when Michael interjected with his idea of help, Verena thought she would collapse in shame right before them.

"No, that is not necessary." Verena pushed away from the tree. "I would like to speak to my cousin." Not surprised that her words did not seem to be enough to convince him, Verena gathered what strength she had left to step away from the tree.

"If you say so."

Verena watched as he gave Rya a lingering kiss.

"I'll see you after work, baby."

Verena pushed back the jealously she did not have the energy to feel, and forced herself to move away from the embracing couple.

Rya was at Verena's side seconds later, wisely saying nothing as she led her in the direction of the dwelling she shared with her half-ling.

Once they were inside, Verena collapsed onto the nearest place she could land, a strange pallet she had once heard Rya call a sofa. Moments later, a glass was placed into her palms and brought to her lips.

"Toca," Rya told her as she stared into her eyes, worry pulsing in her own.

Verna drained the contents of the glass and waited for the restorative effects of the drink to give her strength. Toca was an elixir with many uses. She was grateful that Rya had some on hand. As the weakness inside of her began to fade, the energy she had not been able to release pulsated within her, making itself known, warning her that soon her body would not be able to hold this natural passion inside much longer.

"Verena," Rya said, the worry in her eyes reflected in her voice.

Verena sighed. "The Toca has done its job. It is a wonderful elixir, is it not? It can ease almost any ailment."

"Yes, I have used it as a natural way to soothe the nausea I have been experiencing."

"Too bad it had no effect on the plague that killed all our males. If it had," Verena looked straight into her kinswoman's eyes, knowing that she could no longer hide the effects of not having mated with Jordan, "I would not be suffering as I am now."

"Verena, what is it?

Verena opened her mouth to speak, then closed it tight as shame filled her. Unwanted tears rolled down her face.

"Verena, you must tell me this instant."

"I must tell you nothing," Verena burst out, losing her courage. "I am the commander here," she ended on a whisper.

"Yes, you are the commander of this ship, but at this moment you are more than the commander to me," Rya told her, grabbing both hands as she knelt before her. "You are my kinswoman. I have spent more time with you than either your mother or your father. And in all that time I have only once seen tears on your face."

Verena gave a reluctant half-smile and nodded her regal head. "When I lost my footing and fell down the side of Mount Ora, breaking my arm."

"So what have you broken now to cause you such pain?"

Broken. Yes, something inside of her was broken, she realized. Jordan's refusal to accept his fate and perform the Ceremony of Unity with her had broken her heart because she cared for him deeply. But she could not share this with Rya, not yet. Not when she had just discovered this truth. There was something else that had been broken. That, Verena could share with Rya, though it would expose her shame.

"I have broken with tradition. I did not perform the Ceremony of Unity soon after marking Jordan."

"But you have seven days to do so before you even begin to feel the effects."

"I know this. I marked Jordan on the very day we left Earth."

"That is more than twice as long," Rya gasped. "How have you survived this long and why have you waited?"

Rya stood. "You could die. The unsatisfied energy will overwhelm you canceling out your life force. Verena, you will simply fade away if you do not take him."

"I know this also." Verena paused to take a breath, feeling less and less like a commander as she spoke. "Rya, he does not want me." Speaking aloud the truth stirred a restlessness inside her. Verena stood and began to pace up and down in front of her kinswoman, stopping a few moments later only to fall onto the sofa once again. "And I want him to want me."

"It does not matter what he wants. You will not die this day. I will get your half-ling, bring him here and you will perform the Ceremony of Unity and come together in this very place."

"No," Verena whispered, then realized that she was the only one to hear that quietly spoken word as Rya slammed out of the dwelling. Having no energy to stop her, Verena closed her eyes, thinking that her mother would truly be humiliated when she discovered how she had died.

"J.M., what are you looking for?" C1 asked Jordan for the fifth time in ten minutes.

"For the last time, C1, I don't know."

"If you do not know then cease this useless searching and instead devote your time to clearing your mind of this resistance you have of uniting with the commander."

"No can do," Jordan answered automatically, having become accustomed to this argument. "Oh-ho!" he exclaimed a moment later when his fingers discovered an indentation in the wall he had been probing.

"Yes, you must do. This situation has become dire, J.M. This very morning, just before the commander left the chamber, I was able to carefully scan her—"

"I've discovered the mother lode!" Jordan yelled when a gentle swish revealed a small square enclosure with a few interesting looking gadgets inside.

"The scan—"

"What is this thing?" Jordan interrupted.

"Will you cease and listen to what I have to tell you!"

Jordan didn't know if it was C1's tone or the use of the word cease, the same word Verena had used put an end to their lovemaking that caused him to pause and really pay attention. "I'll listen if you tell me what this thing is that I'm holding."

"Gladly! You are holding what you might call a remote control device."

"For what?"

"For—I don't know. If you wait but a moment I will scan it. Then you must listen."

"I said I would, didn't I?" Jordan muttered, not understanding the near panic C1 was getting himself into.

In a matter of seconds C1 rattled, "It is a remote device used to control illusions."

"What does—"

"No more! Listen, J.M.! You must find the commander and perform the Ceremony of Unity. If not, she will likely cease to exist."

"That's ridiculous," Jordan told C1 just as the signal at the entrance sounded.

Rya stormed in, grabbed him by the arm and pulled him across the chamber with the strength of an elephant, declaring, "You must come with me now."

"Where? Why?"

"To my home to save the life of your mate."

CHAPTER 12

Jordan's heart stopped, then accelerated as both Rya's and C1's words penetrated the cloud of disbelief he had been under since C1 had first told him about the possibility of Verena dying if they did not unite. A chill of fear passed through his body as he followed Rya down the bright halls, then passed her, only to have to wait for her to punch in the code at the entrance of the holo-lift.

In the seconds it took for her to reach his side, Jordan recognized that it was fear that was coursing through his body.

Fear for Verena.

Fear for her life.

Fear for how losing her would make him feel.

Then Rya was there punching in the code with no thought of concealing the numbers. Automatically, his mind stored away the seven symbols before pulling Rya behind him into the holo-lift.

"What's wrong with her?" he asked, though he already knew.

"Verena is dying."

"Why?"

"Because you have refused her." A look like none he had never before seen on the normally pleasant-faced Rya overtook her face: anger. Seconds later it was transformed into a frown of worry.

"I had no idea that not putting out would kill her!"

"The passionate energy that naturally develops inside a female after she has chosen and marked her male must be given to that male after the Ceremony of Unity. If not, the energy will clash with her life force. Her body has been overwhelmed by the energy for far too long and has reacted as if it is a sickness, draining itself as it tries to rid her of the excess energy."

"Like someone's autoimmune system attacking itself," Jordan said, remembering that with juvenile diabetes, the body's auto-immune system turns on itself after fighting an infection and loses the ability to create insulin. Verena could actually die from him not 'putting out.'

"Yes, her own body is working against her, draining her life away."

The holo-lift doors opened and Rya darted out with Jordan right behind her. They ran past the construction site to the housing units and stopped at the very first house.

"Let us pause a moment. Be prepared. She was very weak. I found her there." Rya pointed to an oak tree a few feet away. "She barely made it inside my dwelling before collapsing."

Jordan's eyes followed her pointing finger, unable to believe that his strong, regal beauty didn't have the strength to walk a few steps. "I didn't know this would happen." Jordan shook his head. "And I didn't ask to be marked."

"It does not matter if you asked or not. You are the reason she is suffering, and you will save her." Rya moved to go inside, but paused, stared into his face and demanded, "You will tell Verena that you *want* to perform the Ceremony of Unity."

"If that is the only way to save her life, of course I want to," Jordan said, realizing he meant every word. His resistance had died the moment he understood that Verena's life actually was at stake. He had never wanted to hurt her; he had just wanted to go home.

Rya issued him a nod of approval before opening the door. Jordan wasn't prepared for the sight that met him. Verena lay on the sofa curled into a tight ball. He could see and almost feel the pain and tension in her body. Kneeling before her, Jordan glanced at Rya with a plea for help in his eyes.

"More Toca will help," Rya said, leaving to get the drink he remembered from the bet they had made.

Jordan rested a hand on Verena's forehead. It was burning hot, somewhat like a fever, but then again, not. It felt as if a live pulsating energy lay beneath her skin, radiating into his own. He touched her face, her neck, gliding his hand down to her shoulder and past her hip. He felt it everywhere. As he continued to touch her, the energy pulsed into his palm like an intimate caress, arousing him. Jordan stared at his hand as understanding dawned. This passionate energy, as Rya had called it, had to be transferred. It was a way to ensure that a mating *would* happen.

"Jordan?" Verena whispered just as Rya returned with the Toca.

"Good, you are relieving her of some of the energy that is overpowering her. Give her this." Rya thrust a small tube into his hand. "Continue to do as you are doing and I will bring everything that is needed." And then she was gone.

"Jordan, leave. I want no witness to this shameful death."

"It would have been shameful only because it would have been unnecessary. There won't be a death, not if I have anything to say about it. Why didn't you explain all of this to me, Rena?" he asked, his hands continuing their journey across her body, gently, slowly, relieving more of the overpowering energy inside of her. Already her body had began to relax and her muscles to loosen.

"I did not wish to force you. You have anger in your heart. I do not want a mate who does not want me. It does not matter much if I die. My mother has other daughters."

"It matters to me if you die," Jordan told her.

"You do not speak the truth."

"But I do." Jordan lifted her head, pouring the entire contents of the tube into her mouth. Gently, he extended her legs, caressing their smooth length from hip to thigh and knee to ankle with steady strokes that pulsated with an intensity he could barely contain. If this was a taste of the passion she had been holding inside, it was a wonder that she didn't simply *take* him. He definitely had the urge to take her. The overpowering need to touch and taste was an all-consuming thing with no room left for thought. Jordan took a deep breath and, relying on his Karate-do training, managed a slight control of his response to Rena.

Focused once again, he gave her arms the same treatment, leaving Verena stretched before him with a fiery demand that they join together. Allowing himself to partially give in to the urge, he eased onto the sofa and pressed his body against her own, absorbing the heat and passionate energy at every point they connected.

"Then what truth do you speak, Jordan?" she asked in a whisper so unlike her that he could barely connect this voice to the woman he had come to know and care for.

"The truth?" Jordan had to pause to remember what they had been talking about. "The truth is *I* care if you live or die. I want you to live."

"So that my death won't be laid at your feet?"

"No, damn it!" he grunted, attempting to keep his thoughts on the conversation and not give in to the sudden urge to stop her from talking with deep, moist kisses. Hell, he missed kissing her. When was the last time he had kissed her?

"Jordan?"

"It's because," he began, staring at her lips. Jordan's mind was empty of everything except the passion for Rena building up inside of him. This was harder than it should be. Rya had told him what to say. "It's because I just plain want you! I want to perform the Ceremony of Unity." Having said what he knew would make her believe that this was what he wanted, he pulled her even closer, leaving no room for air to separate them as he took her lips in a kiss that sparked a charge inside of him even before his tongue found the soft inside of her cheek, then her tongue, her lips. Each touch sent pulsating waves of pleasure darting through his body, settling into a hardness between his thighs, intensifying to a point where he knew there was no turning back. Jordan, for the first time in his life, lost all control, exploding inside his pants as a tsunami of passion washed over him. As pleasure ebbed and flowed throughout his body, Jordan slowly became aware of the fact that he was now lying on the floor. Within his grasp were Verena's long, bronze fingers.

Opening his eyes, he found Verena's deep, brown gaze on him. Jordan rested on his elbows, resigning himself to the fact that he couldn't do much more than that.

"Thank you, Jordan," she whispered in a voice that was stronger and filled with a huskiness that promised that there was much more to come.

"For what?" he asked, impressed with her words of courtesy and hoping what her voice promised wouldn't kill him.

"For wanting me."

"Oh, the Toca has revived you, I see." Rya came into the house, saving Jordan from replying. He had said enough already. He needed time to think about...*everything*.

187

"Toca and other things," Verena answered Rya, her eyes smiling at him.

Rya nodded at Jordan. "I congratulate you on your diligence in providing relief for your mate." She placed a basket on the floor, then laid three square boxes, a beautiful gold trimmed goblet and two miniature bottles on the coffee table near the sofa. "I will leave you to proceed. Have a long life together, good day." And then once again, she was gone.

The silence that filled the house seemed as uncomfortable as the inside of his pants.

"If you have thought again and wish not to proceed—"

"No!" He rose from the floor, finally having regained enough strength to do so. "I mean, I do wish to proceed. I can't deny that I want you almost as much as I want to go home."

"That sounds promising."

"And I can't let you die."

"I have no wish to. Which leads us back to the Ceremony of Unity. Shall we begin?"

Jordan nodded, wondering at this polite Verena who had somehow merged with the one he knew. "I'm going to need a few minutes to clean up a bit. I wish I had C1 here to get me some clothes."

"That won't be necessary." Verena stood, swayed on her feet a moment before gaining her balance. She reached inside the basket Rya had left. "Ceremonial robes," she announced, holding them out to him. "The facilities here are much like those you were once accustomed to on Earth. Take care of your needs," she told him with a knowing smile. "I will await you here."

Wasting no time, Jordan undressed. After tossing his jeans in a corner, he threw his underwear in the trash bin and methodically went about the business of cleaning and clothing himself in the silky, metallic robes Verena had given him. Leaning against the sink, he took a long look at himself. He was a man who wanted to go home, who wanted to save the men on this ship, and at the same time wanted to save the woman in the next room.

And why was that?

Jordan shook his head, not wanting to answer that question. An answer would force him to make a choice. And right now choices were not an option. Verena would not die because of him. Having already made the only decision he could at this moment, he left the room, leaving for tomorrow the worry about other decisions he would have to make.

Verena held her breath at the sight of Jordan in the traditional ceremonial robes. Immense strength, evident in the firm muscles in his legs and arms, seemed to exude from him. Taking a step forward forced Verena to remember to breathe. She reached for his hand. The instant heat between them was a result of the slightly subdued flow of energy from her to him. Verena searched his face for any sign that he had changed his mind. Reading a steady determination, she guided him to the small table, knelt beside it, easing onto her heels and motioning for him to do the same. Without another word between them, she began the ceremony which had always been done in private, the woman of Vixen and her mate the only two in attendance. Chanting a pledge that spoke of the sacredness of unity, Verena's heart swelled with emotion as the meaning behind the words she had been taught so long ago that she could not remember learning them penetrated her soul. A deep pride in her choice of mate rushed over her. She did not know what troubles they would meet but she was comforted to know that Jordan would be behind her through them all.

As she opened the first box, Verena felt Jordan's eyes on her. The open box revealed a smooth leaf from the macog tree found only at the crest of Mount Ora on Vixen. A treasure lay in its center, a dollop of the creamy, fragrant sap from this rare tree.

Verena positioned Jordan's hands palm up, spread the sap onto her fingers and rubbed it into his open palms. Speaking in Vixen she said, "That your life will be devoted to soothing and comforting your mate."

Jordan's hands stiffened beneath hers for a moment, making her wonder if he understood her words, but that, she knew, was not possible. He grasped her fingers, turned her hands palms up and repeated the phrase and the action until the last of the sap was rubbed into her hands. Startled, Verena looked into his eyes. Sure that this had never happened before, Verena didn't quite know what to do about this shift in the traditional Ceremony of Unity. Besides, she hadn't recovered enough strength to protest.

What did it matter? she asked herself. No one was here to see that, once again, she had veered from tradition. Verena nodded, feeling the energy growing between them once again in anticipation of her right to celebrate their unity after the ceremony. She proceeded to open the second wooden box. Inside this box were seeds crushed into powder from the flower of the macog tree. It was said to have powers of fertility resulting in the birth of many daughters.

"That daughters are plentiful and sons are accepted," Verena said as she sprinkled a pinch of the powder into the gold tinted goblet.

"That sons and daughters are equally welcomed," Jordan smoothly said in Vixen, adding a pinch of powder into the goblet.

Verena inhaled sharply, folding her arms in shock. Too overwhelmed with her need to join with him and determined to get through the ceremony, she could not stop to think on how and why he had learned her language. Instead, Verena handed Jordan one of the tiny bottles, taking one herself to pour into the goblet.

"Water from planet Vixen flowing into this glass will flow into each of us." She paused as he perfectly repeated the phrase, pouring the contents of his bottle into the goblet.

"To keep us connected to Vixen, its daughters and all its glorious charms," Verena added.

Jordan remained silent, which was what was expected of a male during the entire ceremony. How ironic that this was the only portion of the ceremony that Jordan followed as tradition dictated and that he probably did it to show that Vixen's charms could not entice him. If he felt this way, then Verena had no choice but to charm him herself. She lifted the goblet, her eyes gazing into his with a challenge as she swirled the contents. Rising to her knees, she placed a finger inside the goblet and stirred. Lifting her finger to her lips, she sucked the liquid from her finger, her eyes never breaking contact with his. Another dip of her finger drew his eyes to her action. She leaned into him, raising her finger to his lips. Jordan pulled it into his mouth, drawing from her the passion that had once again grown into a need for fulfillment, building up in the pit of her stomach and pulsating through her blood. Almost overcome with the need to take him, to give him the gift of the passion exclusively designed for him, Verena eased back onto her heels and then stood.

"I hope that's the end of the ceremony," Jordan said, taking her hand as he began to rise.

Laying a hand on his shoulder, Verena silently urged him back down. "Almost." She released him to open the last box. Inside was a shearing device. She fitted it into the palm of her hand and kneeling behind him, pulled Jordan into her, his firm back just inches from her breasts. Her free arm wrapped around his chest.

His fingers grazed her arms.

Verena smiled, realizing that Jordan had to participate in some way. He could not remain motionless as males were expected to. And she had not expected him to.

"I'm about to lose my hair," he quietly stated.

"Yes."

"I wonder how I'll look as a bald man?"

"Beautiful."

"Beautiful?"

"Yes. Hush. Relax," she whispered into his ear as the passion flowed between them. Verena waited until she felt its rhythm and began to chant in Vixen, "United for life, united under the sign of the Crescent," over and over again as she guided the shears across his head, taking time to form the symbol of her family at the back of his head.

The gentle hum of the shears and her chanting ended, leaving the room silent. Jordan reached a hand above him to capture her own, removing the shearing device and replacing it in the third box.

Seconds later Jordan faced her. Knee to shoulder their bodies met. Verena pressed into him, the rhythm of passion demanding a primal beat, her softness burning into the hard-fast need she had created in him. Wrapping his arms around her, he answered the rhythm, claiming her mouth for the kiss she craved, the kiss she would use to channel passionate energy into her mate. The heat of his breath was a pulsating pull joining their lips, giving her tongue access to dance with his in a wild, desperate need. He wanted her, and the knowledge sent a tremendous tremor through her, pooling at her groin. She could wait no longer to join with him. Jordan was hers. Leaning into him as she deepened the kiss, Verena found herself flush against him, flesh to flesh, their robes somehow open, giving her hands freedom to roam across his muscular body, hers to touch and feel, but only for a moment. Her body demanded more. Straddling him, her hands pressed against his shoulders, Verena rose to claim her mate in the way Vixen tradition demanded, only to feel herself shifting forward.

Jordan's hands were at her waist and he was moving her. Verena noted his passion-filled eyes only for a moment. His hot breath and then his tongue and teeth at her breasts pulled her eyes closed so that her only focus was the pulsating heat at her breasts spreading to her loins with the speed of light, culminating between her thighs as a breathtaking tremor of astounding pleasure pulsating her entire being, leaving her sated yet wanting as she collapsed on top of her mate. Then without her knowing how it happened, Jordan towered above her, his body poised to claim her. Somewhere, a protest to this shifting of positions, this untraditional first mating, rang inside her head. But then, his fingers were parting her thighs, opening her moist heat, probing and filling her with expert ease only to leave her a moment later panting for more. Which he gave, thrusting into her once, twice, as they roared each others' name in the midst of blind passion.

Jordan woke up from the best sleep he had had since being taken away from Earth. The warmth of Verena's gentle breath moving across his chest sent a shaft of wanting that hit him hard between his legs. Suppressing a groan, he eased away from her, disgusted with himself, the choice he had been forced to make and his complete lack of control.

Two strokes. That was all it had taken. Each and every time he was inside her his body convulsed with astonishing speed, pulling from him the most staggering fulfillment of his life, as if he belonged exactly where he was for all eternity, making love to Verena, his mate.

Mate.

He turned away from her and stared at the wall, avoiding looking at her beautiful face and luscious body he now knew so intimately.

Mate!

He had a mate, a wife, an alien spouse. No matter how he said it, he was bound to her, but only for the moment.

He had a mission.

One that Jordan was determined to see through. This unity thing coupled with an unbelievable night of love-making—no, *mating* with her—done only to save her life, was just a detour. A detour he had taken at least a half a dozen times before losing count. But not again.

Never again.

Jordan stood and walked to the other side of the room. She could already be pregnant, he realized. The heat, the tension and the pure pleasure of it all had made him forget that procreation was the objective of these women of Vixen.

He wouldn't forget again. If she was pregnant, Jordan wasn't exactly sure what he'd do. He wouldn't make the mistake of leaving a kid of his to be raised without a father, that's for sure. He'd probably have to steal the baby if that was the case, especially if it was a boy. No son of his was going to be raised as a second-class citizen of Vixen. Hey, if it was a boy, they'd probably give him away without a second thought; a girl he would have to kidnap.

Jordan shook his head free of issues he might not even have to face. He went into the bathroom and pulled on his jeans. His hand encountered a solid object in his back pocket. Pulling out the slim instrument, Jordan remembered that C1 had said it was a remote that controlled illusions.

Illusions.

Three steps took Jordan to the bathroom window. His eyes absorbed all that the sisters of Vixen had created to dupe the men into believing that they were still on Earth.

It was all an illusion.

This room, the entire house was an illusion. Glancing down at the remote, he stared at the strange symbols running down the center of the slim device, two of which he recognized from his lessons with C1: :/: meant on and /:/ off. The button lit up as his thumb caressed the 'on' symbol with a sense of hope. It couldn't be this easy. Pointing the remote at the toilet, he pressed a symbol he didn't recognize. Nothing happen. As his thumb traveled down, hope faded with each failure. Pausing over the last, Jordan prayed that something would happen. He could not believe that he would have such a gift land in his lap and be unable to use it. The toilet shimmered and disappeared in an instant.

Just as hope flooded his veins, he realized he needed to use the toilet, which he had just made disappear. Jordan played with the control until it appeared again. He suppressed his excitement so as not to risk waking Verena. He used the toilet, then went to wash his hands, staring at his reflection in the mirror. The sign of Verena's possession was staring him right in the face. He swiped at his freshly shaved head. She had possessed him but he had proven that he had also possessed her. He had taken control of their lovemaking over and over again.

Turning away from the memory, he peered out the window again. In the pale dawn light, he focused on a huge oak tree. In his hand he still held the remote. He pointed the control and watched the huge oak disappear and then reappear according to his wishes. In his hands was the proof that would get the men on his side.

Pulling on his pants and boots and tossing his shirt across his shoulders, he grabbed a hard hat he found at the door and silently left the house, not daring to even glance Verena's way. Seeing her would force him to stop and think, and this was a time for action. He jogged toward the trailer in the hope of meeting Bruce or one of the other guys. It didn't matter. He was making this plan up as he went. Entering the trailer he was ecstatic to see Bruce already at a desk working.

"Good morning," Jordan said, trying to slow the rapid push of adrenaline coursing through him.

"Morning yourself, boss man. What are you doing here so early?"

"Hoping to meet with the crew before work gets started today," he answered. "I have to give a preliminary status report."

"Then you'll have to talk to Susie."

"She around?" Jordan twisted his head, hoping *not* to find the Bruce's mate.

"No, this is Wednesday. She won't be in 'til noon. She's got some kind of club thing going on with the other women."

"Good." More than good, Jordan thought. Things were falling so easily into place he started to wonder.

"Why would that be good? Susie is the foreman. She's the one you have to talk to. You're not trying to push her aside because she's a women, are you? I support women in the workplace—"

"No, that's not what I'm saying," Jordan interrupted, realizing that Bruce could either be his biggest adversary or his biggest support. "I only meant that it was nice that she took time out for herself. We all need to do that, and I'm sure that you can give me an update and gather the men for an early meeting. I need to relay some general information."

Bruce stared at him a minute before asking, "General information?"

"General information that you can share with Suvan when she gets back," Jordan threw out as his mind buzzed with how to explain their kidnapping, spaceships and men used as baby-making machines.

"No problem." Bruce stood. Moving past Jordan and pausing at the door, he asked, "No secretary today?"

"No, she's otherwise occupied," Jordan said. A picture of a completely sated, naked Verena flashed inside his head before he pushed the image aside. Sure that she needed time to recover, Jordan expected her to be absent for quite some time.

He walked to the window of the trailer, amazed at the instant hardness produced by the mere thought of Verena and the passion they had shared.

Seeing the men slowly leaving the temporary homes scattered across the open field pulled his mind away from Verena and toward freedom. Excitement and apprehension pumped through his veins as he anticipated the men's reaction. A pinch of sadness hung at the edges of his thoughts, though he refused to consciously acknowledge it. His focus should stay centered on revealing the truth without being discovered and going forward with the steps necessary to take control of the ship.

"One thing at a time," he muttered to himself as the men filed into the trailer, laughing and talking, filling it to capacity. All the masculine energy and the brotherhood of testosterone diminished Jordan's minute concern about being a white man telling a room of fifty black men what to do. But in fact that wasn't what he was going to do. He held essential information, but *they*, all the men inside this room, including himself, had to decide together what action to take. He would just have to use his diplomatic skills to steer them into the idea of instant takeover.

199

"Alright, men, the boss man wants to have a word," Bruce announced.

Every face turned toward Jordan with a look of expectation. A huge question hung in the air. There would soon be some answers and more questions than he would know how to answer. Taking the remote out of his pocket, he gently slapped it against his palm and began. "What I'm about to tell you will come as a shock. This information affects every one of us, putting us all in the same boat that we'll have to guide and hold steady together."

"What's this about? It doesn't sound like you're asking for a status report to me," Bruce told him in a loud whisper.

"Sounds more like we're about to lose our cushy, high-paying jobs with benefits," someone on the other side of Bruce added.

"I knew this was all too good to be true," Big John, the man Jordan knew to be Zytai's husband, growled. The comments threatened Jordan's hope of bringing the men together. He had to do this quickly, so that they didn't have time to draw conclusions before he had even begun to explain.

"Give me a second and I'll tell all of you what this is about. In a way it does affect your jobs because all of this *has* been too good to be true. Every benefit you have received has a price, and that price is your freedom." Jordan paused a second. "I'm asking that you listen, hear all the facts before you make assumptions. Have an open mind. Don't let disbelief cloud the truth." Drawing in a deep breath, Jordan explained in short calm statements their predicament. The second he finished talking the room was silent.

"What are you talking about?" Bruce asked.

Zytai's husband stood, all six-foot-five of him, and asked, "Are you expecting us to believe that load of sh—"

"Yes," Jordan quietly interrupted.

"Who are you?"

"An FBI agent specializing in alien contact. After studying the ship from afar, I came on board to investigate and the ship took off."

"Right."

"Some agent."

"He's not an agent. He's probably some kind of crazy sci-fi-Star-Wars-Trekkie," someone else said before the room exploded with noise.

Jordan's eyes scanned the trailer as the men had a good laugh at his expense. Bits and pieces of their comments floated to him.

"—alien women."

"We got us a group of sperm stealers!"

"Spaceship? How could this be a spaceship?"

Through it all Bruce sat with his arms folded, an amused look on his face. Feeling that enough time had passed, Jordan turned to Bruce and requested that he get the men's attention, knowing that they would respond to Bruce much quicker than to him. Throwing Jordan a condescending look of pity, he gave a shrill whistle.

"I can prove it," Jordan quietly said.

"Then prove it," Michael said before anyone else could open their mouths.

Jordan pointed the remote at the table in the middle of a room. There was a thump when someone who had been leaning on the table hit the floor, then a few surprised grunts.

"What happened?"

"How'd you do that?"

"Somebody take that thing from him!"

Swinging his arm in a wide arc, Jordan pointed the remote at the men. He had been hoping to keep the demonstration down to a minimum so that it wouldn't be seen by any of the women, but now he had no choice but to give a grand demonstration.

"I'll tell you what it is. This little device is a bit of Vixen technology. It controls the many illusions you have been living in for the last few weeks. That table wasn't really there, neither is that phone." He made it appear and disappear. "Or that computer." He performed the same routine. "Or—" Jordan paused for dramatic effect, "this trailer."

The men stood in amazement looking at the trees around them and up at the sky. Seconds later, they were covered once again by walls and a roof.

"Government testing, that's what you're doing to us. You've been giving us drugs and now we're hallucinating."

Jordan sighed as a few men nodded their head in agreement. Seeing the mixed reactions in the group, Jordan turned to Michael. "What do you think?"

"I—well, I…" He nervously looked around. "What I think is that something strange is going on and you telling us that our women are aliens doesn't feel too out of the box."

"Like how tall all of them are."

"This whole bald-headed look they like."

"The secrecy."

"The sex."

"Oh man, the sex is the best I've ever had and she wants it all the time."

"That's out of the box."

"And too good to be true."

"That's because Vixen women have the ability to enhance sex for their partner. At least for the partner they have chosen."

"Man, you have an answer for everything," a solemn young man muttered.

Zytai's mate asked, "Chosen? Impossible. I picked the lady. I wanted her and I plan on asking her to marry me."

"Zytai chose you and according to them, you are already married. Almost all of you have been chosen, marked and taken advantage of by these women."

"If we've been taken advantage of, then let 'em keep doing it."

"They intend to, for the rest of your lives, on a planet called Vixen, unless we do something about it."

The room again erupted with noise that abruptly stopped when the door opened. Suvan stood in the doorway. Surprise flashed on her face when she took in the crowded confines of the trailer.

203

"Why are you all in here? There's work to be done. Bruce, what's going on?"

"You tell me," Bruce answered as he stepped toward the woman he was crazy about. Before she could answer, the door opened again.

"Michael, I couldn't find your hard hat—" Rya was saying as she walked into the trailer.

"Because I borrowed it," Jordan said, tapping his head.

"What is Jordan doing here?" Suvan asked Rya.

"I don't know but this should not be happening."

"Have a seat, ladies," Jordan offered as two men stood.

"Yes, please sit," Bruce directed.

"What have you done, Jordan?" Suvan asked, her eyes alarmed. "Where is the commander?"

"I've explained the situation. And the commander is exactly where I left her. Alive and well."

Suvan visibly relaxed. Jordan felt a bit insulted that Suvan would think that he would hurt Verena.

"And the men believe you?"

"Of course. This little device helped them see that I was telling the truth." Jordan caused the trailer to disappear and reappear once more.

Rya and Suvan stared at each other in horror. A heavy sigh poured out of Suvan. "You have only created a problem. The men should not have been told," she said in a loud whisper, loud enough for Bruce to hear though Jordan didn't think that was her intent.

"So, it's true," Bruce said, his normally boisterous voice a heavy admonishment that spread to every ear.

"Yes, but that does not mean I do not care for you. I made you my mate and—"

"You made me?" Bruce leaned into her as Michael stood grim-faced next to Rya. "You didn't make me. You took from me. You took my home from me. You took my lo—. You took my life away." Bruce stood, his eyes scanning the room. "I say we take it all back!"

The men hooted in agreement. Jordan almost felt sorry for Rya and Suvan. Of all the women of Vixen he'd met, these were the two he had actually come to like. Well, of course there was Verena, but what he felt for her was a ton more than 'like.'

"We need to make a plan, but first I suggest that that you search the women. They must have some way of communicating with the others, and we can't have them warning the crew. Bruce, Michael, I think you should probably do the honors. The rest of us will step outside a minute."

"*The Twilight Zone*. That's it, man, I feel like we're in *The Twilight Zone*," Jordan heard above the other mutterings coming from the exiting men.

"Jordan, wait!" Rya called out to him. "You did perform the ceremony. You did save Verena."

"Didn't you see her in the house?"

"I thought her to be exhausted from your first night together."

"So she is," Jordan said, sliding the hard hat from his head. "I couldn't let her die because of me."

205

"They got you, too," Bruce said through gritted teeth. "And you knew."

"Only because I was marked and discovered that performing the ceremony and mating with Verena the Commander was the only way to save her life."

"And I thank you," Rya said, turning to Michael with a stiff neck, holding back a flood of tears. "Do what you must," she said, her feet spread wide, her hands on her hips. Jordan watched as Suvan took a similar pose and the men searched them, finding a number of interesting things they piled high on the table.

"My God!" Michael yelled, his hands at Rya's sides. "You're pregnant. I almost forgot. You're pregnant with my baby. You can't have him."

"I most certainly am and will have *her*."

"You guys had better come quick. I couldn't stop 'em. The rest of the guys are storming the bar," Briceson poked his head inside to say.

"That is where the sisters are meeting," Suvan explained. "I only stopped to see Bruce this morning."

"Why?" Bruce asked.

"I had yet to kiss you good morning."

"Oh, right."

"Hey, there's a confrontation about to take place out there," Briceson reminded them.

"Michael, stand guard. Bruce, Briceson come with me," Jordan said. Bruce nodded, accepting Jordan's role as leader. Jordan was relieved to have Bruce as an ally and not the adversary he could have been.

The bar was a chaotic scene. All of the women were not present but the ones who were were giving as good as they got. The men who had not found their mates guarded the doors while verbal mini-wars raged in every corner, at every table, and in every open space.

This was not how Jordan had envisioned their takeover. They couldn't win this way. Soon Verena would be informed and...

"Jordan, what have you done?"

Jordan turned to find *his* mate regally standing behind him, a look of distinct displeasure in her eyes as she took in the chaos.

"Not enough, obviously," he answered, noting the amusement that had begun to creep into her eyes. Turning back to the chaos, Jordan discovered the reason for the change in her expression. The verbal warfare had ended as the women resorted to a more physical form of retaliation. Long elegant fingers caressed the hands, muscled shoulders and rough faces of the outraged men. Angry voices turned into grunts, growls and even a moan or two as the women used their powers to subdue the men. A hush spread throughout the room as slowly every man began to conform to this sinister method of surrender.

"Jordan," Verena said behind him, a brush of her fingers sending a pulsating wave of pleasure through him.

Jordan jumped away from her touch, spinning around to face her.

"I forgive you. Come, let us discuss this so that we can start again," Verena said.

The pull of her eyes, her touch and the memory of the night they had shared dulled his senses. Jordan felt himself moving into her embrace.

"Do we look like that with our women?" Jordan heard Briceson ask in a loud whisper.

Taking a step back, Jordan shook his head to clear his mind of the promise of passion, refocusing on this one chance to gain their freedom.

"This is ridiculous!" Bruce yelled, giving Jordan a different focus.

"Silence," Verena ordered, her tone surprising Bruce into giving her what she commanded.

Taking a sweeping glance around the room, Jordan tasted failure. It was harsh and bitter. His head hung low in defeat even as his mind searched for a way to turn it around. *How* could he turn it around when the women preyed on a man's sexual hunger to subdue him into submission? How could he just break this unnatural hold the women had on them?

"Jordan!" Bruce yelled from across the room.

Verena directed one of her most commanding looks at Bruce. "Suvan will hear of this," she said before turning back to Jordan.

"Susie has already heard a whole lot from me and will be hearing more once I get back to her."

"Where is she?" Verena asked, real concern on her face.

"Suvan and Rya are being safely guarded," Jordan answered, continuing to back away from Verena. He glanced at the men who were now attempting to pull a few of the entrapped victims away from the women. Bruce held his hand out, his thumb wildly moving as if clicking an imaginary remote.

A split second later, Jordan grinned as understanding dawned. He raised his eyes to Verena, allowing her to read triumph in his own before lifting the remote and clicking it at the bar. The entire length of mahogany disappeared, sending Calvin and a beautiful Vixen sprawling to the floor. A dazed Calvin was pulled away by Bruce. Jordan pointed and clicked at tables and chairs that disappeared with the speed of light, disrupting the hold the women had on the men. Bruce and Briceson and a few of the other men swooped in to collect and revive the men with a spray of water in the face, a shake, and even a slap on the head. Like a synchronized attack, Jordan removed every illusion as Bruce gathered and regrouped the men, organizing them to surround the dazed women. The room became a dazzling silver dome with the disappearance of all illusions.

In a matter of moments all the men had been separated from the women and a human wall surrounded the Vixens, those without their mates standing closest to the women.

"Jordan, stop this at once!" Verena commanded.

"I can't."

"You must!"

As Verena stared into his eyes, Jordan felt the pull of pleasure, the need to go to her, to touch her.

"You will obey me," she whispered.

Those words were enough to shake him out of the magnetic hold she had on him.

"Jordan, my man, we could use some help over here," Bruce was saying.

"I can feel her pulling at me," Joe was saying.

"I can't take too much more of this," Nick moaned.

"Damn, she did choose me," Big John muttered, feeling Zytai's fingers reaching out to him.

The few whose mates were not in the crowd were having a tough time holding the men to the barrier. And Jordan knew exactly what they were feeling as Verena circled him.

Verena could not believe what was happening. After Jordan had freely come to her, she'd thought that she had won.

That he understood his place.

He understood nothing.

He had created an unnecessary problem. Anger stirred inside her as she circled him. Knowing that she should call immediately for reinforcements, still Verena held back. She wanted, no, she needed to show Jordan, to show the other males, that it was *she* who was in control.

"Find a way to make a net or some handcuffs or something," Suvan's mate yelled out to Jordan.

Having no doubt that her mate had enough intelligence to figure it out, Verena lunged at him, missing entirely as he dodged to the side and manipulated the remote to cause a rainstorm to appear. The rain doused the men, somehow giving them the control they needed to resist. Verena maneuvered herself behind Jordan, her fingers brushing his shoulders as she lunged once again for him. He sidestepped and pointed the remote in her direction. The next instant a large hairless beast stood before her, causing her to trip and fall ungracefully to the ground that had remained Earthlike and was now quite muddy from the rain. The beast squealed and dashed away, a pink curly tail their final view. Admitting defeat, Verena called for reinforcements just as Jordan created the handcuffs Suvan's mate had called for. Before her very eyes, her mate was tossing the contraptions to the males with a great deal of glee. What a disappointment she was to her mother, Verena thought.

"Cease!" she demanded as Bruce and a few others attempted, quite unsuccessfully, to attach the handcuffs to her fellow sisters. At that same moment the ship tilted with a sudden jerky movement.

"Explain," Verena commanded, fearing that something worse than a revolt of their mates was at hand.

"We are under attack, Commander," a voice answered.

"Who?"

"The Gargantums."

"Those smelly beasts? Sisters, take your posts." The women moved with a disciplined speed that belied the notion that the men had even had a chance of subduing them for more than a moment or two..

"Intruders on board," the same voice announced.

"That's Tora, that's my girl," Joe muttered. "What's she talking about and where the hell is she?"

"What's going on?" Jordan demanded.

"An invasion. Stay here," Verena answered as she sped past him.

"That's not happening," Jordan told her, reaching for her arm, turning her to face him. The touch caused a reaction that affected them both despite the threat looming over their heads.

"That *is* what will happen," Verena stated in her most commander-like voice.

"We're not gonna sit and hide," a deep voice declared.

"Who are these invaders?" someone else asked.

"Whoever they are, they're gonna be invaders getting their butts kicked," yet another man promised.

"Your lives could be in danger," Verena told them, taking in the comments and the determination on their faces as she tried to decide how best to keep them out of the way. The ship tilted again, throwing her against Jordan.

"Can't be any worse than what we're dealing with," Jordan muttered as he helped her steady herself. Verena felt determination begin inside of her and noted that same look of determination on her mate's face. This was going to be difficult. She had to find a way to keep the males out of harm's way.

The ship tilted yet again. Verena pushed herself away from Jordan. "As you wish," she declared, knowing that she had no time to deal with contrary males and thinking that perhaps experience was the best teacher. Verena dashed across the room to the same panel the other women had disappeared behind a few moments before.

"Follow them. This could be a trick," she heard. She could feel Jordan hot on her heels.

"Wouldn't be the first time we fell for one either," Joe muttered.

Jordan, Bruce and Briceson led the men into the narrow hallway. With unwavering resolve, they moved as one, barely keeping up with Verena, let alone the other women who had left before her. At a curve in the hallway Verena disappeared. Her long flowing ceremonial robes were the last thing Jordan saw as she vanished behind a swishing door.

"Damn it." Bruce slammed a fist against the metal, voicing Jordan's exact sentiments.

"Knew it was a trick," Joe grumbled, sinking to the floor.

"Let's ram our way in," Big John yelled, giving action to his suggestion by clearing a path and running into the door that now resembled a wall. The door gave but not in the way that was expected. It thinned, stretching and becoming transparent. Big John sprang back into the room, knocking down a bunch of the men like pins in a bowling alley.

"Krylogin." Jordan explained his experience with the special metal.

When the ribbing and laughter died down, the sudden hush in the room allowed Verena's voice to be heard. "Be gone, you stench-infested being. We have no interest in you or any offer you might have."

"But I do, mighty sister of Vixen. I understand that you need males to survive and here we are," a deep, gravely voice answered with firm conviction.

Males? These Gargantums were males, males willing to mate with the sisters of Vixen? This information sent a brief feeling of relief through Jordan, an extremely brief feeling of relief. He did not like the idea of some upstart species showing up to claim his woman. A warm sense of peace descended on him, and a quirky smile took over his mouth as he whispered to himself, "My woman." Verena *was* his woman.

"Who the hell is that and what is he talking about?" Big John said in a harsh whisper, pulling Jordan back to the immediate problem at hand.

"What he better not be talking about is laying a hand on my Susie," Bruce growled.

Other men echoed similar sentiments, voicing what Jordan felt himself. "Are you saying that you want to keep these women? Stay connected to them? Mate? Live the rest of your lives on another planet?"

"We didn't say all that, but hey, man, it's a possibility," one of the men whispered.

Murmured agreements left a subdued tension in the air.

"Okay then, we can decide what to do with the women and about this situation after we take care of the Gargantums."

Bruce hushed the men as Verena's voice came into the hall once more. Jordan was intent on not only hearing what she was saying but trying to detect any level of fear or anxiety, or pain. *He had better not hurt her...* Jordan forced himself to focus.

"And you think that we, the sisters of Vixen, have stooped to mating with animals?" Jordan was proud of the steady confidence that rang out even through the wall. Whatever creature it was on the other side of the wall could not possibly think that it was claiming *his woman.*

His woman.

His mouth lifted into a quirky smirk once again. Who'd of thought?

Verena, *his woman.*

"Man we've got to get in there," Briceson was saying.

"Sounds like they're trying to take what's *not* theirs."

"And what's ours."

"We can't let that happen."

"We have gotta save them."

"Release me!"

The strong, solid command he heard sent a chilling fright down Jordan's spine. Verena was in trouble.

"When I'm ready, Mighty-one," a hoarse, gravelly voice answered and laughed with a menace that heated Jordan's spine.

Without even thinking about what he was doing, Jordan pounded into the wall, his fisted hands creating a hole, his hands stretching, reaching for a neck, some hair, anything to beat to a bloody pulp.

He didn't make contact with his foe. Gentle fingers briefly connected with his. It was Verena. Her presence washed over him and her voice eased into his head.

"Be calm, all will be well."

An instant later his hand was thrust back into the room. Jordan stumbled backwards, losing his balance before he was steadied by a few of the men.

"What happened?" Bruce asked.

"Verena pushed me away."

"Man, what's that stench?" someone asked just as Jordan noticed it himself.

"Must be whatever it is on the other side of this wall."

"They smell as bad as they are."

"Nothing worse than a man trying to steal another man's woman."

"Nothing worse than a man who doesn't understand no."

"Oh no! He, it or whatever that is, is gonna understand," Jordan declared, gathering the men closer as a plan began to form in his head. Verena was in danger and he was going to protect her. He hadn't saved her life to let something happen to her now.

When Jordan's hands appeared in the wall Verena's heart had jumped. As the arrival of Suvan and Rya, escorted by two of their invaders, distracted Gorg, the leader of this savage race who had overtaken their ship, Verena had done the only thing she could think of. She'd shoved his hands back into the other side of the wall, savoring his touch but a moment and sending him a soothing message before pushing him away with all her might. The Gargantums did not know that the males were on the ship and Verena hoped to keep it that way. It was the only way to protect them. The Gargantums were a barely civilized, hairy bunch residing on the fringes of acceptability and had no regard or respect for the females of their kind. That fact alone was enough for the sisters of Vixen to hold them in contempt, but there were other layers of unacceptable behavior that kept them as outcasts.

"Come," Gorg, the leader, commanded, pushing his shaggy body against her own. The stench of unwashed, damp fur filled her nostrils, sickening her. Verena gagged inwardly. Refusing to lose control, she pulled the scent of Jordan from her memory.

"Come where?" Verena asked as other Gargantums filled the room. Rya and Suvan eyed them with equal disgust. A brief moment was all she needed with her sisters to formulate a plan of action, but Gorg was smarter than he looked or smelled.

"Get them out of here. Look them over, choose one for yourself, but keep them away from the Mighty-one."

"I only came to inform you that the ship is ours," one of the Gargantums said. The other stood silent, rubbing one brown, matted, furry hand over the other in anticipation.

"Of course it's ours!"

"Not for long," Verena whispered, her voice low but steady as she stared into the bushy face of her enemy, finding solid dark eyes that bore through her with deep hatred.

"No, Mighty-one? I win," he said, grabbing her close once again. "It was I who came up with the idea to do away with all those weak little males. It was easy enough to find a sickness that would quickly terminate their lives, leaving the strong sisters of Vixen without a way to survive. Of course everyone in the last two galaxies knows the enjoyment you give and take as you mate and the pride you take in reproducing. Well, you can now joyfully mate and reproduce with us," he growled.

CHAPTER 13

Hours.

Verena held back a sigh.

Long, frustrating hours of silently sitting on the bridge of her ship, unable to control its destination as Gorg dashed from one display to another.

Exactly three vile, nauseating, nostril-offending hours later, Verena still found that she was unable to extract herself from her current circumstance. Separated from her sisters and kept under close watch by Gorg and another very disgruntled Gargantum, Verena had little choice but to do no more than wait for an opportunity to act.

So far she had accomplished little other than to ensure that Jordan and all the other men were safe. Satisfied that she had accomplished at least that much, Verena briefly considered the talk she and her mate would have when all this was over.

Jordan.

She saw his face, consumed with concern and care as he eased her suffering both before and after the Ceremony of Unity; then she saw it charged with determination as he used the illusion device to cause havoc and chaos just before the Gargantums invaded. Something had twisted inside her as she witnessed proof that Jordan's determination to return to Earth had not died after the ceremony and the long, pleasurable night they had spent together.

A sudden revelation shook her. The pulsating need that twisted inside her to oust her enemy and deliver a fitting punishment must be the way Jordan felt about them all. Which was why he could not accept his fate. The very idea that she had caused Jordan this type of anxiety and frustration made her heart twist with remorse.

And still he'd come to her.

He'd saved her.

Which had to mean that Jordan truly cared for her.

"Come, it is time to rest."

Gorg's command pulled her away from her troubling thoughts. Despair and joy should not be allowed to co-exist.

"Come!" her captor repeated, his paw pulling at her arm.

Verena's skin felt as if it were crawling with vermin. She turned toward Gorg, unable and unwilling to hide the disgust on her face.

"Lead the way, Mighty-one." Thrusting his arm out, Gorg waited all of two seconds before growling, "Move!"

"I would if I had any knowledge of where you wish to go. I am certain that the destination must be lingering somewhere beneath that layer of fur covering your brain," Verena said, venting a little of the justified frustration *she* was feeling. Gorg's expression changed from anger to puzzlement, then to a smug look of satisfaction. "Lingering? Yes, there will be a lot of lingering. And where do I, the future mate of the commander, wish to linger? Your chambers, of course. I will say this only once more: Lead the way, Mighty-one."

Verena took the longest route to her chambers, hoping that she might encounter one of her sisters but also to keep secret the fact that the ship's bridge was fairly close to her chambers. Many minutes later Verena stopped at the door to her own private sanctuary. The anticipation that she had most recently come to feel upon entering was gone. She felt as if she stood before a black hole that had pulled from her all the happiness and joy of life.

"Step back. I must enter first. Superior beings have that privilege." He stomped past her, entering the room with his stench lagging behind.

There before her stood the beast who had not only taken over her ship, but had murdered half of her race. Soon, Verena promised herself, Gorg would experience the wrath of the sisters of Vixen.

Attempting to keep useless emotions from over-whelming her, Verena turned her head, searching for a bit of clean air so that she could inhale a deep, calming breath. Anger and frustration rushed over her as she stared at Gorg's back. With sheer determination, Verena willed away the useless feelings that would not free her, her sisters or protect their mates.

Her mate. She could not keep him out of her mind, especially since she was coming to understand him.

Jordan.

What was he doing now? A slow smile spread across her mouth as she pictured him. Verena was certain that he wasn't cowering in some corner waiting for rescue. Then her smile faded into a worried frown. He was probably planning wild scenes of revolt that would get the men captured and anger Gorg. They would all be at his mercy. He would not hesitate to give them a death sentence, just as he had not hesitated to infect every Vixen male.

"Enter!" Gorg demanded, bringing Verena back to the present.

Stepping forward, she moved to the middle of the room. The door swooshing closed behind her felt like a trap. She was trapped in her chambers with a beast.

Now she knew exactly how Jordan had felt about her. No wonder he had been so resistant. But she could not dwell on it now.

Later, when they were all free.

Verena found herself choking and sputtering at the odor, the stench that completely enveloped her as Gorg circled her. He offended all of her senses.

He paused to watch her until her spasms subsided. "You will get used to the unique scent that surrounds the Gargantums." He paused, a sneer stretching the fur on his face, "As well as all other things."

The memory of saying something quite similar to Jordan as she insisted that he would come to accept his fate flashed through her brain. Tossing that particular revelation aside along with the others, Verena concentrated on her enemy. He was moving about *her* chamber, touching *her* things.

"These instruments interest me."

Verena forced herself to focus on his words as he continued.

"But I will not bother asking you their purpose. Your brain could not possibly hold that much knowledge."

Despite knowing that he was deliberately taunting her, picking at her pride, since the vast knowledge of the sisters of Vixen was known far and wide, his words deepened her anger, and his deep, gritty voice pricked her nerves. Verena folded her arms and remained silent, determined the insults would not make a visible mark.

"I'm sure that with my superior abilities I can figure it all out on my own. After all, I have outwitted you once before, and on quite a grand scale."

His grin widened as he stepped forward, stopping a mere inch from her, peering into her face. A greedy, superior gloating aura surrounded him.

"Get out of my presence. Go into the side chamber where you belong."

When she only stood and stared, Gorg went on, "Is that not where you Vixens store your mates until you have a need for them?"

"Need?" Verena asked as she came to grips with her rising anger, concentrating more on diminishing the effects of Gorg's insults than the impact of his words.

"A physical need."

"A physical need?" Verena absently repeated.

"Your skill in echoing my words has been noted. Maybe you wish to stay out here with me. I believe I could rally up a physical urge or two."

Processing his meaning, she slowly backed into the side chamber, her eyes relaying the revulsion and disgust she felt. He might have taken over her ship and dictated a minor command, but he would not win this battle. Transmitting every thought and feeling she had for him

223

and his followers, Verena held the hard, cruel eyes of her enemy. His tiny pupils widened, a second's fear appearing before he turned away with a derisive, nervous bellow that did little to fool her into believing that she had not bred a morsel of concern inside his puny brain.

Standing in the middle of the side chamber, Verena forced her body to release the frustrated tension that been growing with her inability to control her circumstances. It had further escalated when she watched the beast throw his filthy fur covered body onto her sleeping pallet. So appalled was she by the sight of him infecting her most personal space that it took a moment for her to realize that C1 was calling her by name in a forceful, demanding manner.

C1.

He was only a computer.

"Commander!

But then he was Jordan's companion and, like so many other things involving her mate, not an ordinary computer.

"Commander! You must pay heed!"

"I am. I am here and attentive now."

"That is the most wonderful news I have heard in the last hour. Commander, I am most pleased to see that you are well and that you and J.M. have finally united—"

C1's voice abruptly halted only to return a few seconds later.

"Pardon my sudden rudeness, Commander, but J.M. seems to believe that congratulations should be postponed—" the computer began again. "Yes, I will tell her." he said, speaking to some unknown person.

Not just any unknown person, she realized. "Jordan. C1, you are speaking to Jordan!" Verna began to move about the room.

"Yes, and he wishes you to—"

"Tell him he must stay hidden until we can find a way to regain the ship!" she demanded, pacing the tiny space.

"He—"

"Tell him that this race of beasts is heartless and dangerous!" She stopped, frustrated by the confines of the chamber. How did a male endure such confinement, she wondered.

"Commander—"

"Jordan and the men must remain hidden!"

"Mighty she-force!" C1 yelled. J.M. on one side was demanding that he give instructions to the commander who on the other side was demanding the complete opposite.

"C1!" both voices bellowed, vibrating C1's circuitry.

"Silence!" C1 demanded, surprising them all. After a moment, C1 used sensors to check the state of the Gargantum reclining on the commander's pallet. Despite the disruption, the beast was sleeping. "You are both lucky to have not awakened the enemy. Jordan, if you will remain silent I will convey your message." C1 paused, obviously listening to Jordan.

"Allow me to hear what Jordan is saying!" Verena demanded. "I command him to take no action."

"Commander, you may convey this message yourself if you take a few steps to the rear of the chamber and place your back against the wall."

Verena did not hesitate to do as C1 suggested. She was probably the first sister of Vixen to follow the dictates of her mate through his computer. One moment she was pressed against the wall of the chamber and the next she was pressed against the warm, hard flesh of her mate.

"Jordan!" Verena twisted to face him. "Are you safe? Are you are unharmed?" Even as she asked the questions, her hands roamed his body to seek their own assurance.

"Are you?" Jordan asked, not waiting for a response but checking for himself, stopping her roaming hands to pull her tight against him. Feeling her long, warm body crushed into him relieved his fear and worry. Leaning back to peer into her beautiful face he brushed the tiny tight curls behind her ears, gently moved his lips over hers. When his tongue requested entrance, it was quickly given and he reached deep into her heated mouth, pulling all that was her inside himself. This kiss wasn't one taken or given by force, or as a means of relief or salvation, but a symbol of what he felt her. His lips and tongue hungrily translated a truth he'd revolted against, a truth that he had denied.

He was in love.

He was in love with his captor.

"Hmm-huh," echoed around them.

"I know, C1. I couldn't help myself."

"So, in this case it is acceptable to waste time mauling your mate when you could not give me a moment to congratulate—"

"I apologize," Jordan told the computer.

"Jordan." Verena pressed a finger behind his ear. "You have discovered how to activate the communications device to speak with C1 away from our chambers."

"Forgive me, Commander. It was I who activated the device when I realized the ship was being taken over. I also took the liberty to enhance its function so that anyone within a few meters can hear my voice as well. But it was J.M.'s idea to attempt to contact you."

"All true, and now that we've gotten Verena free, let's get on with it!" Jordan said, anxious to continue with their plan.

"Get on with what? Jordan what's happening? How did you release me? And what scheme have you and C1 devised?"

Jordan held up the illusionary device that he'd used to cause so much havoc a few hours ago. "I created a door, pulled you through it and into my arms. Magically, you are free."

"Freedom is a state I never wish to lose again. Quick, we do not have much time. Gorg will soon realize that I am gone, though he will have no idea how, and he will sound the alarm."

Verena was down the sparkling hall and around a bend before she realized that Jordan had not followed. "Come, Jordan, we must stay together."

"But first you must see this."

"See what? We do not have a moment to waste."

"See step one in our ingenious plan to take back the ship and run the beasts out of town." Jordan pointed the

227

device at the wall. A small circular hole appeared in the wall. "Take a look."

Verena placed her eye on at the hole and was surprised to see the interior of Jordan's chamber and beyond into her own.

"What do you see?"

"Your chamber and mine and the foul creature contaminating my pallet. What is this about? We are wasting time."

"Who do you see?" Jordan asked, "besides the foul creature contaminating your pallet?"

"Jordan, this is a waste of precious time."

"Scan the chamber," Jordan prompted again. "Who else do you see?"

"Besides the smelly beast? I have know idea who you expect—"

"Well?"

"It is I."

"Not the real you. Only an illusion, thanks to this little device."

"This is step one in your plan?"

"Yes, to release everyone without our enemies realizing that you have been released."

"Brilliant."

"Thank you. Now if you will lead me to where we can find more of these little babies we can get started with step two of our plan—"

"—to take back the ship and run the beasts out of town," C1 interrupted. "Enough talk, J.M. It is a time for action."

"Exactly, C1," Verena answered, moving once again down the hallway. "Come, my mate. We will follow this corridor. It will lead us to every sister's private chambers. Every Sister has such a device. Tell me, how do we know that they are being held in their chambers?"

"My buddy C1."

"I have sensed the presence of every sister of Vixen. Not one was lost."

"And how do they fare?"

"Strong and powerful as usual," C1 answered.

Verena released a sigh of relief. "But wait." She stopped and Jordan nearly crashed into her. "Where are the other men?" Verena turned to him, her hands resting on his firm, solid shoulders, feelings of mutual respect and reassurance flowing between them.

Jordan smiled into her face. "You said men, not males."

"And so they are. Now please tell me they are still in hiding. If the Gargantums have captured them, they are in grave danger, especially if it is known that you are our mates. Jordan, it was these beasts who infected our males with that deadly disease. They exterminated half my race to join with us."

The revulsion was plain on her face. If the odor the Gargantums carried hadn't been enough of a repulsion, his brief exposure to their personalities and Verena's revelation sealed his opinion. "Don't worry, the Gargantums will get what they deserve. As for the men…C1? Where are they?"

"Approximately fifty meters behind you."

"Perfect timing."

In no time the hall vibrated with strong men who emitted the same strength and determination Verena had experienced with her sisters united in battle.

"Jordan, man, you were able to get her out!" Bruce said in a loud whisper.

"It worked."

A quiet rumble of approval marked their first success.

"What are we waiting for? I've got a wife and kid I need to save." Michael pushed his way to the front.

"You are Rya's mate," Verena said.

Michael nodded. "Point me in the right direction."

"Ten meters forward. Her chambers are closest to mine. We are kin."

"I know," Michael answered, taking the device from Jordan.

The large contingent of rescuers moved on silent feet as C1 directed Michael to Rya. Michael pulled her through the door and possessively into his arms.

"Michael. What are you—? Quick, go. You must hide. They will kill you if they know you are my mate."

"Rya, be calm.

"Verena!"

Rya reached out a long graceful arm and pulled her into the embrace because Michael was not letting her go.

"All will be well," Verena continued. "Our mates have a scheme. A plan that has already progressed to—" Verena turned to Jordan.

"Step two."

"Step two," she repeated, her eyes smiling at him in complete confidence.

"Then we must proceed in all haste." Rya returned the smile.

"Your illusion device, can you access it?" Verena asked.

"Yes, that abominable beast has left my chamber to relieve another of his kind on the bridge. He gloated that he was taking over my duties, as if he—"

"Sweetheart, it's okay," Michael said. "No one can ever replace you."

"Although this is touching," Big John jumped in, "we've got some serious rescuing to do. I'm itching to have Zytai back where she belongs."

"He's right, let's get this plan rollin'," someone else muttered.

"Yes, we must take back the ship and run the beasts out of town," C1 declared.

"Right, but this is going to take some time. C1 can easily find everyone. Once each sister is located I can stand near a chamber. C1 will let each sister know that rescue is on the way through my communications device." Jordan tapped his ear. "But the amplification will allow C1 to talk to only one sister at a time."

"I have a much quicker method of communication," Verena said.

"How?" Jordan asked.

"Vixen explorers are trained to communicate in a special way. When two sisters are together, they have the means to communicate with all," Rya answered.

"That is why they kept us apart," Verena explained.

Jordan nodded, remembering the Gargantum, Gorg, giving that exact command.

"Wait a second!" Big John's voice rumbled quietly. "How do we know that they're doing what they say they're doing? I want Zytai back so I can have it out with her but that doesn't mean that I trust her or any of you."

"You do not trust us?" Verena turned to the men to ask.

Heads shook, defiant eyes bore into her and voices quietly but firmly responded with various forms of no.

"We have given you no reason to trust us. I have come to understand that, but now we are forced to work together and if we are ever going to be able to 'have it out,' we must trust each other. You began this plan, but we must proceed together in the most efficient manner."

"Yes, we need action to take back the ship and run the beasts out of town!" C1 interjected.

"C1," Jordan warned. Jordan turned toward the men hoping to defuse the situation. He understood exactly how they felt. They had been in charge. They had planned the rescue. Allowing the sisters to get involved would give them the upper hand again.

"Jordan, do you trust me?"

Jordan looked into her face. The 'no' he was about to utter died in his throat because, surprise, surprise, he did trust her.

She smiled at him, a smile that made her face radiant, a smile that held gratitude and love. She loved him?

"This manner of communication is also one that you can experience with your mates."

"What are you talking about now?" Bruce asked. "I've never experienced anything like that with Susie!" Bruce turned to the other men. "Any of you?"

More negative responses were provoking those in the hallway into a field primed for mutiny.

"Jordan has."

"*I* have? When?"

"Just a moment ago to some degree, but most definitely so when I pushed your hands back through the wall, after Gorg threatened me."

"You did?"

"Where are my recently learned manners? I have yet to thank you for that show of protection," resounded inside his head, though Verena's mouth never moved. "I spoke to you then to protect you. You spoke to me also. You told me no," she then said for all to hear.

She had, Jordan realized. He had heard her voice. "She did," Jordan confirmed. "I just didn't realize that her voice was inside my head."

"Then why haven't our women spoken to any of us that way?" Briceson asked.

"It was one of our secrets."

"More like lies," Big John said.

"What?" Michael jumped.

"It's true, Michael," Rya said.

"What was that all about?" Bruce asked.

"They're telling the truth." Michael looked from Rya to the men. "She just spoke to me that way."

"The sisters speak the truth. I didn't offer this alternative because we were using the resources at hand," C1 informed them. "We must act now. Must I remind you once again that enough time has been wasted?"

"C1, my friend, you're getting a little smart in the mouth but when you're right, you're right," Jordan said.

"I also agree with C1," Verena said.

"Commander! You agree with me, a mere male companion? I am—"

"It *is* time for action," Jordan interrupted. What he said now would determine their success and their future. "We have to work together. We must allow the sisters to do their thing, under the condition that we will not be treated as prisoners and that we will be free when all of this is over."

"Agreed," Verena immediately responded with calm authority.

"But, Commander," Rya gasped.

"We have no other option. We have been unjust. Our actions have been as heinous as those of the Gargantums."

"I wouldn't go that far…" The heavy voice of Suvan's mate faded as Verena pressed her palms against Rya's, combining their minds to reach out to their sisters.

Jordan watched as they stood together. The men behind him were watchful and suspicious. A gentle hum began to emit from them. Jordan focused on Verena. The serenity of her face clearly evolved into authority as she issued a command he could hear as plain as day. "Hear me, sisters of Vixen. We will regain the ship but you must heed my command. Claim the illusion device within your chambers. If you are not guarded, use it to create a duplicate of yourself. Also, create a portal into the corridor and meet your fellow sisters as well as your mates and future mates who have devised this ingenious plan."

Jordan turned to the men. "It's done."

"I still don't like this."

"We don't have much choice."

"At least this will buy our freedom."

"Freedom bought or not, my choice is made. I'm staying with Rya," Michael said, effectively shocking the men into silence.

One by one the sisters of Vixen began to emerge into the hallway.

"Zytai, lead a contingent of sisters to the engine room, stay hidden and await future instructions."

"I'm coming with you," Big John said.

"Calvin, Earl, Joe and Briceson, go with 'em!" Bruce said, his eyes scanning the hall.

Verena issued orders sending sisters to strategic areas of the ship. Bruce and Jordan directed a few of the men to join each group.

"C1, how many sisters are out?"

"Forty-five, J.M."

"Suvan's one of the five missing," Bruce said. "I think I'm gonna have to kick some Gargantum butt."

"Rya, stay with Bruce and Michael to aid in rescuing the other sisters. Then bring them to the private holding room outside the bridge. I'm sure it has remained inaccessible to our enemy, " Verena commanded, turning to Jordan who nodded his consent.

"C1 has already identified those who remain," Jordan added before moving to join Verena.

Jordan and Verena had only gone a few feet when they heard the gravelly voices of two Gargantums. Without a second's pause Jordan created a silvery wall to hide behind.

Another click of the device allowed both him and Verena a good look at the enemy through twin peepholes. Jordan watched as they turned the corner, one Gargantum shoving the other.

"Stupid ship," one growled. "I thought this was the right path."

"Stupid, stupid. You couldn't find your way out of a tree a hand's length from the ground."

There was a scuffle and more shoving before the voices faded.

"We must go back and try to get through the other way. It's longer but hopefully more secure," Verena advised.

Jordan nodded as he followed her back down the hall where they had left the others.

"Rya and Michael have found and released four of the trapped sisters," C1 informed them. "All except Suvan."

"Susie. Where the hell is Susie!" Bruce grabbed Jordan by the shoulder nearly screaming in his ear. "C1, if she's where you said she is, why hasn't she gotten away?"

"She is exactly where I have reported," C1 answered.

"Then she must be—" Fear twisted Bruce's face. A second later he took the illusion device from Michael and headed back to the spot where C1 had reported Suvan to be.

"I must warn you," C1 interjected.

"I'm warning you." Bruce said in a deadly quiet voice. "Just be quiet. I'm going to save her."

"Is she alive, C1?" Verena asked.

"Yes, but barely. This must have happened recently. All the sisters who were trapped were in good health ten minutes ago."

"Rya, stay and attend Suvan. I must get to the bridge."

"I'll stay with Rya," Michael said.

"Jordan?"

"I'll stay. Bruce might need me and C1."

"If this corridor becomes crowded with Gargantums, use that beautiful mind of yours to stay safe."

"You do the same," Jordan said, giving her a hard kiss before handing her one of the devices, watching as her lithe body disappeared down the corridor.

Suddenly a crashing sound filled the empty hall.

"That is the direction you must go," C1 said. "Twenty meters to your right."

"I know." Bruce was there and had already created a peephole. His tense body relayed the news that it was as bad as they had expected.

"Susie's on the floor. She's bleeding. I can't tell if she's alive or dead."

"She is alive, Bruce. Be assured of that," C1 said.

"That thing looks like some kind of Bigfoot. He's throwing stuff around and wrecking the place."

A tremendous growl shook the wall.

"I'm going in." Bruce pointed the device at the wall.

"Wait, go in low. Make a small opening. Once you get inside, disguise yourself as the wall or a chair or something. That'll surprise him."

"Man, he's gonna be surprised."

Bruce did as Jordan suggested. A few agonizing minutes later, a howl of rage filled the corridor. Seconds later Bruce came out holding an unconscious Suvan in his arms. "He sounded the alarm before I could stop him, but he won't be sounding any more alarms, not ever again."

"What's that god-awful smell?" Michael whispered.

"It's ten times worse in there," Bruce said, leaning against the wall to adjust Suvan more comfortably in his arms.

"Five Gargantums are approaching," C1 announced.

"Making the smell five times more powerful," Jordan muttered. "Quick, where's the device?"

"I just had it in my hand. I must have dropped it inside." Bruce twisted his head toward the opening in the wall.

"Rya, whatever happens you need to get Suvan to the doctor." Jordan said before ducking into the door Bruce had made to get Suvan out. Just inside, on the floor was the device. The odor hit him before he caught sight of the Gargantum lying a few feet away. The thing did look like Bigfoot or Sasquatch or whatever they were called. Hearing the others approaching, an idea popped into Jordan's head. He dashed back into the hall. "We'll look like them," Jordan said as he pointed the illusion device at Rya, Michael and Bruce, then on himself before using it to close the opening not a second too soon.

"What are you doing here? Didn't you hear the alarm? Get to your post," the Gargantum standing in the forefront growled.

"Alarm? What alarm?" Jordan asked, stalling.

"That sound we heard?" Rya asked, the first to realize what Jordan had done. "I thought it was only a trick. Those stupid sisters of Vixen should know better than think we'd fall for something that obvious."

"No, we're not that stupid," Michael joined in.

The Gargantum grunted. The others echoed the sound. Jordan stared at the leader through his brand new bushy eyebrows, hoping that he wouldn't ask for name, rank and serial number. Bruce shifted Suvan's weight. Rya grunted in reply. He and the others quickly followed Rya's example by adding a few grunts of their own.

"What's wrong with that Vixen?"

"Got too rough with this one," Bruce answered.

"There is no mating until we reach our planet. That was the order. The Universal Council will not be able to touch us once we reach our own planet."

"There was no mating. We were *playing*. Almost done her in. I'm taking her to the healer," Bruce said. "That way she'll be healed up real nice for mating when we do get back to the planet."

The hall shook with a raunchy, vulgar sound that was a mix between a laugh and a gravelly growl.

"And where are you the rest of you going?" the lead Gargantum asked, his eyes boring into each of them.

Jordan hesitated only a second. "We got to see the healer ourselves," came out of his mouth. He knew that he would have to have some explanation for all of them walking away together. He had no intention of separating, not if they could help it. "The food sucks. It's made us all sick."

"We know, too fresh."

"You are new recruits then? This is your first journey?"

They all nodded.

"You gotta learn to deal with the challenges of space voyage. But we just might have some pity on you. Some of us have found some real food."

"It's been fermenting a good while," a voice in the back of the furry group bellowed.

"Be in the dining quarters in one hour's time if you want any. It'll do more for you than that Vixen healer possibly can. They couldn't even save their own males from death. They won't be able to do a thing for what ails you."

Good information. Definitely something they could use to their advantage.

"Will there even be enough food? I mean, how many of us will be there?"

"There's enough for all. But we're only inviting a select few."

Smart question, Michael, Jordan thought as the group began to walk away. "I'm not interested unless the commander's going to be there!" Jordan lowered his voice to a deep shout, hoping to hear that he would be there.

"Ambitious."

Jordan nodded, adding a grunt for good measure, hoping that by not responding verbally he could avoid prolonging the interaction.

"Maybe he will and maybe he won't. Now get out of my sight before we decide to toss you out into space. Might be fun to see you spinning around out there, unable to take a breath, suffocating and finally surrendering to death," he said in a deadly serious tone, his fur standing on end. The atmosphere heated with violent intent.

The four of them didn't waste time leaving. They were silent until reaching the healer's quarters.

"Talk about unstable, moody creatures," Michael muttered.

"They are unpredictable. They can be pleasant one moment and violently brutal the next. Look at what one of them did to Suvan," Rya noted as they entered the healer's chambers. "Though Denee is not here, I can make Suvan more comfortable and convince her to drink a bit of Toca. Bruce, you must find Sister Denee, the healer, and bring her back. Take the device. The rest of us should be safe here."

With C1's help Jordan led Bruce through the ship, encountering no one along the way. They found the healer hiding near the ship's engine room with a few of her assistants and two of the men keeping surveillance and awaiting orders. Bruce went up to the healer and started to explain the situation as he began to drag Denee away. Jordan and Bruce were instantly jumped, thrown to the ground and held all in a matter of seconds. As Jordan's head hit the ground he felt the communication device pop out from behind his ear. C1 was no longer an aid to him.

"What shall we do with them?" Jordan heard Denee ask.

"I say we kill them," Mark, one of the men pinning Bruce to the ground suggested.

"No, that goes against the healer's oath."

"It goes against common sense. Are you crazy, Mark? It's me, Bruce!"

Jordan was making an attempt to add something to the mix, but the knee on his chest and the body across his abdomen were not allowing enough air to breathe, let alone speak.

"What kind of trick is this? How do you know my name?" Mark asked.

Jordan began to feel a blackness overcoming him as the surreal conversation dragged on. "Verena, it's just a disguise. Tell them we are not Gargantums," was his last thought before the blackness consumed him.

"Verena, it's just a disguise, tell them we are not Gargantum," echoed inside Verena's head, interrupting her thoughts as she visualized the various positions of the enemy from the information gathered by her sisters, the men and C1.

"Jordan!" Verena stood in the close confines of the tiny chamber hidden in a small alcove just off the bridge of the ship, made even smaller by the two sisters and their mates keeping a watchful, secretive eye on the two Gargantums left to operate the ship and the two guards who alternated position every quarter of an hour.

"Tora, come." With the help of Tora, Verena sent forth a message to every sister. "Jordan and one of the men may be disguised as Gargantums. Do not harm them."

"My apologies, Commander," a reply came almost instantly, "they came upon us unexpectedly."

"You have done what you must, I am certain. Is all well, Denee?"

"Your mate must catch his breath and the other is most insistent that I go with him."

"Do so. He is Suvan's mate and she, I suspect, is in great need of your aid."

"Yes, Commander. Once again, I apologize. I should have realized that they were not truly Gargantum. There was no odor surrounding them."

Going back to the schematics of the ship she had drawn on the wall, Verena smiled, relieved that Jordan was well and impressed with his ability to mentally communicate with her when he had just gained knowledge of the skill. He'd spoken to her through his mind, and he had disguised himself as a Gargantum.

How remarkable.

How ingenious.

How exactly what she should have come to expect from him.

Not many minutes later Verena felt his presence beyond the walls of the hidden chamber. He was seeking her whereabouts. As capable as Jordan was, he would not be able to access this room. It responded exclusively to her commands. Feeling him drawing closer, she stood at the hidden entrance and waited. "Place your back to the wall, Jordan," she told him and a moment later she pulled him through the secret entrance. He turned to face her, his disguise still in place.

"You look much more handsome as yourself, Jordan."

"You knew it was me?"

"I would know my mate anywhere."

"That's a good thing, I think." Jordan pointed the device toward himself. Instantly he was transformed.

"Come, you have given me an extraordinary idea. I am blessed to have a mate as brilliant as you."

"It's good to be appreciated," Jordan said, cautious of Verena's approval but nevertheless basking in it. When this was over they would have to talk and settle some things and—He shook his head. Later, when this was over.

"It is so simple, which is what makes it so brilliant. I have discovered that we outnumber the Gargantums by far. I find this unusual, but they are only twenty of them."

"Nineteen now. Bruce took care of one of them."

"Bruce disposed of a Gargantum?"

"Suvan was badly hurt."

"Denee will make her well," Verena said, trying hard to hide her worry for her officer and fellow sister.

"You were saying?" Jordan asked.

"Yes." She paused to track her thoughts. "I was saying that the Gargantums usually travel in much larger packs."

"Do they normally attack ships?"

"That is also unusual, for we are in open space. Gargantums usually remain on the outskirts, only attacking those who venture too close to their home planet."

"Everything about this attack is unusual, but we'll wait to pick it apart until after we've caught them all, which should be a piece of cake since we outnumber them five to one," Jordan said.

"Strange, but I think I understood most of what you were saying."

Jordan laughed. "I'll give you a few lessons on figurative language when all this is over. Tell me about this simply brilliant plan inspired by me."

"We will use the illusion devices," she began, "to disguise ourselves as Gargantums and reclaim our ship, a section at a time if necessary."

"Step three in our plan."

"Yes, and we will capture these beasts as we recapture each area of the ship."

"Step four."

Verena nodded. "We will simultaneously begin in the engine room and on the bridge."

"So that we will instantly have control of the ship through the power source and the guidance system."

"Exactly." She beamed up him. "Then we will strategically overpower pockets of patrols at the greatest distance apart."

"To reduce the risk of those being captured warning others."

"Precisely." Verena twisted to look up at him. She felt as if she had been speaking to Zeda, her strategic defense officer. Pride filled her. It felt so much more powerful than dominance.

"They won't know what hit them," Jordan said, wrapping his arms around her and pulling her into his body.

Startled, Verena stiffened. Never having had or even witnessed a serious conference between mates, she was not sure if this behavior was appropriate.

"What's wrong?" he whispered in her ear.

"Nothing." Verena sighed. The warmth of his breath in her ear felt quite appropriate. "To imagine that I expected you not to think, that I assumed that you were simple-minded."

"Commander! Jordan!" C1 said, static filling the air. Jordan touched the communication device he had reinserted behind his ear hoping to clear away the static. "Large masses of the enemy are moving about." C1 continued rattling off their position just as Verena began receiving messages from every hidden post on the ship. She made changes on the wall, adjusting and readjusting as the enemy moved.

"Where are they going?" Verena hissed.

"My guess is to get something to eat."

"Jordan, this is a time for seriousness. Why would they…" Verena's voice trailed off as she listened to reports and gave commands. "How did you know?"

Jordan pointed to his head. At the widening of her beautiful eyes, he admitted, "Actually, I was coming to tell you about an interesting conversation I had with a few Gargantums. They seem to hate fresh food and have somehow discovered some food that meets their standards."

"I had forgotten. They eat only spoiled or rotten food, which I am certain adds to their nasty aroma."

"Which could be a problem for our plan. Visually changing into one of them will only take a push of a button. Smelling like one will be a challenge."

Folding her arms, Verena stood quietly, lost in thought. "The refuse chamber."

"Are you suggesting that we wallow in filth?"

"Yes."

"Then let's move on to step three."

CHAPTER 14

All was in readiness.

The sisters of Vixen and the men of Earth waited together in alcoves, air ducts and impossibly tight corners, all hidden from view but ready to go into battle.

Jordan led a group of five disguised as Gargantums to the dining quarters. Despite their own horrible smell, acquired by rolling in piles of trash, the stench coming from the dinning quarters reached them long before they got near the entrance.

"Are you sure there's just ten of them in there?" Bruce muttered.

"According to C1. And that's more than half of them. Four are in or near the bridge, four more are in the engine room. These guys are supposed to be patrolling the halls."

"That's eighteen," Michael said, having missed the briefing as he argued with Rya about joining the fight in her present condition. "Where's the other one?"

"In Verena's chambers. Sleeping like the dead, which is why these guys aren't where they're supposed to be, making our job much easier," Jordan answered.

They stepped in, pausing at the entrance. Jordan scanned the room. Few were eating but there were scattered remains of rotten food, stale bread and unrecognizable mush thrown on tables, the floor and even the walls. "Try not to breathe too deeply and grunt every now and then," he told Zytai and Big John, who were part of the group.

Everyone grunted in reply.

"The puny ones have arrived!" the Gargantum who seemed to be the leader announced.

Jordan grunted. A delayed series of grunts followed.

"Too late!"

Unsure of what the Gargantum meant by 'too late,' Jordan stood stock-still. Had they given themselves away already? Was the grunting supposed to be synchronized? He could feel the tension rising among the five of them. Slowly pulling in a deep stench-filled breath, Jordan forced himself to relax, drawing from the teachings of Karate-do.

That same gravel-like snort he'd heard earlier shook the room as all ten howled with mirthless humor.

"Nothing left but a platter for our commander."

Food. They were late for the food. Jordan looked at each member of his group and shrugged his shoulders. "I see food."

"What are you talking about, you puny fur-ball?" The remark came from the same insulting Gargantum. Those around him seemed to smirk, as if they were in on some unknown joke.

"There's food all over, everywhere." Jordan pointed to the floor, then smacked his hand on a wall and proceeded to lick away the contents.

"Hey, bread!" Bruce shouted, dashing across the room and carefully placing himself into position. "The mold is perfect."

249

"Don't touch it." A huge Gargantum towered over Bruce.

Bruce grunted, "It's on the floor."

"Exactly where I left it."

"If you want this delicious morsel, you have to catch me to get it." Bruce grabbed the bread and dashed to the far end of the room and through the doors leading to the kitchen, the beast howling behind him.

"I'll catch you and beat it out of your stealing hands," it roared.

"I'm coming to help you with that." Another stood and began lumbering behind them.

Their plan wasn't working out exactly the way they had anticipated but Jordan was nevertheless satisfied. They each had planned on dealing with two Gargantums. Jordan was sure Bruce would have no problem handling the two chasing him. Jordan stooped to pick up what looked like a chicken bone.

"Not bothering to help your friend?" the leader grumbled.

Jordan shrugged his shoulders. From the corner of his eye he spotted Zytai, Big John and Michael fanning out, supposedly looking for food.

"I'm liking you better and better, fur-ball. We might just let you live," the Gargantum announced.

The room shook with an animalistic war cry as the Gargantums separated and pounded toward each of them. Jordan didn't waste time in using the illusion device he'd strapped to his arm and hidden under the matted fur that covered him. A giant hole big enough to contain one of their huge bodies appeared in the floor just in time for the first unlucky beast to tumble into it. Another click of a button and the hole tightened, making it impossible to reach the deadly-looking swords and mace-like weapons they carried.

"Give me that!" the leader roared, hopping over the next hole Jordan had made.

Jordan ran. Hot, rotten breath hammered down his back as he dodged his enemy. A heavy paw swiped at him as he jumped over the head of a Gargantum trapped by one of the others. Hoping everyone else was having better luck than he was, Jordan kept running, this time dodging a sword that sliced past his ear. His heart pounding, he dashed past overthrown tables and chairs and behind a high metal shelf, effectively trapping himself. Jordan could hear the Gargantum's harsh breathing. This had to be what if felt like to be stalked like an animal.

"Think. Think," he told himself. "Verena's says you're brilliant. Prove it."

The shelf began to shake. Unknown heavy objects rattled, threatening to fall on top of him. Pointing the device at himself, Jordan jumped out of his hiding place and yelled the first thing that came to mind, "Boo-ga boo-ga!"

The hairy beast froze, giving Jordan the moment he needed to take him by surprise with a kick in the chest that sent him reeling backwards. Bruce and Big John came out of nowhere to toss a net over their prey and drag him, feet first, across the room.

251

"Where'd you get the net?" Jordan asked between gasping breaths.

"These are great," Bruce said by way of explanation, holding up one of the illusion devices.

"Release me!"

"We plan on it. Right into that little hole I designed just for you."

"What have you done to my men?"

"They're taking a much needed rest," Zytai said, displaying the inoculators used to deliver the sleep-inducing injections they had each been given.

Jordan widened the hole as they tossed the leader in, then tightened it so that he was nice and secure.

"Gorg put you up to this. How did he discover that we planned to take the ship and the women?"

"Nope. It wasn't Gorg, my friend."

"I am no friend of yours. The name is Bock. What are you?"

"I'm just a man from Earth working with the sisters of Vixen to put you in your place. Would you like to take a look at the rest of us?" Jordan asked.

"Why not?" Michael answered when Bock's only response was a hostile stare. In an instant Michael transformed himself. Zytai, Big John and Bruce did the same.

"We men from Earth have a problem with creatures that try to take what's ours," Big John said, taking the inoculators from Zytai to send Bock to la-la land.

Finally having caught his breath, Jordan scanned the spectacle of hairy heads protruding from the floor. A knot began to loosen in his stomach, and he burst out with an incredulous guffaw, triggering an uncontrollable laugh fest among the five of them.

Pulling himself together, Jordan asked Bruce, "The ones that chased you into the kitchen?"

"They look as ridiculous as the rest of them."

"Good. C1, are you there?"

"We have taken back the ship. When shall we run the beasts out of town?"

"We shall run them to face the Universal Council," Zytai answered.

"How are the others?" Jordan asked.

"They have successfully subdued the enemy. All except Gorg."

"What?" Though slightly alarmed to hear this bit of news, Jordan was not worried about Verena. As her mate he would sense if she was in any sort of danger. And right now he was sensing a strong degree of pride and relief.

"Gorg is dead."

"What?" Jordan asked again.

"The healer has determined that he was poisoned."

"Probably by his own men," Bruce muttered.

"According to Bock, they were planning a mutiny," Michael added.

"I am not surprised. These beasts have a reputation for ruthlessness and betrayal," Zytai declared.

"All of them?" Big John asked.

"Everyone that I have met."

"Seems strange."

"Why do you say so?"

"Well, from my experience, to judge a whole race of people by the actions of a few is unfair."

"You know nothing of this kind, John." Zytai folded her arms, making Jordan realize that this action was most likely a Vixen trait.

"We've just fought together and we won. Let's not fight with each other. We've got better things to do," Big John suggested.

"I agree, but first we must report to the commander," Zytai said as they walked away, Bruce following not far behind.

"Bruce, where are you going?" Jordan asked.

"I just realized that I've got better things to do too. I have to see how Susie's doing. She'll be looking for me."

"And I have to check on that hardheaded mate of mine," Michael said, leaving Jordan alone with a roomful of hairy heads.

Without warning, laughter rolled from the bottom of Jordan's belly once again.

"Jordan, do you wish for me to call for the commander or possibly the healer?" C1 asked.

"No, I don't need either. Besides, Verena's just where she needs to be, doing exactly what she needs to be doing, commanding her ship. Don't worry about me. I'm just releasing a small amount of tension."

"If you say so."

"I say so. And if you don't mind, I'd love for you to keep me company as I guard these nasty critters."

"My pleasure, J.M."

"No, the pleasure's all mine, C1." Into the silence that followed Jordan added, "I've missed you, my friend."

C1 sighed, "It's good to be missed. Now, what shall we talk about?"

Hours later, after Verena met with her crew and made sure that the prisoners were secured in the brig, it was time to face the next challenge, one that arose from feelings she had never experienced before. Apprehension, nervousness and fear flowed freely through her as she walked toward the dining quarters where the men and sisters were set to meet.

Entering the room, now returned to its natural state, Verena searched for Jordan. It was impossible to locate him, not because of the crowd but because Jordan had blocked her ability to sense him. She paused in her search, closed her eyes and inhaled deeply. The fact that Jordan had deliberately blocked her was troubling. She had not shared the knowledge of this ability that the sisters of Vixen had used for years to keep their mates safe and yes, ignorant of certain things. But he had somehow discovered this ability. Her brilliant mate had learned of it entirely on his own.

"Verena."

Turning at the sound of his voice, she cautiously faced him, unable to sense his mood or intent. "Jordan," Verena nodded, feeling stiff and formal. She looked into his eyes, but only very briefly.

Afraid.

255

She was afraid of what she might see in his eyes.

"Did you and the sisters have a productive meeting?"

"Yes," Verena answered, uncomfortable with the unusual coldness in his voice.

"Then shall we get started?" he asked.

Verena nodded once again.

Having experienced the degradation of being held against her will and forced to obey the dictates of another, she understood exactly what she had put Jordan through. Perhaps that was where this coldness originated. *Her* adversary was dead, and those with him captured and awaiting punishment. Could she expect Jordan to want to have a life with someone he had considered his adversary?

They had planned and fought together, but only out of necessity and only for a brief moment in time. It could be that the emotions that she had read in him mere hours ago had been the result of the circumstances surrounding them.

Verena searched his face for some small sign. Reaching out once more with her mind left her disappointed. Jordan refused to give her access to his mood or thoughts. Other than knowing that he was physically well, she could not read him at all.

Standing before the group of sisters and men, Verena collected herself. Her mission was at stake. All sisters of Vixen depended on her to provide mates and therefore offspring so that they would survive as a race. During their meeting, every sister on board had agreed that these Earth men could not be forced into the exact roles Vixen males had served. There would be changes and adjustments, but they were all willing to make them, even to challenge tradition to keep their mates. So Verena could not allow her personal failure with Jordan to place everyone's future, most specifically her crew's future, at risk. Like the other explorer missions she would return to Vixen providing mates, though not the hundred mates she had initially been required to obtain, and perhaps not all of the fifty who were here. Verena hoped that she could convince most of the men to stay. Her eyes landed on Rya and Michael, giving her some assurance that it was possible.

"Sisters of Vixen and men of Earth," Verena began. "We have united as one and have achieved a great victory!"

"That's right, sister girl!" someone yelled.

"I thank you, my sisters, for your strength, steadfastness and loyalty, as always."

The men began shouting and raising fisted arms up and down into the air, preventing her from continuing. Verena turned to Jordan, a question on her face.

"It's a form of appreciation."

When the noise diminished, Verena continued. "Your enthusiasm, men of Earth, is noted and reciprocated, for you, with your unique talents, energy and determination have been an integral part of this victory. We hope you will wish to remain a part of our life."

No shouts or fisted movements followed this part of her speech. Eyes bore into her in much the same manner as when she had been rescued from her chamber. This silence rang like a death knell to her mission. Jordan's hard expression confirmed that all was not going well. Verena tasted failure. Its unfamiliar sourness filled her mouth.

"Is that a fancy way of saying that you're backing out of your promise?"

"Backing?" Verena scanned the room, finding many disgruntled faces. The enthusiasm had turned into distrust and anger.

"Are you trying to avoid the real issue here?" someone else asked.

"Yeah, what about keeping your word?"

"Are you lying to us?"

"Again!"

Shock froze her completely.

"It's something I'd like to know myself," Jordan whispered in her ear, at the same time motioning for the men to settle down.

When the room was silent Verena quietly took in the appalled faces of her sisters and the leery ones of the men. If they were to come together as one, they had a long road to travel before they gained enough knowledge and understanding of each other.

"Men, we have given you no reason to trust us, but know this. Though a sister of Vixen's word is rarely given, once a promise is made it is held. There will be no backing."

"Backing out," Jordan whispered.

"There will be no backing out," Verena repeated, noticing a brief softness in his face.

"Then what were you trying to say?" Calvin asked, a hard look in his eyes.

"That though we have treated you unjustly—"

"How?" Jordan whispered.

"By taking you away from your home world without your knowledge," she continued as if Jordan hadn't whispered the question into her ear.

"And?" he prompted. This time his warm breath blew directly into her ear stirring a two-way spark of awareness between them.

"And attempting to force you to live in our world without your consent. We ask your forgiveness and request you try to understand our dilemma." Verena went on to explain about the plague and their desperate search.

"Seems to me," Briceson said, "if you had paid more attention to the men of your world you might have been able to stop this plague before it wiped them out."

A hum of disagreement rose, the sisters protesting this statement.

"We did not ignore our males."

"They were honored and cherished."

"And kept safe."

"Apparently not safe enough. Sisters, we have to admit, as kin, we were neglectful," Verena stated, remembering her father and the manner in which her mother treated him, how she and her kin sisters expected everything from him but rarely thought about his needs. He had been sick for weeks before they had even realized it and dead within a day's time after that. "Not with evil intent, but in the name of protection and selfishness we made it easy for an enemy to attack those we loved."

Verena stood quiet a moment, allowing her words to land and take root, stir memories and find truth. "While we and our foresisters have failed our mates in the past, we have no intention of failing them now. We are requesting that you remain with us, live in our world, aiding in our quest to remain a vibrant, proud race for many generations to come."

Her last words seemed to echo inside the chamber only to be smothered by the sudden verbal exchanges taking place as men of Earth and sisters of Vixen began to discuss their futures.

"You kept your word," Jordan whispered, much further away than before.

"I had no intention of doing anything other than that."

"I know, I mean, I sensed your intent when you made the promise. But then—"

"But then what, Jordan?"

"You and your sisters went off and had a private meeting. I thought that you had only made the promise to free us because you'd do anything you could to get your ship back and complete your mission."

Verena shook her head, saddened by the idea that he thought so poorly of her. But what else should she expect? "I met with my crew out of necessity. I needed to be sure that all were willing to adjust to the challenge of having an Earth man as a mate without forcing them into the mold of the past."

"That would be an adjustment," Jordan said with a strange chuckle.

"I have not been able to sense anything from you, Jordan. Not since realizing that you were safe after regaining control of the ship."

"I know, we need to talk about that."

"Commander," Bruce interrupted. "There are a few things we need to discuss."

"Certainly," Verena answered, giving her attention to Bruce, wishing he had waited a few seconds to make his request.

"What is your planet like?"

"It is much like your planet Earth," Verena began. Jordan listened with half a mind as she patiently answered every question thrown at her. Soon Rya, Suvan and Zytai joined her, standing at her side, a panel of sisters intent on keeping their mates, Verena included. But did he want to be kept?

Jordan took a step back. He was exhausted. The past twenty-four hours had taken a toll on him and the energy he was using to block Verena out of his mind was sapping what little strength he had left.

Earlier, as he sat guarding the Gargantums, his mind had wandered toward his future, that of the men and the sisters, and he found himself second-guessing his own judgment. Should he have believed Verena? Did he truly trust her? Was it all a lie? Apparently it wasn't. But where would it all leave them?

"Men, please know that there will be challenges if you choose to stay with your mates and live your life as a Vixen. In the past, men have not been treated as you expect to be treated but you have helped to open our eyes to the error of this way of thinking. Maybe you can become the catalyst for change on our planet. With that said, I will leave it up to you to make your own decision to claim Vixen as your new home or be returned to your planet."

"When do you need to know?" Bruce asked.

"By the morrow."

"You don't have to wait till then for me," Bruce announced, going up to Suvan. "Susie's my life now. That hurricane took my parents and sister and destroyed my home and theirs. I'm ready to make a new life in a completely different place."

"I'm not living anywhere Zytai is not," Big John began, walking to the front of the room as soon as Bruce had finished. "There's nothing for me on Earth. I didn't have a family to lose because I haven't had one since I was seventeen years old. I'm willing to take you on, baby. The challenge can't be worst than floating down the street on the roof of your house in the scorching August heat of New Orleans."

"Well, I've got something to go back to!" Mark declared. "My parents need help getting their lives back together. And I had plans to rebuild my business. This was just a job to help me get back on my feet after the disaster."

And so it went. In the end thirty-nine men decided to become men of Vixen; the others were determined to go home.

Verena reiterated her promise to return those men who wished to go back to Earth immediately after delivering the prisoners to the Universal Council. Once decisions were made and recorded, Jordan quietly left the dining quarters. He needed some sleep and some time to clear his head. How else would he be able to make a decision that would literally change his world?

"Commander, I must speak to you a moment." Suvan effectively pulled Verena away from thoughts that were quickly depressing her.

"Yes, Suvan."

"This report lists the men who will remain as Vixens and those who will return to Earth. This graphic…" The screen changed before Verena could read the names. Her eyes were blurry from lack of sleep. "Commander?" Suvan asked.

"Proceed."

"This graphic displays each union, those that will remain intact and those that will be severed, as well as unions that are being performed at this very moment."

"We've met with some successes but have doomed others."

"It seems that way, but we do so without tainting our honor."

"You are wise, Suvan. I wish I had paid more heed to your counsel and been less arrogant at the start of this mission."

"You have learned a great deal, Commander, we all have," Suvan said, handing the reporting instrument to Verena.

"Thank you." Verena reached for the device, promising herself that she would read it thoroughly when she wasn't feeling so exhausted. "Now it is time to rest. I will be in my chambers."

Suvan paused. "Before you take this, how shall I record Jordan?"

"Has he not given you an answer?" Verena asked, realizing that her quick glance at the names on the chart and her watery vision had less to do with tiredness than avoiding the knowledge of Jordan's decision.

"No, Commander."

"I have no knowledge of his wishes."

"I—"

"Do not worry on my account."

"But Commander, I only wish to say…"

"I will speak with Jordan and record his decision on the appropriate chart." Verna took the instrument from Suvan's hands and quickly moved out of the dining quarters, but not quickly enough to miss hearing her words.

"I am sorry, Commander."

Suvan's pity followed her down the corridor and into her chambers. A commander should not be pitied. Verena refused to be pitied. The chamber was empty. Of course Jordan would not be here. He wished to be anywhere she was not. Hadn't she made that same wish about Gorg? Turning to her pallet, she felt her skin crawl as she remembered Gorg throwing himself onto it and then dying there. As exhausted as she was, she could not rest there. Going into Jordan's chamber, Verena lowered herself to the floor and rested her head on her folded arms.

"Commander, do you wish—"

"I wish to be left alone, C1," Verena muttered as sleep came to take her away from the hollowness she felt at the prospect of life without Jordan.

"As you wish," C1 said, following the commander's desire, to some degree at least. J.M. had issued just such a request not long before. But as a loyal friend and servant he had to do more than leave them alone.

C1 monitored their life signs, kept a constant surveillance of the temperature of both of the areas each had chosen as their resting place so that they would be as comfortable as possible. Then C1 waited, saying on alert until one or the other awakened. He had to do something about the state they were in or they would lose each other forever.

Many hours later, Jordan's erratic breathing and accelerated heart rate drew C1's attention.

"Whoa!" Jordan sat up, his heart pounding inside his chest.

"J.M.?"

"Hey." Jordan took a quick succession of breaths. "C1, what's happening?"

"Nothing beyond me allowing you to sleep until you felt better than a slug on the bottom of an old man's shoe."

"Ha, I told you that, didn't I?" Jordan pulled in a long breath, trying to even out his respiration.

"Yes, and do you?"

"Do I what?"

"Feel better than a slug on the bottom of an old man's shoe."

"Yeah, much better, but I woke up to one hell of a dream."

"About your father?"

"My father, the Gargantums, the sisters," he paused, "Verena."

"Speaking of the commander..."

"I'm not ready to speak of her, C1, not yet, my friend."

"Later?"

"Much later."

"Then that is how it shall be, but later is when I will insist that you do speak of her."

"Deal."

Before C1 could respond, Rya and Michael burst through the door and into the room, laughing, kissing and hanging all over each other, obviously not noticing him.

Jordan stood, hoping to interrupt them before they elevated to the next step of intimacy right in front of him. "Look guys."

"Jordan!" Rya said, stepping away from Michael, folding her arms, obviously embarrassed.

"Hey," Michael said, sliding an arm around her waist and looking the exact opposite of embarrassed.

They were looking way too happy for Jordan to deal with right now. "I didn't know you'd be here," Jordan began to explain. "I was only looking for a quiet place to sleep. I figured since everything's over you'd be staying in Rya's chambers. I guess I was wrong."

"No, I mean we are staying there," Rya began, "in my chambers."

"We were just looking for some variety," Michael said, raising an eyebrow at Rya.

"And to collect a few items belonging to Michael," she added.

"I'll leave you to it." Jordan moved toward the open door they had burst through.

"Stay a moment," Rya suggested. "We'll not drive you away. I know this room holds moments as precious to you as they are to us."

Rya continued talking as Jordan went back to his seat on the sofa in the living room where he had performed the Ceremony of Unity with Verena, had saved her life and had the most gratifying sexual experience of his life. Rya's lips were still moving but Jordan didn't hear a word. Unable to bring himself to enter Verena's chambers, he had searched for a quiet place to rest and had come directly here. He hadn't thought to ask himself why. Holding his face in his hands, he asked the question now.

"Why?"

"Why don't you tell me why?" Michael asked.

Jordan jumped. "I almost forgot you were here. Where's Rya?"

"She went to get you some Toca. She thought you might need it. She's worried about you and Verena."

"Toca won't help what's bothering me."

"And what's that?"

267

"Do you really want to know?

"Since we're kin and all since we married cousins, maybe I can help you out."

Jordan shook his head.

"If nothing else it'll make Rya feel better to know that I tried."

"Scattered brains," Jordan finally answered, figuring it couldn't hurt to get another man's perspective.

"Tell me about it."

"Actually, Michael, I think you need to tell me about it." Jordan stood and began pacing. "I mean, before any of us had even *considered* staying with the sisters you had already made the decision."

"Not as quick as you're saying. I went through stages, just like you're doing now. I was mad as hell and as hurt as a little puppy being kicked around. And I felt like an absolute fool."

"I would have never known."

"There was a lot happening in a small amount time. It makes you go through those stages kind of quick."

"Then why am I still in them?" Jordan asked, barely believing that he was having this conversation. "Nobody else had any problems making a decision."

"The way I see it, you've got a little more you're dealing with than the rest of us. You were the only one who one knew all along what was happening. You hated Verena before realizing that you didn't want to hate her anymore."

"Maybe."

Sensing that Jordan didn't want to talk about his feelings for Verena, Michael backtracked. "As for me, I realized in the midst of it all that there was something stronger than the anger and the hurt I was feeling."

"Obviously not a desire to go home."

"That was there but my love for Rya was stronger because, Jordan, I've found the Universal Truth."

"And what's that?"

"The Universal Truth? It's love. And I've found that with Rya."

"Yeah, Rya's special." Jordan chose to latch onto the only part of the conversation he felt comfortable commenting on. "I liked her from the start."

"What are you saying?" Michael asked, looking at him sideways.

"I like her as a person, nothing more. She's very sweet."

"She *is* sweet, which makes me lucky, but so are you."

"Humm," was all Jordan could say to that.

"What's gotten into you, Jordan? What happened to the guy who ran around making things disappear to show us where we were? Where's the guy who rammed his way through a solid door? Take control. Take charge of what you want. Allow yourself to be lucky!"

"Who says I'm not?"

"Are you looking beyond the pain?"

"You think I'm not looking?" Jordan stood. "I've been trained to look."

"If you're hiding out here, then you're not looking."

Without saying another word, Jordan left the mobile home where he and Verena had become one, making love for the first time one long, heated night. He was going to look beyond the pain and the first place he planned on looking was Verena's eyes.

"Jordan," Rya called as he dashed past her and across the open field. "Where are you going?

"To find my Universal Truth."

Jordan's Universal Truth smacked him right between the eyes the moment he stepped into his chamber. There she lay in the middle of the tiny room she had assigned to him, banished him to, saved him from and entered early one morning as he bared himself and his soul to her. He didn't even have to look into her eyes to discover his truth. Finding her sound asleep in his chamber was enough.

He deserved to love her.

His admission of that fact and his ability to accept it had been miles apart.

Jordan's commitment to the men and his determination to return to Earth had stood in the way of his feelings for Verena. Being her enemy first had not left room for any truths until everything had been resolved.

And all had been resolved except matters between them, all because he could not see that he deserved to love her.

Removing his shoes and every stitch of clothing, Jordan walked on silent feet to where she lay. He lay behind her, flush against the silkiness of her robes. The energy between them was alive and pulsing.

"Jordan." Verena turned, her face inches from his. "You came."

"I had to."

"Why?"

Opening himself to her, Jordan looked into her eyes, allowing her to read his every emotion.

"You love me. I thought that I was mistaken, but you do love me. Jordan, you must know that I love you too!" Her arms wrapped around him, pulling him closer, simply holding him and allowing feelings to flow through and between them, the energy becoming a pulsating, vibrant need.

"I wanted to talk. I planned for us to talk."

"Yes, we must talk," Verena agreed, pulling him closer, deftly changing positions as her mouth landed on his. Her body melded into him, showing him exactly how expert she had become at kissing. Her tongue brushed against his, arousing a heated friction as she channeled her desire for him. The intense contact enhanced his excitement to the point that he barely registered the fact that Verena held his pulsating manhood between her heated hands, guiding him inside of her, claiming him with one forceful thrust, which was enough to take them both over the edge. He was so embarrassingly, unbelievably amazed that they had exploded together in such a powerful way with so little effort that he didn't know what to say.

So he didn't say anything.

For a very long time he couldn't say anything.

And then he didn't want to say a word as Verena rolled off him to press into his side, her face resting against his chest. There would be time for talking later.

Much later.

Waking to Jordan beside her and with the certainty that he loved her was such a sublime feeling that Verena felt as if a whole new world had been created exclusively for her.

For them.

Burrowing more deeply into Jordan's warmth Verena sighed, inhaled and sighed again. She could stay like this for an eternity.

An eternity, her mind echoed.

But did she have an eternity? Verena sat straight up. The abrupt movement caused her to slip her hand from beneath Jordan's head where it had been trapped. His head banged loudly on the floor of the chamber.

"What the—" Jordan sat up, rubbing the back of his head, half asleep and dazed. Only a few moments before he had been wrapped in complete, sated contentment.

"Jordan, you must tell me now," Verena demanded. A wary but earnest expression of expectation was on her face as she folded her arms.

"Tell you what?" he asked.

"I am sorry about your head!" She reached both hands out to massage the back of his head. "I cannot read your thoughts. You must tell me now."

"That's one of the things we have to talk about. When you want to know something, all you need to do is ask."

Without hesitation she leaned toward him, her forehead pressing into his, "Will you give me your decision? Will you be my mate for an eternity?"

Never had he sensed such vulnerability from her and he didn't have to probe her mind to feel it. He didn't want her to have to probe his for every question, need or desire either.

"Jordan, speak."

"Yes. Of course yes." He kissed her, a brief kiss of assurance. "That's why I came to you. I didn't mean to leave you hanging. I was thinking."

"About?" She leaned back, resting on her heels, her hands on her thighs.

"About reading each other's mind."

"You do not wish for me to know what you are thinking."

"Not always."

"Because sometimes you do not feel love for me."

"Not at all. Where is that coming from? I love you now. I'll love you always."

"I have sensed it in you, I know it's true, but how could you possibly love me *always*?"

"How could I not?"

"I am stubborn and forceful."

"You are a bit rigid."

"My whole race has been rigid for centuries."

"It's not your whole race that I fell in love with, Rena, it's you. And you may be rigid but you're also flexible,

273

caring, courageous and fair. Not to mention one of the most gorgeous women I've ever met."

Placing a hand on his lips to stop the barrage of compliments, she asked, "How can I be both rigid and flexible?"

"You are rigid in following your traditions, but flexible when you realize that they may not fit into every situation."

"Our situation."

"Everyone's situation. By keeping your word you are altering your mission. You are openly challenging Vixen tradition. That takes courage."

"I would be unable to live with myself if I allowed this injustice to continue."

"I would not have been able to live without you, Rena."

"But Jordan, I have oppressed you and treated you as a non-person. I experienced it for myself when Gorg held me captive."

"Did he do something to you? Something you're not telling me about?"

"No, he only did to me what I have done to you. He lauded his dominance over me and forced his will upon me. I did the same to you. And I hated every moment I was forced to endure his presence. That is *why* I cannot understand why you love me."

"Because you are not Gorg. Gorg would have taken you by force once he reached his planet. Would you do that to me?"

When she didn't answer Jordan answered for her. "You almost died because you would not force yourself on me. Do not ever compare yourself to that nasty slime. Promise that you will never do that again."

Verena sat so still and remained so silent Jordan thought she would not make the promise. "I give my word," she said, raising her hand to her chest to make the oath.

"Thank you, Rena. I accept your promise. Please accept the fact that I love you, even when you can't read my thoughts."

"Why do you block them from me?"

"Sometimes it is better to know by talking and communicating. Conversation brings people closer together. I'd like to develop our relationship by talking about how we feel, not just know how we feel."

"So you would never wish to open your mind to me."

"I didn't say that. Before and during the battle with the Gargantums it was reassuring to know where you were, what you were thinking. Then it was appropriate, but not always."

"I am understanding you."

"Then you think we can try talking?"

"If you are willing to leave your world to be my mate for life, I am willing to try anything."

"Anything?"

"I believe that is what I said."

"How about making love—"

"Yes!"

"Slowly, very slowly. I want feel myself inside you for more than a second."

"You have not enjoyed the power of our lovemaking?"

"Enjoyed is an understatement, but there's a time for fast and there's a time for slow."

Pulling her forward so that she was once again on her knees, Jordan released the clasp on her robes, letting the sides drift open. "And right now I'd like to love you very, very slowly." Starting with his hands on her waist, his fingers gently pressed into her skin as he eased his hands between her smooth skin and the soft material. His lips pressed against the skin he had exposed, savoring the silkiness, then inched up her neck only to come back down again to work at removing the robes. He pressed warm, wet kisses at her collar bone, her shoulder, down her side, pausing where her breasts plumped out. He allowed himself to become completely distracted by the round softness as he held the weight of her breasts in his palms, grazing the hard peaks of her nipples with his thumbs.

"Jordan?" A hitch of breath caught in her throat.

His hands left her breasts to glide down past her shapely hips and back up again to hear that breathy catch as he reclaimed her breasts. "Do you like slow?" he asked.

"Yes," she answered as he guided her to the floor. Jordan followed her down, his hands leaving her breasts only to be replaced by the moist heat of his mouth.

Verena felt her body lift, press against him, wanting the fulfillment she knew they'd reach, but not just yet. This slow method was building within her a feeling of closeness. She wanted to linger and wallow in it, in

Jordan. She wanted to participate. Her fingers grazed the hard muscles of his back and traveled across the width of him. His muscles reacted to her touch. After finding the crescent-shaped hair at the nape of his neck, her fingers traveled across his shaven head, which was already covered with a thin fuzz of pale hair. Glancing down at him, she watched as he laved her breasts, her excitement increasing tenfold by the sight.

Suddenly she wanted more.

They could wallow in each other later. Gently lifting his head she told him, "Jordan, slow is not enough. I want more. Kiss me."

"No, Rena, this time we save the kissing for last."

"Why?" She squirmed beneath him.

"Anticipation," he said, making a point to know the feel of her hips, the slant of her waist and the weight of her breast in his hands, continuing the foreplay until he couldn't take it anymore. Lying between her legs, he positioned himself, then entered her with a smooth, easy stroke, savoring the feel, the tightness. Slowly he moved, in and out. Then together they moved with deliberate intent, unhurried strokes that slowly built the tension that would take them over the edge.

"Kiss me, Jordan!" she demanded. "Now!"

Unable to hold out any longer, Jordan gave in to her demand, welcoming the pulsating explosion as their lips touched, magnifying the shared pleasure of their love as they came together as one.

"Rena." Jordan collapsed, resting his head on her breasts. "You are going to kill me."

MISSION

"No, Jordan, it was the anticipation that would have killed us both."

CHAPTER 15

Not wanting to but knowing that she must, Verena laid a gentle kiss on Jordan's forehead and moved to rise. Her foot was trapped in an iron grip before she could move away.

"What was that?"

"A farewell kiss that would not lead into slow or fast lovemaking."

"Why would you want that?" Jordan looked up at her, his gray eyes sleepy and full of promises.

"Because I am the commander of this ship and I have neglected my duties for far too long."

"You needed sleep and some time to engage in other necessary activities with your mate."

"For far too long."

"You're probably right. It's all my fault. I won't keep you from your duties any longer." Jordan released her foot, stood and searched the chamber for his clothes. They each moved around the chamber washing and dressing as if they were an old married couple. Jordan liked the feeling.

"What are your plans for this day?" Verena asked him, just like a wife.

"To explore the ship."

"Let us do so together. And when we are done you can accompany me to the bridge."

"I'd like that."

"But first, I wish to show you something."

Verena took the reporting instrument that Suvan had given her and finding the appropriate screen, asked Jordan, "Do you wish to stay with your mate for eternity or return to Earth?"

"Stay with my mate for eternity, but perhaps visit Earth now and again."

Smiling as she recorded his decision, Verena turned to say, "Visiting Earth in a few years would be something I would like to do as well."

"Who else do you think would like to come?"

"Rya and Michael. Any one of the men and their mates."

"It's something to think about."

"Why don't you do more than think about it. Gather some information. Find out what the men and their mates think and share your findings with me," Verena suggested as they left the chambers.

"That was great!"

"What?"

"You didn't say 'report back to me.' You said to share my findings with you."

"It is not much of a difference."

"Trust me, it is."

They took a tour of the entire ship, starting with the engine room where a few of the men stood head to head with the sisters learning what it took to run the ship. Everywhere he went, the kitchens, the medical chamber, the science lab, there were scenes similar to what he'd witnessed in the engine room. All the sisters had truly meant what they said about treating the men as equals. Jordan hoped the sisters of Vixen inhabiting their planet would be as open.

As he trailed Verena, the detailed knowledge she had of every operation aboard her ship impressed him more and more. She wasn't a figurehead who simply commanded others. Verena's comments showed that she had insight regarding every aspect of running the ship and *could* do her officers' jobs.

"You know everything about this ship, don't you?" Jordan asked as they entered the portal that would lead them to the brig.

"I've held a position as an explorer since before reaching adulthood."

"As a child. Was that unusual?"

"Very. My mother would not hear of it. Very young children simply do not go into space to learn about becoming an explorer, especially not me. It was my father who convinced her."

"A *man* had influence? How did he do it?"

"Steady persuasion."

"Ah, the idea that running water can eventually wear away rock."

"Somewhat like that." She paused, folding her arms, a pensive expression on her face. "I miss my father," she quietly said.

"I know you do."

"I wish I could see him again, if only long enough to tell him how much I appreciate all he did for me as a child."

"I'm sure he knew," Jordan told her, unfolding her arms, taking one of her hands in his and giving it a squeeze. "Tell me about your early explorations," he asked to change the subject and lighten the suddenly solemn mood.

"They were only short trips. We orbited Vixen, visited the moons and traveled to a few nearby planets."

"Sounds like fun."

"I learned a great deal. My experiences gave me an advantage when I was finally old enough to begin training."

Having made it to the entrance of the brig, Verena released his hand to question the guards. "Come," Verena motioned to him a moment later.

"Where are we going?" Jordan asked, nodding to Zeda, the security officer who followed along behind them. He had worked with her, and some of the men and sisters, to transfer the prisoners the day before.

"To question one of the prisoners," Verena answered. "Most have been questioned, but I left orders that this one was to be questioned by me."

"You're talking about Bock?"

"With your assistance."

"Zeda, have all the others been placed in the containment modules?"

"Yes, Commander," Zeda answered as they walked past cells that consisted of holes in the wall meant to confine dangerous prisoners in deep sleep mode for transportation.

Veering to the left and entering another corridor, Zeda took the lead, stopping at a panel to enter a quick succession of symbols. The silvery wall slowly became transparent, giving them a clear view of Bock secured to a chair by thin wires at his ankles and waist. The chair appeared to be bolted to the floor. His heavy paws rested on a sturdy table and each was secured to one of the table's legs by wire.

"Is that wire going to hold him?" Jordan asked as flashes of a documentary he had seen on TV about Sasquatch rolled through his head.

"The wire is made of an alloy unique to Vixen. It is the strongest substance in the known universe. It is impossible to break by sheer force of will."

"Good to know."

"Kill me, kill me now!" Bock growled, raising his head to peer up at them.

"You are a murderer, we are not," Verena answered.

He lifted his head, a raised bushy eyebrow no indication that he disputed the charge. "I'd rather die then be forced to deal with *them*."

"You have no choice. The Universal Council will deliver justice."

"I have no worries in dealing with the council. I wish I had to deal only with them."

"Who else do you have to concern yourself with?"

"The others."

"What others?" Verena asked.

Jordan listened intently.

"The others that share my home world but hide away and live like frightened little animals instead of the mighty ones that we are!"

"You are saying that the Gargantums share their world with another species."

"I am speaking of the others that *are* my species."

283

"Then you fear retribution for taking the life of one of your own kind."

"I loathe the thought of their kind of punishment. I do not fear them. I loathe them all!" he roared. "They are a cowardly bunch."

"I have not met a Gargantum who fits this description."

"You have not met all Gargantums. You have only met those brave enough to venture out into the universe and *interact* with others."

Verena signaled to Zeda, who quickly went back to the panel. The wall became translucent as Bock shouted, "Get me to the Universal Council before they come for us!" The panel converted into an opaque wall blocking him and all sound.

"What do you make of this?"

"It is obviously a ploy. We know that all Gargantums are ruthless and have no care for order and no known system of justice," Zeda said.

"True," Verena said, her last word lingering in the corridor. Verena looked up a moment later. "Jordan, you seem to be lost in thought. What do you think of Bock's ranting?"

"This may sound strange to you but I've got a feeling he's not ranting."

"A *feeling*?" Zeda asked, a touch of condemnation in her tone obviously left over from her previous opinion of males in general.

They had a ways to go, Jordan realized, deciding to ignore the tone.

"A bit more than a feeling. The Gargantums remind me of a legend."

"A legend, such as a story? Should we be wasting our time discussing a story?" Zeda asked.

Taken aback by her nastiness when just yesterday they'd worked as a team, Jordan went on as if she hadn't interrupted. "The Bigfoot legend describes a beast who looks remarkably like a Gargantum. Though they are huge they have never been known to hurt anyone. As a matter of fact, Bigfoot has been notorious for hiding or running away when they encounter anyone."

"Sound like 'the others' Bock has described."

"Or a child's story you have conveniently made up to impress your mate!" Zeda said between clenched teeth.

"Zeda, that is enough. You are conducting yourself in an unbecoming manner and you have insulted my mate for the last time."

"Yes, Commander. I apologize to you both," she immediately replied. A moment later she asked, "May I be excused?"

At Verena's nod, Zeda moved to go back the way they had come. "Call her back, Rena. Something's wrong. She didn't act this way yesterday."

Without questioning him and without attempting to read his mind, Verena did as he asked. "Zeda, return."

Reluctantly she turned back, her head in a position Jordan had never seen a sister of Vixen hold. Her chin on her chest, she stood before them.

"What is wrong, Zeda?"

Without lifting her head she asked. "Must I answer, Commander?"

"Yes, your unusual behavior makes it necessary."

"My mate is returning to Earth," she began, continuing in a rush of words that oozed with hurt and anger. "I despise him for leaving. I despise all Earth men. I despise hurricanes and families and the thought that I will never bear a child and have a family of my own because my mate for life will be living on a planet on the other side of the universe."

Setting aside her role as commander, Verena became a fellow sister. She opened her arms and wrapped them around one who hurt so badly that she had begun to act like someone other than herself.

A few minutes later Zeda took a step back. "I did not mean to release such anger. Forgive my outburst. I will return to my post if that meets your approval."

"Certainly," Verena answered.

"Zeda." Jordan stopped her from leaving. "Have you spoken with your mate? Maybe you two could come up with some alternative."

Zeda shook her head. "I do not believe such an alternative exists."

As she walked away Jordan asked, "What did she mean by never having a family of her own? Surely she would be able to find a mate somewhere in the universe."

"Once a sister of Vixen chooses a mate he is hers for life. That is why, I am certain, Gorg killed all Vixen males. He wanted to be certain that all women were free of their mates. That we were all desperate and needy."

"If I hadn't decided to stay with you—"

"I would have had only memories of you to last a lifetime. I would not have been able to join with anyone else. My body, my mind and my soul would have rejected anyone as long as you were alive somewhere in the universe."

"We should tell the men."

"No sister of Vixen wishes a male to be coerced into a union."

"But that is exactly what you were doing before."

"And we were unjust. The men have made their decisions, we will not beg."

"Is it pride that's standing in the way?"

"Jordan."

"There must be some way to help."

"There is nothing we can do. Let us continue our discussion. You were speaking of Bigfoot."

"Yeah," Jordan answered. Deciding that they would revisit this subject later, he forced himself to refocus on the previous one. "We were discussing Bigfoot. Well, there have been reported cases of Bigfoot or Sasquatch, as some people call them, being spotted almost immediately after strange lights appeared in the sky. My team and I investigated a time or two but never found anything concrete to support the claims, but I'm thinking that maybe the Gargantums *are* the Sasquatch who visited Earth."

"Why would they do that? The Bigfoot you have described does not behave as the Gargantums we know."

"That's just it! Maybe you have not met all Gargantums. Maybe the Sasquatch are the others Bock just told us about."

"He spoke as if they were different from him."

"On Earth we have many races of people. Maybe that is also true of the Gargantums. Something Big John said stayed in the back of my mind. One race of people should not be judged by a few. There may be Gargantums like Bigfoot who are peaceful and reclusive, which is why no one has met any. On Earth we can't seem to get a decent picture of one to verify that they exist. Those like Bock are violent, dangerous and un-welcomed. What if they've tainted the name of all Gargantums?"

"Your mind works in wondrous ways making connections I would not have thought possible. What you say makes sense, but how do we verify that it is true?"

"Why don't we let them find us? Bock had the impression that they were out looking for him and his men. Is there any way we can send out a signal that would inform them that we have their prisoners?"

"What if it's all a ploy to lead other Gargantums to us in order to continue what they have started? I must think about the safety of everyone on board."

"Yes, you must. That's your job as commander of the ship. But what if it isn't a ploy? This could be an opportunity to reach out to a species you have never truly known."

"I must discuss this with my officers," Verena said, her mind already churning with the steps that would need to be taken to insure that all who were on board were safe if they proceeded with this plan. Noticing that Jordan was not walking at her side, Verena turned back to find him standing at the wall. She was not surprised to see that the panel was clear and that he was staring at Bock.

"I need to ask him one more question," Jordan said by way of explanation when she stood beside him once again. Verena waited as he asked, "Tell me why a beast as huge as yourself can be so frightened at the sight of me that it caused you to be captured."

"Will my answer get me to the Universal Council faster?"

"Maybe."

"There have been stories of your kind hunting and slaughtering Gargantums. Seeing one of you startled me into remembering those childhood myths."

With that Jordan programmed the panel to convert the wall.

"You continue to impress me, Jordan. Have I told you that I am proud to have you as my mate?"

"I believe you have, but I don't mind hearing it again."

"I am proud to have you as a mate. And I thank you for your counsel."

"I appreciate the chance to give it."

Verena nodded as they left the brig. "I must speak with my officers. You may continue to explore the ship and perhaps speak to the men about their thoughts on a future visit to Earth in a few years' time."

"That sounds good. Shall we meet for lunch?"

Verena smiled before saying, "It is a date."

❦

MISSION

A few hours later, feeling like a househusband, Jordan arranged the covered plates of food on a small table. "Do you think I have everything, C1?"

"It will be a perfect mid-day meal."

"Thanks," Jordan said, appreciating his help. "And thanks for keeping a low profile yesterday. We needed that time alone to straighten a few things out."

"I'm pleased with the outcome."

"So am I. Now Rena will be here in a minute. I love you, C1, but time with my mate means time with my mate."

"J.M., you love me?"

"Like a brother."

"That fact has been noted and recorded."

"Good."

"Jordan," Verena said, sweeping into the chamber with her robes flowing behind her. "We have decided to contact the Gargantums. A signal has already been transmitted. Zeda has created a defensive plan to prevent an invasion, but of course we won't be contending with a revolt of our mates as we were when Gorg and his men invaded our ship. Suvan is organizing a contingent of men to ensure that all have a role on board the ship. Why are you staring at me?" she finally took a breath to ask.

"Because I missed you, and you're beautiful and you're mine to stare at." He pulled her into his arms to deliver a kiss that began as sweet appreciation but quickly escalated into a frenzy that had them pulling at each other's clothes. Verena pushed Jordan into one of the chairs at the table.

Her breathing was in rhythm with his as she eased his hard member into her. She paused midway, staring into his eyes.

"What are you doing?" Jordan asked. Her heat and tightness surrounding him were almost his undoing.

"Savoring the feel of you inside of me."

"For how long?" Jordan asked, his hands at her waist. He was dying to pull her down so that she would take all of him, but she had humored him last night. Rena had let him savor. He could do the same for her. "Please tell me it won't be too long."

"It has been long enough," Verena answered. Taking all of him, she rested flush against him for a moment. Then her hips moved up and down, claiming him with her body as her lips delivered a kiss that pulsed with the power of her love for him.

"I love you too, baby. How I love you," Jordan told her, his breathing slowly coming back to normal. "I wasn't expecting that."

"But it is a moment we have both savored."

"How about another?" Jordan stood, holding her to him, keeping them connected, and headed into the side chamber. "Shower mode, C1."

The door closed and the room began to fill with hot, soapy water. They spent the next five minutes washing each other, which led to another bout of lovemaking minus the savoring. Completely sated, they rinsed and dressed, finally sitting down to eat.

"It's probably cold."

"Not so, Jordan," C1 interjected. "Realizing that lunch would be delayed, I kept the meal warm by transmitting a low heat to the covers protecting the food. "

"Thanks, C1." Jordan smiled as he pulled a chair out for Rena.

"Your diligence is appreciated," Verena added.

"I will leave you to your own company. If I am needed, call out my name. My sensors will then respond."

"Thank you," they answered together. Their laughter was interrupted by a signal at the entrance to the chamber.

"Enter," Verena called.

"Commander," Zeda said, "I do not wish to disturb you, but it seems that I am."

"It seems that you all are," Verena said, noticing nine other sisters behind Zeda.

"We wish to speak to you also," Tora said. "On behalf of ourselves."

"Of course. Jordan, would you mind giving us a moment?"

"Commander, I wish for Jordan to stay," Zeda said before he could rise from the table.

"Yes, I believe that it was because of him that we have discovered a solution to our problem," Tora noted.

"An alternative," Zeda added.

"Jordan?" Verena looked at him with suspicion.

"I'm not sure what they're talking about." Jordan wondered if the seed he'd planted had sprouted.

"You may begin," Verena stated.

"We seek your permission to become citizens of Earth," Zeda began, the other sisters standing firmly beside her. "It is an alternative that will satisfy all concerned."

"Our mates will get their wish to return to Earth," Tora said.

"And we will spend our lives with the mates we were destined to have. It is Vi-she," said another sister Jordan did not know other than that she was Calvin's mate.

"Will you not miss your home world?"

"Just as the men will visit Earth, we can return to Vixen."

"And what do your mates think of this?"

"Commander, it was their idea."

Verena looked at Jordan again for another brief moment before returning her attention to the sisters.

"Vi-she is powerful. Your attachment to your mates is much the same. You have my support."

Each sister came forward to seal the understanding between them with an oath. When all were gone Verena turned to her mate, who wore a suspicious look of innocence on his face. "Jordan, what did you do?"

"I did nothing."

"This is one time that I am wishing that I could read what is in your mind."

"All you have to do is ask."

"I have. All you must do is reply."

"Do you want to kiss me instead?" When all he got was an exasperated look accompanied by folded arms, he knew he wasn't going to get out of this without some kind of explanation. "It was all very innocent. If you remember, you told me that I could collect some information regarding the men returning to Earth to visit. Well, when I asked Briceson I didn't realize that he was one of the men returning to Earth permanently. He said to me, 'If the men can come back to visit Earth what's keeping their mates from going to Earth with them and visiting Vixen every few years. The same ship could make the journey.' I told him I didn't know."

"What other information did you relay?"

"There was nothing else."

"Jordan, I have noted the manner in which you speak when you are hiding something. I do not have to read your mind to know this. Remember that I am the one who sat through listening to hours of boring facts trying to understand you. And now that I do, you must tell me what you are not saying."

Knowing it was useless, Jordan admitted, "I told him I didn't know, but that he should ask his mate himself."

"And you had no idea his mate was Zeda, the sister to whom who you gave a suggestion to seek an alternative solution?"

"And she did. Did I do something wrong? Did I coerce anyone?"

"You did not, but you are wise and you are sly, my mate. Come, let us eat."

Hours later, after spending the afternoon on the bridge and having a light dinner, they lay on a pallet in the side chamber, having made love the slow way, which was still faster than Jordan had ever experienced in his life. But also more powerful than any he'd experienced in his life. Jordan was beginning to believe in the power of Vi-she. What force other than destiny could have brought them together to share such powerful feelings? He wasn't just talking about the amazing physical pleasure they gave each other. Each hour, each minute, Jordan was falling deeper and deeper in love with his mate.

Propping himself on his elbow, he pulled her closer, pressing soft kisses on her forehead, her nose, her eyelids. "What are you thinking about?" he asked.

"What makes you think I am thinking?"

"I just know. Now tell me what's on your mind."

"I have become used to your strange way of speaking but still it amuses me. Nothing is on my mind but yes, I have been thinking."

"Go on."

"Your appearance on the bridge received varying reactions, surprise being the most obvious."

"No one ordered me to leave."

"They would not dare. You are the commander's mate. The sisters will follow my example. I lead by my actions."

"I know that from experience," Jordan said, suddenly in the mood for a bit of fast, explosive lovemaking. He leaned down to claim her mouth.

"J.M., you may wish to—"

"C1, no one said your name."

"Leave or we will think you a bothersome computer," Verena said. Both of them laughed as if she had made the most hilarious joke in the world. They were laughing so loudly that they did not hear the signal announcing an unexpected arrival.

"Verenavella, what in the name of Vixen are you doing?" a voice called in her native language.

"Mother!" Verena made a kind of screeching sound Jordan had never heard from her before.

"Mother?" Jordan whispered, handing Verena her robes, which she used to cover herself, partially at least.

"What are you doing frolicking in your mate's side chamber? That is beneath the expectations of a commander and far beneath that of a princess. Clothe yourself and meet me in your conferring room."

"Yes, Mother."

"Was that really your mother?" Jordan asked as he helped her get into her robes, which wasn't as easy as taking her out of them. Her arms were literally shaking. Pulling her into his embrace, he held her until she stopped.

"Are you frightened of her?"

"No, surprised, and nervous about the coming battle. My mother is one who holds tightly to traditions, and as queen of Vixen—"

"Queen? Then you really are a princess."

"Yes."

"Why didn't you tell me?"

"It is not so important. I am the second youngest of six, almost last in line for the throne. I will never become queen, which is the only reason my mother relented and allowed me to become an explorer."

"Commander," a voice called into the chamber.

"Speak," Verena answered, arranging her robes.

"Your Queen Mother is awaiting you. She insists that you come to her immediately."

"I am on my way."

"Commander, I apologize for not following protocol and informing you of the Queen's arrival but she insisted that I not disturb you."

"Do not concern yourself," Verena said as she left the room.

"A princess," Jordan whispered, pulling on a pair of pants. "Why didn't she tell me? C1," Jordan called out, "why didn't you tell me Verena was a princess?"

"I did not have access to that information."

"Then it is a secret."

"Perhaps."

Wanting to go to her but surmising that it was best for Verena to speak to her mother alone, Jordan paced up and down the chamber until she returned.

"How did it go?"

"As well as your first meeting."

"I didn't actually meet her."

"You will on the morrow and then you will wish that she were not your kin," Verena said, leading them to the side chamber.

"You've had a long, hard day. Let's sleep on your pallet, it's softer."

"I do not wish to."

"Why?"

"Please, do not ask questions. I have just been bombarded with them."

"Is it because of me? Just tell me yes or no."

"Great Vixen, no! It is because of me. I can only see that beast Gorg falling onto my pallet and me finding him dead and rotting."

"Rotting? Rena, he had only been dead a few hours."

"He smelled as if he were rotting."

"He smelled that way when he was alive!" Jordan laughed; she laughed right along with him.

"Thank you for lifting my spirits. Now come with me so that I can rest."

Jordan joined her on his small pallet, wrapping his arms around her and wondering what the next day would bring.

He didn't have to wait long to find out.

In what felt like minutes later, Jordan woke to the shrill sound of the door signaling an unexpected arrival. "I did not activate the locks. Truly I did not think she would be up before me," Verena mumbled before rising.

"Still abed and in inappropriate places," the Queen said in her native tongue. She stood at the entrance of the side chamber, as tall and regal as Verena. Her face was beautiful but cold and hard.

"Any place where my mate can be found is appropriate," Verena responded in English.

"Such thinking. Where is your pride? Never mind, just tell me, what are you about this day?"

"Many things, Mother, but firstly I wish to introduce you to my mate. Queen Reza sovereign of Vixen and all her treasures, meet Jordan, your new son."

"He is pale and much too big," she said, walking back toward the entrance before Jordan could step forward to say a word of greeting. "I will meet you in the dining quarters."

"Mother, *that* was inappropriate," Verena called, locking the door.

"Unlock this door, Verenavella. This behavior is unbecoming to a princess."

"I will unlock the door after you have properly greeted my mate."

"Rena, it's okay. You don't have to do this," Jordan told her.

"I must. If the leader of Vixen cannot come to terms with the way life must proceed, then we won't have a chance when we get back to the planet."

As the Queen just stood there, her back to them, Verena went about the business of washing and dressing for the day. Jordan did the same. When they were ready to leave, Verena asked, "Mother, why are you here?"

"I am here because of my concern for you. I read the report about the Gargantums overtaking the *Vixen II*, my daughter's ship. Being the brave sister of Vixen that you are, you fought back and regained control."

"With the help of our mates, Jordan in particular. I was held captive and he released me. Do him the courtesy of greeting him."

"Of course," she said as if she'd had no problem with the idea before. "Greetings," she said to him.

"Greetings," Jordan replied. Not quite sure what was expected, he gave a sort of half bow.

"Step number one," Verena whispered.

Her mother turned away, taking graceful steps toward the door, sure that Verena had unlocked it. Reaching the threshold, she turned to say, "What foolishness were you uttering? You could not mean that males helped you to overcome the Gargantums? I don't believe I understood you."

"You are correct, Mother, you do not understand. Take a good look around this ship and make an attempt to understand what is happening."

CHAPTER 16

The war was on and Jordan wasn't sure who was winning. It was a silent war but one filled with tension and resistance. Jordan didn't start it, he barely participated in it, but he was a part of it anyway. It had been a week since Verena's mother had come on board, and in the week she had uttered only one word to him on numerous occasions, "Greetings."

She spoke to Verena excessively but in Vixen, which prompted Jordan to begin his lessons with C1 again.

Jordan sat in the side chamber in the middle of a lesson now. A movement in the outer chamber caught his attention. Verena, who had only left a few minutes ago to make her morning rounds, had returned, with Queen Reza right behind her. Jordan caught Rena's eye, winked at her and continued his lesson. Queen Reza ignored him. "I guess I'll get my daily greeting later, C1. "

"That was excellent, J.M. You speak Vixen extremely well for a beginner."

"It's because I take what I've learn and apply it by teaching the other men. Let's keep moving, it'll keep my mind off the shrew. How could she have ever ruled a planet?" Jordan asked, continuing to practice his new language.

"According to my recent research, Queen Reza is considered one of the most loved and fair rulers."

"That fairness and love obviously didn't extend to motherhood."

"Maybe that is why the commander chose not to recognize her status as princess in her command of the *Vixen II*."

"Knowing Rena, it probably had more to do with pride and making her way without royal connections. I don't think I blame her. Why don't we run through words dealing with family," Jordan suggested, getting back into the lesson.

"You have finally begun to teach your mate his proper place," Queen Reza was saying, waving her hand at the side chamber as if it was of no importance.

"Jordan is in the side chamber because that is where he wishes to be at this moment." Verena caught his eye and he made the one-eyed blink he called a wink. Verena, unable to wink, blinked both her eyes at him and smiled.

"What are you searching for?" her mother asked, observing the exchange and purposely attempting to break it.

"A report that I must download to the central unit and transfer to the central base. We are just within range to make that communication."

"Tell that pale one of yours to find it so that we can talk."

Verena sighed, her mind exhausted from the derogatory comments that constantly came out of her mother's mouth. Verena had been taught to respect her mother, to revere the queen, but those teachings were being erased by her excessive behavior. Her mother had always spoken her mind and been a forceful presence, but her behavior since she had been on board was beyond anything Verena had experienced before.

"Verenavella, go on, tell him what needs to be done so that we can continue our conversation."

"Mother, you do not wish to talk to me, you only wish to badger me," Verena told her, feeling frustration begin to build within her. Unable to immediately find the report Suvan had given to her, Verena had no time or inclination to deal with her mother right now. "I will not bother Jordan, he is busy."

"Busy? He is sitting there playing with his toy! You are creating problems within your union. We will never survive as a race if this is an example of how we will live!"

"Problems within my union? What of the problem within yours? I know that Jordan is busy because I know exactly what he is doing because we speak to each other. Perhaps if you had spent time speaking to my father instead of ignoring him you would have noticed that he was ill and we would have had time to do something about saving him and every male Vixen on the planet."

A stricken expression such as Verena had never seen before took over her mother's face before it quickly became a hard, cold mask. "I now know exactly how you feel. You blame me for that tragedy." And she was gone.

Verena sat at the small table and placed her hands on her face. She normally had more control. Too much had happened in so little time. She needed to contact her kin sisters. Soon they would be in range; then she could get some insight into her mother's excessive behavior.

"You were looking for this?" Jordan asked, kneeling before her.

"Yes." Verena took the report from his hands. "Did you hear?"

"Most of it. You looked like you needed some rescuing and I was coming to do the job, but you pretty much handled it yourself."

"I did not mean to say what I said."

"But you had been thinking it?"

"And I believe it, but I do not solely blame my mother. I blame all sisters of Vixen and their blind insistence in following tradition so strongly."

"Then you have to tell her that."

"I will. She is acting extremely rigid. She is not the same woman she was before my father died. Before all the males died."

"Circumstances can change a person. Your mother is the ruler of a planet that has experienced something probably no other planet has dealt with before."

"How can you be so understanding when she has been so horrible to you?"

"I don't take it personally. I've learned from my own experiences not to take certain things personally. Come, I'll walk you to the bridge. I have to meet with the men for their lesson."

"Commander." Zytai's voice came into the chamber.

"Speak."

"We have made contract with a Gargantum ship requesting permission to speak with you."

Thirty minutes later Verena, Rya, Zytai, Suvan, Zeda and Jordan stood in the transferring room awaiting the arrival of a Gargantum named Bing and his assistant, Zorg, on board the *Vixen II*.

"Are you sure you want me here?" Jordan whispered to Verena.

"I am certain."

Two very large, very clean, odor-free Gargantums appeared before them. "Greetings." Verena approached them.

"Greetings," was the soft response from the huge creatures.

Verena introduced everyone. Sensing that the Gargantums seemed uncomfortable, she asked Zytai and Rya to go back to their other duties. "Would you like refreshments as we meet to discuss the matter of the prisoners?"

"Refreshments will not be necessary. We would like to see the prisoners," Bing answered in a soft, even tone.

"But wouldn't you care to discuss the situation?"

"We care to apologize for the atrocities inflicted on your world and aboard this ship. We learned of Gorg's plan but were unable to stop him."

"Gorg is dead. His own men poisoned him. We believe Bock had a great deal to do with that."

"May we see the prisoners?" the smaller of the two asked.

"You may, but we wish to speak about this matter in great detail."

"I understand."

MISSION

Though obviously uncomfortable, the Gargantums sat and spoke with them.

"So, you are saying that the Gargantums we have encountered are part of a group who have disconnected with you," Verena summed up.

"They have turned their back on our ways and live on an isolated part of the planet. They have nothing to do with us. We had not understood that they were causing pain and harm to others. If we had known this they would have been contained."

"How?" Verena asked.

"Deep beneath our planet are the caves of desolation. They would survive, but alone and without light of day."

"I have never met Gargantums such as you. Explain to me, what are your ways? Why did this group want to break away from you?" Suvan asked.

"We are peaceful and live quietly among ourselves. We explore but do not wish to interfere in the lives of others. We do not make ourselves known. Gorg and others like him do not agree."

"May we see the prisoners now?" Zorg asked again.

"We have a dilemma," Verena began. "The Universal Council has ordered that the prisoners be brought to stand trial for all the crimes they have committed."

"We would see to their punishment."

Verena nodded to Suvan who continued, "We are certain that you would see to their punishment, but these Gargantums have harmed many and all wish to see them brought to justice. If you take them and hide them away, how will those who have been offended be satisfied with their punishment?"

"You do not take our word?"

"We do not know of your word. We only know of the Gargantums we have met."

"But those of Bock's ilk do not represent all Gargantums."

"They have." Verena let that thought hang in the air. "I invite you to come to the Universal Council, present yourselves and allow other species to know the true ways of the Gargantums."

"Those who see us will not be like you," Bing said. "They will attack and imprison us before knowing that we are not the ones who harmed them."

"We will offer protection. If we, the species hurt the most by some of your kind, support you, others will not harm you."

"We will speak to our council and contact you once again," Bing said, standing, obviously ready to leave.

Satisfied with the manner in which the meeting had progressed, they also rose to leave. Unable to help himself, Jordan walked up to Bing. "Have you ever visited Earth?"

"Yes, many times. I did not want to pry but I suspected that you were from that lovely planet. You are an interesting species. We apologize for frightening you."

"No problem," Jordan answered, amazed to be privy to inside information on the Bigfoot legend. This was only the beginning. He could learn more from the direct source. Hopefully they would do as Verena suggested, opening the door to meeting other species despite their inherit shyness.

MISSION

Just as the Gargantums were transferring to their own ship, Queen Reza burst into the room.

"Verenavella! Are those Gargantums? Why have you not contained them? They will be loose to harm and kill others!"

"Mother, the Gargantums we hold are the criminals. These are not. Not all things are as they seem. If you will come with me and listen, I will explain all there is to explain."

Briefly hugging Verena to his side, Jordan gave her a kiss on the cheek, whispered, "Good luck," and left her to deal with her mother.

Hours later, walking into the dining quarters to get a drink, Jordan spotted Queen Reza. Preparing himself for the next battle, he did not pause but walked straight to her and gave her a half bow as he said, "Greetings."

"Greetings," she returned and as Jordan walked past she called out, "I must have a word with you."

"Certainly," Jordan answered, unsure of what had happened to bring this miracle about.

"To Verena's chambers," she said.

Jordan followed her and stood at the door as she continued in, pausing at Verena's pallet with folded arms. "I have had a long talk with my daughter."

"Yes," Jordan said, thinking that if he said more she would clam up and say nothing or if he started talking he'd tell her off and say way too much.

"She is fond of you."

"As I am of her."

"Even though you are large and pale."

"So I have been told."

"I have decided to accept you as my daughter's mate."

Jordan nodded and was about to reply when from behind him Rena answered for him, "That is very gracious of you, Mother, considering that you have no choice in the matter."

"I have choices."

"We have had very few choices and yet I have made a very wise one," Verna said, moving to stand next to Jordan.

"Humph," was all her mother said.

"Mother, I know."

"What do you know?"

"I have spoken to Valleah."

"And your oldest kin sister has revealed to you that I am no longer acting queen of Vixen, that I have released myself from the throne."

"Yes, but why, Mother?"

"The other ships returned with new males. I could not bear watching the spectacle of it all. Traditions broken, males taking positions meant for sisters, speaking out. The changes were everywhere. Valleah insists that the changes were necessary, that she knew what was good for Vixen's future."

"Exactly what sort of changes?"

Queen Reza sighed. "The same changes I have encountered here. I can no longer escape the truth. Vixen will never be the same. We will never regain what was lost and the fault is mine."

"As I told you earlier, Mother, the fault belongs to every sister of Vixen. We have always been strong and when given

309

a task we see it through. I have been truly impressed with my sisters' ability to adjust to a different role for the men in our lives here on the *Vixen II*. From what I understand from you, it is the same on our planet. We will learn from our mistakes and truly become one with our mates to sustain and keep Vixen a strong, vibrant planet."

"We men are willing to try. How about you, Queen Reza?"

"Simply Reza will do. Unlike you, I have no choice in the matter," she said, walking to the door, pausing at the threshold. "This mission did not turn out the way we planned."

As the door closed behind her mother, Verena wrapped her arms around Jordan and pulled him close. "She's right, you know. The mission didn't turn out the way we expected, but happened just the way it should have."

"Of course, it was Vi-she," Jordan agreed.

"Ah, destiny. I wonder what else Vi-she has in store for us?"

"Right now, I'd say replacing an unpleasant memory with a pleasant one." Jordan nodded toward her pallet.

A thoughtful expression on her face, she asked, "Slow or fast?"

"Both," Jordan answered, pulling her backwards to land on the softness of the pallet. He proceeded to erase all thought of conflict from her mind.

Not long after, as they recovered from the intense power of their lovemaking, Jordan studied their entwined hands. Each of their fingers was a separate entity but now they were joined; they had come together as one.

"You know what I just realized?" he asked.

"No, tell me."

"We were both on separate missions when we met but now we're on the same mission."

"What mission is that?"

"The mission of living a wonderful life together. Our mission."

"Our mission," Verena agreed, "is off to a great start."

EPILOGUE

"Open your eyes to your new life."

Doing just that, Jordan opened his eyes to the sight of his beautiful mate. "That phrase used to scare the hell out of me."

"What does it do to you now?"

"Offers me promise, anticipation, a whole new world."

"That is exactly what I wish you to see, my world, our whole new world. Rise. Vixen can be seen from the observation deck."

Tossing on robes, they left the chamber, making their way down the silvery corridor to a panel that led them to the observation deck where they had spent much time in the last month. There had been hours spent speaking and planning with the men, with the sisters, with the men and sisters together, with her mother, with the Gargantums. And most often, hours alone with Jordan when all was quiet, the ship guarded and run by a small contingent as all others slept. This had become their special place to plan and think about their future.

"There," Verena said, pointing to the huge orb floating in the sky that couldn't be mistaken as anything other than a planet. Three moons were visible in the distance.

"It's huge, much larger than Earth, and spectacular."

"Are you impressed?"

"I'm impressed with all things Vixen, your strength, flexibility, compassion and forgiveness. Have I told you how impressed I am with your alliance with the Gargantums?"

"You have. They are a gentle species with the misfortune of having a few renegade members of their society. This alliance will allow us to learn from each other."

"I'm grateful that that's the only alliance they are forming. If Gorg and Bock had had gotten their way, you would be trapped with one of them as a mate."

Verena shivered with revulsion. "I can not envision such a horrible life." She envisioned a much more pleasant one. A picture of herself and Jordan and their offspring entered her mind.

"So, are you going to tell me?"

"Tell you what?"

"The wonderful news you brought me her to say."

"I brought you here to share the first sight of our home."

"And to share that spectacular view with the spectacular news that we're going to have a baby."

"How did you know?"

"I don't really know. I simply knew."

"Are you happy?"

"Extremely happy. How about you?"

"Relieved and pleased."

"Relieved?"

"There was a time that you were adamant about not having a child with me. I thought that some of those feelings might have lingered within you."

"Not at all. They died as my love for you grew."

"As mine has grown for you." Turning into his embrace, Verena wrapped her arms around his neck. "I look forward to keeping my eyes open as we continue our new life together."

"Wide open," Jordan said as they looked out at the planet where their new life would begin.

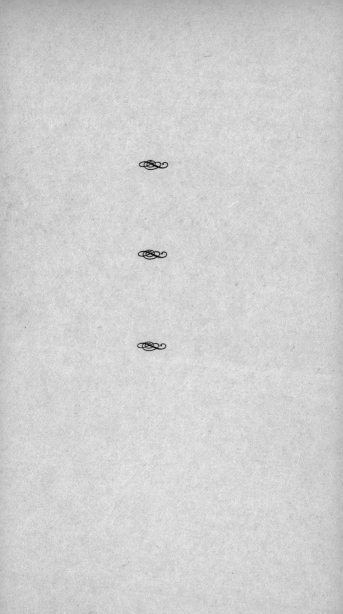

ABOUT THE AUTHOR

Pamela Leigh Starr, a wife and mother of three children, works to aid teachers in creating readers and, hopefully, future fans in her occupation as a staff trainer for an educational publishing company. Mr. Starr traces the beginning of her love for writing back to her very first creation entitled *The Terrifying Night,* which was a twenty page comedic thriller illustrated by a fellow 7th grade classmate. Long after this first attempt, Ms. Starr found the courage to develop love stories that were both thrilling and romantic and she continues to do just this. She has fallen in love with presenting the never-ending cycle of two people who meet, open their hearts and then find their way to love.

MISSION

2007 Publication Schedule

January

Corporate Seduction
A.C. Arthur
ISBN-13: 978-1-58571-238-0
ISBN-10: 1-58571-238-8
$9.95

A Taste of Temptation
Reneé Alexis
ISBN-13: 978-1-58571-207-6
ISBN-10: 1-58571-207-8
$9.95

February

The Perfect Frame
Beverly Clark
ISBN-13: 978-1-58571-240-3
ISBN-10: 1-58571-240-X
$9.95

Ebony Angel
Deatri King-Bey
ISBN-13: 978-1-58571-239-7
ISBN-10: 1-58571-239-6
$9.95

March

Sweet Sensations
Gwendolyn Bolton
ISBN-13: 978-1-58571-206-9
ISBN-10: 1-58571-206-X
$9.95

Crush
Crystal Hubbard
ISBN-13: 978-1-58571-243-4
ISBN-10: 1-58571-243-4
$9.95

April

Secret Thunder
Annetta P. Lee
ISBN-13: 978-1-58571-204-5
ISBN-10: 1-58571-204-3
$9.95

Blood Seduction
J.M. Jeffries
ISBN-13: 978-1-58571-237-3
ISBN-10: 1-58571-237-X
$9.95

May

Lies Too Long
Pamela Ridley
ISBN-13: 978-1-58571-246-5
ISBN-10: 1-58571-246-9
$13.95

Two Sides to Every Story
Dyanne Davis
ISBN-13: 978-1-58571-248-9
ISBN-10: 1-58571-248-5
$9.95

June

One of These Days
Michele Sudler
ISBN-13: 978-1-58571-249-6
ISBN-10: 1-58571-249-3
$9.95

Who's That Lady?
Andrea Jackson
ISBN-13: 978-1-58571-190-1
ISBN-10: 1-58571-190-X
$9.95

2007 Publication Schedule (continued)

July

Heart of the Phoenix
A.C. Arthur
ISBN-13: 978-1-58571-242-7
ISBN-10: 1-58571-242-6
$9.95

Do Over
Celya Bowers
ISBN-13: 978-1-58571-241-0
ISBN-10: 1-58571-241-8
$9.95

It's Not Over Yet
J.J. Michael
ISBN-13: 978-1-58571-245-8
ISBN-10: 1-58571-245-0
$9.95

August

The Fires Within
Beverly Clark
ISBN-13: 978-1-58571-244-1
ISBN-10: 1-58571-244-2
$9.95

Stolen Kisses
Dominiqua Douglas
ISBN-13: 978-1-58571-247-2
ISBN-10: 1-58571-247-7
$9.95

September

Small Whispers
Annetta P. Lee
ISBN-13: 978-158571-251-9
ISBN-10: 1-58571-251-5
$6.99

Always You
Crystal Hubbard
ISBN-13: 978-158571-252-6
ISBN-10: 1-58571-252-3
$6.99

October

Not His Type
Chamein Canton
ISBN-13: 978-158571-253-3
ISBN-10: 1-58571-253-1
$6.99

Many Shades of Gray
Dyanne Davis
ISBN-13: 978-158571-254-0
ISBN-10: 1-58571-254-X
$6.99

November

When I'm With You
LaConnie Taylor-Jones
ISBN-13: 978-158571-250-2
ISBN-10: 1-58571-250-7
$6.99

Mission
Pamela Leigh Starr
ISBN-13: 978-158571-255-7
ISBN-10: 1-58571-255-8
$6.99

December

One in A Million
Barbara Keaton
ISBN-13: 978-158571-257-1
ISBN-10: 1-58571-257-4
$6.99

The Foursome
Celya Bowers
ISBN-13: 978-158571-256-4
ISBN-10: 1-58571-256-6
$6.99

Other Genesis Press, Inc. Titles

Other Genesis Press, Inc. Titles (continued)

Bodyguard	Andrea Jackson	$9.95
Boss of Me	Diana Nyad	$8.95
Bound by Love	Beverly Clark	$8.95
Breeze	Robin Hampton Allen	$10.95
Broken	Dar Tomlinson	$24.95
By Design	Barbara Keaton	$8.95
Cajun Heat	Charlene Berry	$8.95
Careless Whispers	Rochelle Alers	$8.95
Cats & Other Tales	Marilyn Wagner	$8.95
Caught in a Trap	Andre Michelle	$8.95
Caught Up In the Rapture	Lisa G. Riley	$9.95
Cautious Heart	Cheris F Hodges	$8.95
Chances	Pamela Leigh Starr	$8.95
Cherish the Flame	Beverly Clark	$8.95
Class Reunion	Irma Jenkins/	
	John Brown	$12.95
Code Name: Diva	J.M. Jeffries	$9.95
Conquering Dr. Wexler's Heart	Kimberley White	$9.95
Crossing Paths, Tempting Memories	Dorothy Elizabeth Love	$9.95
Cypress Whisperings	Phyllis Hamilton	$8.95
Dark Embrace	Crystal Wilson Harris	$8.95
Dark Storm Rising	Chinelu Moore	$10.95
Daughter of the Wind	Joan Xian	$8.95
Deadly Sacrifice	Jack Kean	$22.95
Designer Passion	Dar Tomlinson	$8.95
Dreamtective	Liz Swados	$5.95
Ebony Butterfly II	Delilah Dawson	$14.95
Echoes of Yesterday	Beverly Clark	$9.95

Other Genesis Press, Inc. Titles (continued)

Eden's Garden	Elizabeth Rose	$8.95
Everlastin' Love	Gay G. Gunn	$8.95
Everlasting Moments	Dorothy Elizabeth Love	$8.95
Everything and More	Sinclair Lebeau	$8.95
Everything but Love	Natalie Dunbar	$8.95
Eve's Prescription	Edwina Martin Arnold	$8.95
Falling	Natalie Dunbar	$9.95
Fate	Pamela Leigh Starr	$8.95
Finding Isabella	A.J. Garrotto	$8.95
Forbidden Quest	Dar Tomlinson	$10.95
Forever Love	Wanda Y. Thomas	$8.95
From the Ashes	Kathleen Suzanne	$8.95
	Jeanne Sumerix	
Gentle Yearning	Rochelle Alers	$10.95
Glory of Love	Sinclair LeBeau	$10.95
Go Gentle into that Good Night	Malcom Boyd	$12.95
Goldengroove	Mary Beth Craft	$16.95
Groove, Bang, and Jive	Steve Cannon	$8.99
Hand in Glove	Andrea Jackson	$9.95
Hard to Love	Kimberley White	$9.95
Hart & Soul	Angie Daniels	$8.95
Heartbeat	Stephanie Bedwell-Grime	$8.95
Hearts Remember	M. Loui Quezada	$8.95
Hidden Memories	Robin Allen	$10.95
Higher Ground	Leah Latimer	$19.95
Hitler, the War, and the Pope	Ronald Rychiak	$26.95
How to Write a Romance	Kathryn Falk	$18.95
I Married a Reclining Chair	Lisa M. Fuhs	$8.95
Indigo After Dark Vol. I	Nia Dixon/Angelique	$10.95

Other Genesis Press, Inc. Titles (continued)

Indigo After Dark Vol. II	Dolores Bundy/ Cole Riley	$10.95
Indigo After Dark Vol. III	Montana Blue/ Coco Morena	$10.95
Indigo After Dark Vol. IV	Cassandra Colt/ Diana Richeaux	$14.95
Indigo After Dark Vol. V	Delilah Dawson	$14.95
Icie	Pamela Leigh Starr	$8.95
I'll Be Your Shelter	Giselle Carmichael	$8.95
I'll Paint a Sun	A.J. Garrotto	$9.95
Illusions	Pamela Leigh Starr	$8.95
Indiscretions	Donna Hill	$8.95
Intentional Mistakes	Michele Sudler	$9.95
Interlude	Donna Hill	$8.95
Intimate Intentions	Angie Daniels	$8.95
Jolie's Surrender	Edwina Martin-Arnold	$8.95
Kiss or Keep	Debra Phillips	$8.95
Lace	Giselle Carmichael	$9.95
Last Train to Memphis	Elsa Cook	$12.95
Lasting Valor	Ken Olsen	$24.95
Let Us Prey	Hunter Lundy	$25.95
Life Is Never As It Seems	J.J. Michael	$12.95
Lighter Shade of Brown	Vicki Andrews	$8.95
Love Always	Mildred E. Riley	$10.95
Love Doesn't Come Easy	Charlyne Dickerson	$8.95
Love Unveiled	Gloria Greene	$10.95
Love's Deception	Charlene Berry	$10.95
Love's Destiny	M. Loui Quezada	$8.95
Mae's Promise	Melody Walcott	$8.95

Other Genesis Press, Inc. Titles (continued)

Other Genesis Press, Inc. Titles (continued)

Path of Thorns	Annetta P. Lee	$9.95
Peace Be Still	Colette Haywood	$12.95
Picture Perfect	Reon Carter	$8.95
Playing for Keeps	Stephanie Salinas	$8.95
Pride & Joi	Gay G. Gunn	$15.95
Pride & Joi	Gay G. Gunn	$8.95
Promises to Keep	Alicia Wiggins	$8.95
Quiet Storm	Donna Hill	$10.95
Reckless Surrender	Rochelle Alers	$6.95
Red Polka Dot in a World of Plaid	Varian Johnson	$12.95
Reluctant Captive	Joyce Jackson	$8.95
Rendezvous with Fate	Jeanne Sumerix	$8.95
Revelations	Cheris F. Hodges	$8.95
Rivers of the Soul	Leslie Esdaile	$8.95
Rocky Mountain Romance	Kathleen Suzanne	$8.95
Rooms of the Heart	Donna Hill	$8.95
Rough on Rats and Tough on Cats	Chris Parker	$12.95
Secret Library Vol. 1	Nina Sheridan	$18.95
Secret Library Vol. 2	Cassandra Colt	$8.95
Shades of Brown	Denise Becker	$8.95
Shades of Desire	Monica White	$8.95
Shadows in the Moonlight	Jeanne Sumerix	$8.95
Sin	Crystal Rhodes	$8.95
So Amazing	Sinclair LeBeau	$8.95
Somebody's Someone	Sinclair LeBeau	$8.95
Someone to Love	Alicia Wiggins	$8.95
Song in the Park	Martin Brant	$15.95

Other Genesis Press, Inc. Titles (continued)

Soul Eyes	Wayne L. Wilson	$12.95
Soul to Soul	Donna Hill	$8.95
Southern Comfort	J.M. Jeffries	$8.95
Still the Storm	Sharon Robinson	$8.95
Still Waters Run Deep	Leslie Esdaile	$8.95
Stories to Excite You	Anna Forrest/Divine	$14.95
Subtle Secrets	Wanda Y. Thomas	$8.95
Suddenly You	Crystal Hubbard	$9.95
Sweet Repercussions	Kimberley White	$9.95
Sweet Tomorrows	Kimberly White	$8.95
Taken by You	Dorothy Elizabeth Love	$9.95
Tattooed Tears	T. T. Henderson	$8.95
The Color Line	Lizzette Grayson Carter	$9.95
The Color of Trouble	Dyanne Davis	$8.95
The Disappearance of Allison Jones	Kayla Perrin	$5.95
The Honey Dipper's Legacy	Pannell-Allen	$14.95
The Joker's Love Tune	Sidney Rickman	$15.95
The Little Pretender	Barbara Cartland	$10.95
The Love We Had	Natalie Dunbar	$8.95
The Man Who Could Fly	Bob & Milana Beamon	$18.95
The Missing Link	Charlyne Dickerson	$8.95
The Price of Love	Sinclair LeBeau	$8.95
The Smoking Life	Ilene Barth	$29.95
The Words of the Pitcher	Kei Swanson	$8.95
Three Wishes	Seressia Glass	$8.95
Ties That Bind	Kathleen Suzanne	$8.95
Tiger Woods	Libby Hughes	$5.95
Time is of the Essence	Angie Daniels	$9.95

Other Genesis Press, Inc. Titles (continued)

Timeless Devotion	Bella McFarland	$9.95
Tomorrow's Promise	Leslie Esdaile	$8.95
Truly Inseparable	Wanda Y. Thomas	$8.95
Unbreak My Heart	Dar Tomlinson	$8.95
Uncommon Prayer	Kenneth Swanson	$9.95
Unconditional	A.C. Arthur	$9.95
Unconditional Love	Alicia Wiggins	$8.95
Until Death Do Us Part	Susan Paul	$8.95
Vows of Passion	Bella McFarland	$9.95
Wedding Gown	Dyanne Davis	$8.95
What's Under Benjamin's Bed	Sandra Schaffer	$8.95
When Dreams Float	Dorothy Elizabeth Love	$8.95
Whispers in the Night	Dorothy Elizabeth Love	$8.95
Whispers in the Sand	LaFlorya Gauthier	$10.95
Wild Ravens	Altonya Washington	$9.95
Yesterday Is Gone	Beverly Clark	$10.95
Yesterday's Dreams, Tomorrow's Promises	Reon Laudat	$8.95
Your Precious Love	Sinclair LeBeau	$8.95

Order Form

Mail to: Genesis Press, Inc.
P.O. Box 101
Columbus, MS 39703

Name _____
Address _____
City/State _____ Zip _____
Telephone _____

Ship to (if different from above)
Name _____
Address _____
City/State _____ Zip _____
Telephone _____

Credit Card Information
Credit Card # _____ ☐ Visa ☐ Mastercard
Expiration Date (mm/yy) _____ ☐ AmEx ☐ Discover

Qty.	Author	Title	Price	Total

Use this order

form, or call

1-888-INDIGO-1

Total for books	
Shipping and handling:	
$5 first two books,	
$1 each additional book	
Total S & H	
Total amount enclosed	

Mississippi residents add 7% sales tax

Visit www.genesis-press.com for latest releases and excerpts.